A CAPITOL OFFENSE

'Tis the talk and not the intrigue that's the crime.

GEORGE GRANVILLE

The She Gallants

A

Capitol Offense

an entertainment by

JOCELYN DAVEY

NEW YORK: ALFRED · A · KNOPF

1956

L.C. catalog card number: 56-7210

© Jocelyn Davey, 1956

THIS IS A BORZOI BOOK
PUBLISHED BY ALFRED A. KNOPF, INC.

FIRST AMERICAN EDITION

A CAPITOL OFFENSE

NEED THE AUTHOR AVER, *what must be obvious: that the Embassy described in these pages is a piece of whole cloth draped over a very dignified institution? The author has been having a little fun, and invites the reader to take part in this fantasy in the same spirit. The events which take place and the characters concerned bear no relation to reality.*

ONE

"About suffering they were never wrong
The Old Masters: how well they understood
Its human situation: how it takes place
While someone else is eating, or opening a
window, or just walking dully along . . ."
W. H. AUDEN

I

SITTING back in his cab on the way to the Embassy,
Ambrose recalled again his intense delight at the
Washington Airport when the negro porter, seizing his
bags, had welcomed him to America with his hearty: "Yes,
suh!" There was all the warmth of the world in that
greeting. It was not only the negro. The air-hostess, on the
plane from New York, had shown the same spirit in her own
devoted way, and so had the man at the desk who had so
patiently and sympathetically sorted out his ticket problem.

As always on visits to this country, he felt the active force
that lay behind the welcome. People were polite enough at
Oxford, and were helpful too; but the mark of it, as of all
English politeness, was a desire that you should never feel
intruded upon. Very nice. But the opposite—when friendship was the aim—could be nice too. You were to be
welcomed in. Even the glorious November sunshine of
Rock Creek Park, through which they were driving, was
more assertive than its pale English counterpart. America
had not drifted into being. It had made itself felt by force of
character, and wanted you to know it.

Now the taxi had turned into the Embassy gates, and
there at the Chancery door—yes, it was still old Needham.
How pleasant.

7

"You know your room, Mr Usher," said Needham, when they had exchanged greetings. "The same room, sir, and you have Miss Hope-Little again. Like old times, sir. Are you glad to be back?"

Was he? He hardly knew. He had been instructed, so he had come. That perhaps was what was really so attractive about these missions. You never stopped to add up units of pleasure and displeasure. Poor old Bentham would have been shocked. Utilitarianism didn't apply. You just did what you were told.

"Yes, indeed, I am delighted, delighted. The same room, eh? Splendid, splendid."

As he bubbled on effusively to old Needham, he could feel himself back, for a moment, with his College porter at St Mary's, and then he knew immediately where the satisfaction lay in this sudden flight to Washington. It was good to be lifted up forcibly every now and then from the inner contemplative life at Oxford and dropped into the world of action. He had pretended to be reluctant when Hepworth, now Under-Secretary at the Foreign Office, had suggested, in his apparently casual way, that he might like the job, yet it was an offer he was unconsciously waiting for. He needed to break away every so often not only from the sybaritic comforts of his Fellowship, but even more from the assumptions that surrounded one at Oxford—that there was an inner rationality in existence that would offer up its secret to the explorer—that contemplation or logical argument took one to a higher plane of reality—that this was, in fact, the only reality worth bothering about. They all needed to get away from it.

Lawrence was, of course, the supreme example, first turning to All Souls from the high adventure of Arab politics, and then giving it up to live as an aircraftman. Some of Ambrose's colleagues at St Mary's could keep in balance by a month's climbing in Switzerland once a year.

8

For him the call to action was satisfied by this sudden immersion into political affairs. Behind it was an unspoken question. Could he understand the secret of the moral imperative unless it emerged from the world outside his study?

There was something else he recognized, coming back to Washington. An Englishman had a special place here. Washington was complete unto itself, as small to encompass as a cocktail party, but with the whole world epitomized in each gathering or policy decision. And at the centre of this peculiar world stood the British Embassy. There was something very satisfying in being an Englishman at the Court of George Washington in this particular era. There was no place where Britain was more respected or more despised. One felt here at the same time Britain's great strength and her appalling weakness—both equally true—and so perhaps one had a chance here of making some synthesis of the peculiar contradiction.

But it was even more than this. It was his *personal* position that Ambrose Usher, coming back to Washington, found so ironic and satisfying. The Embassy, stately and spacious, was the symbol of historic Britain, and all who worked here were looked on as symbols in the first place and human beings only in the second. What was he as a symbol? There was no one here more British or less British than he was. His family had been immigrants to England when he was fourteen, and he spoke any number of European languages as mother-tongues. "Usher" was merely an English way of writing "Uscze", the little Yugoslav town in which his family had lived for about two hundred years. Before this there had been sojournings in Greece; before that in Spain. He was a wanderer, whose identification with England was so secure precisely because its foundations were in full view all the time—like a building of Le Corbusier, he thought, the pillars on the ground floor looking a bit naked. This in fact

9

was the kind of Embassy they would build in Washington to-day if Lutyens' brick mansion were burnt down—something like London's Festival Hall, probably. This was the way England wanted the world to look at her, and the way she looked at herself, bringing her foundations out into the open for examination.

It was nice to be greeted at the Embassy door so warmly by old Needham, and he smiled back cheerfully. Needham, who had been porter for as long as anyone could remember, did not normally melt into warmth at the sight of a visitor. With grave and measured mien, he examined you slowly, warily, while he arranged for you to be guided to the right room. This was right, too, thought Ambrose. How proper it was, in these days of haste and extemporization, that a visitor to the British Embassy should make immediate contact, at the door, with the long-term view of British diplomacy. Needham had the long-term view. He was probably fitting your visiting into the long-established categories of British foreign policy. How did it affect the Eastern Question? Was it something to do with the North-West Frontier? It's probably the whiskers, thought Ambrose, looking at Needham's long drooping Victorian moustaches. He speaks for another age. Yet there's wisdom too in that ancient face. He has seen it all before. Nothing can surprise him, and nothing escapes him. What was it that someone had once said: "It is easier for a rich man to enter Heaven than to pass through the eye of a Needham."

Aloud he was still gossiping with the porter in the peculiarly rapid, happy-go-lucky style of conversation that was his hallmark.

"Yes, yes, I am glad to be back. Everything the same, no doubt? The young full of follies, the old incorrigible? Janus still guarding the door? Nothing changes. I have the same stable. Well, I must get to it. Miss Hope-Little is waiting with the harness, eh?"

Needham smiled warmly. It was the same strange Mr Usher, and he accepted him—this small, rather tubby bespectacled figure, with his baggy flannels and little goatee beard—into the elegant orbit of the Embassy.

Ambrose gave him a cheerful wave of the hand, and proceeded on his way, a bulging brief-case under his arm, and peering happily at the familiar world around him. Hopping down the corridor, and turning sharply at the corner, he tripped over something, and, looking down, saw a beautifully sleek Siamese cat under his feet.

"Why, Palmerston!" he exclaimed, bending down to tickle the cat's ear. "Truly a royal welcome! How are all the souls of dead ambassadors?"

Palmerston purred loudly, and rubbed his head against Ambrose's leg.

"I see Palmerston remembers you."

Ambrose looked up and rose to his feet, extending his hand warmly to the gaunt female that towered over him.

"Miss Hope-Little! Yes, he remembers. Could he forget? We have had so many philosophic discussions. The nature of being. He proved to me that there is no such thing. Only the nature of being a cat. Everything else is unnatural."

"Mr Usher! You haven't changed."

"Ah yes, Miss Hope-Little. I *have* changed. Back at Oxford we are very serious, dealing with abstractions. Only here we can be frivolous, dealing with the fate of nations."

They were walking together towards his old room on the third floor, Palmerston following happily behind them. Miss Hope-Little, from her great height, looked down on Ambrose protectively. She, like Needham, had been at the Embassy for years, and to the young attachés was "an old war-horse". Shapeless in her eternal tweeds, and rasping in voice, she seemed without much human affection. But she was a first-rate secretary and was passed around for special jobs. She had been with Ambrose when he served at the Embassy during the war, working on all kinds of mysterious supply questions. The real mystery perhaps had been how a philosopher could be so interested—and so efficient—on business matters. People said it was an instinct. Working with intercepts and reading hundreds of diplomatic reports and foreign newspapers, he could smell out, somehow, where they might pick up some raw material they needed, pre-empt a supply of oil from German hands, or seize a cargo of food trying to slip through the blockade. Yet there was no real mystery. It was precisely the philosopher in him that allowed him to apply his mind objectively. He was never personally involved. He reserved his real self for the real world, the world of ideas.

But the secret of his charm was that no one suspected it. To the world around him, he was involved in everything. He talked with everybody, as he was going along, about what he was doing. When someone visited him, he would pick up a piece of paper from his desk and laugh about it, dictating a minute to the patient Miss Hope-Little, and constantly appealing to the visitor for comments. "Ah, here is the text of Senator Braunschweig's speech. The Senator doesn't like us. I have to tell the Minister of Munitions what it all means, you know, or his feelings will be hurt. Let's try, Miss Hope-Little. 'If the Senator is successful in securing an adverse vote in the Committee on the proposal to include this item in Lend-Lease, it will be due less to his desire to assuage the Nordic sympathies of his Milwaukee constituents than to a Samsonian compulsion on his part to bring something down in ruins, having correctly discovered that while the great American public has no objection to a politician being blind—especially if he has a weakness for the other sex, as Samson had—it takes to its heart only those who can exalt such blindness into a career . . .' "

"Hearst, the American Homer," the visitor might inject.

"Exactly, exactly. Where are we, Miss Hope-Little? 'into a career, so that Hearst, the American Homer, weaves a folk-tale no less effective, in selling papers, because it confirms...' Let me see ..."

"Their innermost fears?"

"Ah yes, 'their secret fears, no less appealing because it could plunge them into catastrophe while filling their hearts with ...' What shall we say?"

"A transcendent joy?"

"Let's say, 'with a transforming pride'."

The visitor loved all this. He had no idea if it was serious, but he felt, when he left, that he himself had been particularly brilliant that afternoon. It was all so fast that he had hardly time to catch his breath. And all through the talk, Ambrose had been on the telephone with other callers too, trying out different ideas, everything with a kind of mock seriousness whose tone one had to echo.

Only Miss Hope-Little never echoed it. She brooded over the scene grimly and watchfully. While not actually disapproving, she felt, perhaps, that her boss gave himself too much to everybody, not realizing that this kind of active dialectic was essential to him. Perhaps her role was precisely to be on guard. She seemed on guard already as they climbed the stairs and walked down the corridor to his room.

As they approached the door, Ambrose bowed her into the room with a sweep of his black battered trilby.

"This is a great moment, Miss Hope-Little. Like General MacArthur, *I have returned.* We await a summons, I take it, from His Excellency. What are we going to do? A clean desk, empty baskets, bare ruined shelves where late the sweet files lay. Do we know anything?"

Miss Hope-Little was severe. "I'm sure *you* know, Mr Usher. I haven't been told anything. Just that I'm to work with you. But there *is* a message from H.E. You're to telephone him as soon as you arrive."

"Yes, yes, I feared it. The bell, *that summons thee to heaven or to hell*. What did the poet say? *Il faut souffrir pour être belle*. Alexander Bell, of course."

"Shall I call the Private Office?" Miss Hope-Little was patiently stroking Palmerston's head. He had leapt to the empty desk and was purring loudly. It was clear that Miss Hope-Little had at least one very human side to her nature. She adored cats, and of all cats, Palmerston, one would say, was the supreme.

"No, no. That would never do. When the Ambassador is an admiral, we must be sticklers for naval etiquette. I shall pipe myself aboard the flagship. How do we like the Admiral, by the way?" he asked, as he lifted the receiver.

"Well," said Miss Hope-Little cautiously. "It's not the same, of course, as when Lord Halifax was Ambassador."

The switchboard had answered, and Ambrose recognized the voice. "This—is London," he announced, with heavy drama. In the old days, they had anxiously listened every night to Edward R. Murrow's broadcast from the beleagured capital, and his sepulchral introduction had become an affectionate tribute.

Mrs Osgood, the old telephone-operator, had no difficulty in identifying her caller. "Welcome back, Mr Usher," she said. "It's so nice to hear your voice. I heard you were coming. Can I get you a number?"

"Not *a* number, Mrs Osgood. *The* number. Can you put me in touch, by the magic you use, with the Envoy Extraordinary?"

"I'll give you the Private Office," she answered. "Hold on."

Ambrose held on, smiling happily at Miss Hope-Little as she continued to stroke Palmerston. How she loves that animal, he thought. She would do anything for it, absolutely anything.

A laconic female voice now answered from the Private

Office. "Oh, Mr Usher," said the voice. "The Ambassador says could you come over right away."

"Right away," he assured her, and replaced the receiver. "Odd expression, though, don't you think, Miss Hope-Little? Aren't the adverbs wrong? 'Right quickly' would be better. Ah, well. By the way, while I am gone, do you think . . . might I ask . . . could you try . . . ?" With affected timorousness he produced from his pocket several scraps of paper, covered in an indecipherably small script. "Something I was scribbling in the plane. Notes on a book I have to review for *The Oxford Philosophical Journal*. I can't really make up my mind about it. It's this peculiar existentialism. Not even in the pure form. Strange book. Do you mind? Blanks as usual where you can't follow?"

He was just going through the door when Miss Hope-Little called out.

"Oh, Mr Usher, I quite forgot. There *is* something for you." She produced a large envelope out of her desk drawer. "It's an invitation from the Ambassador to a Guy Fawkes party he's giving to-morrow night."

Ambrose took the beautifully engraved card and looked at it in a dream.

"Did you say a *Guy Fawkes* party? Is this some new ritual? A post-war institution?"

"Oh no," said Miss Hope-Little. "It's the first time one has ever been held here. It just happened very suddenly. Apparently it's going to be quite a big party. All Washington is invited."

"A Guy Fawkes party!" Ambrose could hardly take it in. "I wonder why. To demonstrate that we gave the Americans the word *guy*? This is most peculiar, most peculiar. Yes, Miss Hope-Little, things have certainly changed since His Lordship's day." He was shaking his head as he left to keep his appointment.

Despite the urgency of his summons, Ambrose took a short turn around the trees behind the Annex—the "public" part of the Embassy garden—before presenting himself to Admiral Junius Throttle, V.C., Her Britannic Majesty's Ambassador at Washington. He wanted a moment to himself to settle in. He could still almost feel the plane's engines buzzing in his ears.

The garden seemed to him at its loveliest. Some preferred it in the summer, when everything was drenched in green, and when the great lawns softened the white heat that struck the house in dizzying waves. But Ambrose loved it as it was now in late Fall, the trees strident and shapely, and the blue smoke of burning leaves coming pungently through the mild air. In the summer one saw little but the foliage. Now one could see the building clearly, as Lutyens had intended it to be seen, a great English mansion in a foreign land—an English *pile*, wasn't that the phrase? Pile of what? Well, it didn't matter.

As he stood there, alone and still, breathing in the fragrant air, Ambrose had an acute feeling of being in a world exclusively of his own sensation. For once the empiricist formula seemed capable of being believed in as a working philosophy, something which even its supporters never claimed. There was no "real" world here outside his own sensations, no non-sensible entities that gave a frame to his and to everyone's observations. He was quite ready to accept, for a second, even the extreme and absurd phenomenalist view that what he saw and smelt and heard had no relation even to another hypothetical observer in the same situation. This was his world, with no other existence. What about his own existence as the observer? Well, that's easy. All you need is a second proposition describing the activities of a second observer observing him, and so on *ad infinitum*.

At that moment, something grey suddenly shot into his vision, clawed the branch and leapt down at his feet.

"Why, Palmerston!" cried Ambrose. "You have destroyed my illusions. No you haven't, you support me. You are my second observer. What are you doing here, you nice thing?" He bent down to pat him. "Hunting for wild life, no doubt."

Palmerston purred his reply.

"Ah, I see," said Ambrose. "Just glad to see me back. Well, I am glad to be back."

It is all so peaceful here, he thought. Perhaps too peaceful. Like the war films in which, before an attack, the director lets you hear an unearthly stillness broken only by the sound of birds singing. Well, he hadn't come here for a rest, and things would start popping soon, no doubt, like fireworks.

When he thought of fireworks, he suddenly remembered the Guy Fawkes party the next day, and in another part of the garden he could now see workmen erecting some large structures, presumably for the party. What on earth was the point of it all? he wondered. Had the Ambassador thought it out? After all, it had been a *Catholic* plot to blow up Parliament, and Guy Fawkes Day was an anti-Catholic demonstration. True, it was three hundred years ago, but it would still raise a few eyebrows in the United States. Perhaps the Ambassador subscribed to Father Gerard's theory that there had been no plot at all. The whole thing had been a frame-up—the work of *agents provocateurs*. Or perhaps it was just being introduced to America as an English rite, without significance? At Oxford, it was still fashionable for freshmen to climb the Martyrs' Memorial on Guy Fawkes Day and plant a certain bedroom receptacle on the top spire. Was some young Third Secretary being deputed to place a receptacle on the Embassy chimney-top for old times' sake. If so, the receptacle would have to be carefully chosen. Americans were very susceptible. The Oxford version would never do. A top-hat would perhaps be better.

It was time, really, for him to make his call, and he started now for the door of the Residence. He had never met the Ambassador, but there were enough stories about him to make the prospect quite amusing. The one thing that everybody knew was, of course, his Victoria Cross and wonderful, if peculiar, record in two world wars. The V.C. came from a fabulous exploit in the First World War, in 1917, when he had deliberately rammed and sunk a U-boat with his own crippled destroyer, H.M.S. *Falkland*. It turned out to be the U-boat commanded by Captain Fritz von Hoeflein, the scourge of British shipping, and overnight he had become a hero—the "Falkland Daredevil" was one of his nicknames in the papers. He had carried on in the same vein in the Second World War. In the dog days of 1940 he had cheered everybody up with his thrilling chase of the German raider *Koenigsberg*, the exciting part being that he had consciously followed the Nelson technique of turning a deaf ear to Admiralty instruction to avoid entanglement. There had been some talk of a court-martial, but popular hero-worship made it inadvisable and it had been dropped. A little less blatantly, he had done the same thing in the engagement which had endeared him to the Americans. In command of a cruiser supporting an American raid on the Fuju Islands, he had taken complete charge, without instructions, when the American leading ship was knocked out, and had landed the troops almost without casualty. Returning later to San Francisco, he had been given a parade, repeated when he passed through New York. "Full Throttle" was another of his nicknames. Pretty obvious. The legend was that he was the kind of lone-wolf sea-hawk who didn't care a damn for the enemy or the Admiralty or anybody else.

Everybody knew, when Mr Churchill became Prime Minister, that he would immediately make a change in the post of Ambassador at Washington, and he had done so. What a typical Winston touch, everybody said, to appoint Throttle, a man without any political or diplomatic experience and with more than a hint of that kind of bull-headedness that would make it hard for the experts to advise him. But that was Winston's way. He picked a man for his qualities of character. Throttle was perhaps the only British military figure who was as beloved by Americans as he was by the English. This was the way to re-establish that kind of full-hearted admiration for Britain that had existed during the blitz in 1940. For the few disgruntled who said that Winston could only think in war terms, there were thousands to argue that it was an appointment of genius.

The real story was a little different. Ambrose knew it, but by a miracle it had been kept from the gossip columnists. When Winston became Prime Minister again, in 1951, he had indeed decided to make an unorthodox appointment to Washington, and his choice had fallen on Lord Bosworth, his doughty supporter all through the calamitous 1930's. It was an open secret that Bosworth had been the author of the magnificent *New Letters of Junius*, which had appeared week after week in Lord Weaverhook's *London Dispatch* and done as much to discredit Baldwin and Chamberlain as the original Junius's letters had done to discredit Grafton, nearly two hundred years earlier. Winston and Bosworth had fought the fight from two corners, the former with patriotic pomp, the latter with invective and sarcasm. They had remained intimate friends, and Winston referred to him as *Junius* as often as he called him *Bozzy*.

Winston was doubling as Foreign Secretary at the time of the appointment, running everything from No. 10, to the great annoyance of the Foreign Office. Having decided on Bosworth, he genially told one of his assistants to put up

Junius to the State Department. Most unfortunately, he instructed the official at about that same time to invite Admiral Throttle, for whom he had a genuine admiration, to be Governor of the Mermaid Islands. They were being troublesome and needed a firm naval hand. Alas! Officials are only human. The Junius in Throttle had somehow become dominant. His name had gone to the American Embassy for forwarding to Washington. The State Department had accepted it without question and immediately leaked it to the appropriate channels, so that on the next day there was an enthusiastic editorial in the *Washington Post*, followed by many reminiscent and inaccurate anecdotes of his sea-exploits in the gossip columns. There was nothing to be done but carry through. The Admiral had become Ambassador.

There is one member of the Athenaeum Club in London who claims to have seen—and he speaks of it with awe—the letter that Lord Bosworth addressed to Mr Churchill when he received His Majesty's invitation to become Governor of the Mermaid Islands. One has to remember that Winston had told him, privately, that he was going to send him to Washington. One has to remember also that he was a man with a particular gift for invective, sarcasm and abuse. He sat down, without waiting for an explanation, and wrote for an hour. Winston and he had been close friends and allies, but on such occasions it is not impossible to add old grievances and rumoured delinquencies to the immediate affront. He went into all the imagined motives—and he used a lively imagination—which would cause Winston, at this point, to want to banish him to the Mermaid Islands. No explanations were possible after this letter, and Winston never spoke to him again.

But Winston is a great man.

"Has the letter been destroyed?" Ambrose had asked someone who knew about such things.

"Good gracious no," he answered. "Winston thinks it is one of the most wonderful political letters ever composed. He has written an introduction and commentary on it himself, and it is to be published after they are both dead. He's probably sold it to *Life* in advance."

"And what about the unfortunate official?"

"They had to send him from No. 10, of course, as far away as they could. Winston had a brain-wave. He asked for him to be made executive assistant to the man they finally sent out. . . ."

"To the Mermaid Islands?"

"Exactly. But before he left No. 10, Winston sent for him and told him that he was not at all angry with him. Bosworth you see, had shown himself in his true colours. Throttle is a howling success. 'We are all unconscious instruments of Providence,' he told the unfortunate man."

Certainly Throttle had started his mission with a bang. He had arrived in Britain's latest battleship, and put the Royal Navy on the map again in the United States. He absolutely refused to make any public speeches on Britain's dollar gap, but gave the most entertaining impromptu talks about his experiences in the Navy; everybody loved it. But why a *Guy Fawkes* party? thought Ambrose sadly.

He rang the bell at the Residence, and a footman took charge of him. Up the long, splendid staircase, flanked by massive portraits of English monarchs (including, he noticed with some amusement, one of George III), he thought again about the curious fate that brought people together, from so many odd places, into the symbolic role of acting and speaking for a nation. It's all rather phoney, he decided. Once we stop living *inside* a nation, we cease to exist. We're the second observer, looking on from the outside.

As he came into the study, a huge figure rose from an armchair, and a deep hearty voice welcomed him. No wonder the Americans liked him. He was not one of those tiny, taut-looking sailors. The whole man had a large, comfortable ease about him, crowned by the usual deep blue seaman's eyes.

"Well, here you are," said the Admiral. "I've been wanting to meet you. They told me all about you. You have quite a reputation."

"Alas, only too well deserved, sir," said Ambrose. "I hope I can help, nevertheless."

"Oh yes, you can help. You can tell me what it is all about. I don't understand it, but you look as though you might." Throttle was looking him over, beard and all, and fitting everything together. "Did you have a good journey?"

"I flew, sir, into a wild west wind. Shelley himself would have been airsick. But I am renewed, I am well again."

"Well, it was good of you to come. Who did you see before you left?"

"It was Hepworth who arranged it. But it was all very hurried. We served here together during the war, and we had been at Balliol together. Now that he's gone into politics and become Under-Secretary, he tells me what to do."

"You've given up Government work? Back to normal life?"

"If Oxford can be called normal. I sometimes wonder."

"You sit there in a little backwater, keeping track on England."

"Yes, an oddity. The rest of England is the fleet at sea, and we at Oxford are . . ."

"The Admiralty?"

"More like the naval historian."

"But you like it?"

"I like a change, too."

"Well, we all have to have some escape. I never had any head for philosophy, but I get my relaxation out of

22

chemistry. I always liked it, and I've kept it up. Always had a lab fitted up aboard. I've built one here, too, just below."

"Is there any special field you are interested in?"

"Not particularly. But I like bangs, and colours. I've been experimenting with new types of fireworks."

Fireworks, thought Ambrose. Is this the explanation? Can it be as simple as this?

"I've had your invitation to the Guy Fawkes party, sir," he said. "Are you going to display your own fireworks?"

"That's exactly it, my boy," said the Ambassador, leaning forward happily. "I've really worked out some stunners, and I wanted to see them in action, so I had this idea. Rather good, don't you think? Show the Americans that we still like a bit of fun, eh?"

"It's certainly original," said Ambrose cautiously. "What did the people here think of it?"

"Oh, they are a lot of stuffed shirts. Said the Catholics wouldn't like it. But, damn it, they don't seem to mind in England. Isn't it about time we got over all that stuff, anyway? The man who looks after the British Information Services here, Strangeways, he's quite upset. Says there'll be all kind of trouble. But I got a very friendly letter from the President of the Anti-Popery League."

"There is a theory, you know, sir, that it wasn't a Catholic plot at all. The idea is that Lord Salisbury used a lot of *agents provocateurs* to work up the Catholics to the idea of blowing up Parliament so that he could arrest them and execute them."

"Is that so? Well, now why didn't Strangeways tell me about that? We could use that. Of course, the Anti-Popery League wouldn't like it, but it might show that we are quite impartial about the whole thing. The main thing, after all, is the fireworks. I got an enthusiastic letter from the American Association of Pyrotechnicians. They want to make me an honorary member. That's good, isn't it?"

23

"That's excellent, sir. Have they invited you to attend their Annual Convention?"

"They have. Very clever of you to guess that. I'm thinking of it. There's one other thing. You know the Russians have their big party here on November 7th, and ours is on the 5th. Steal their thunder a bit, eh?"

"Do the advisers like that?"

"I can't say they do. But I've pacified them by agreeing to one thing. I wanted to have a bonfire, like we do at home, and burn a Guy, in the traditional way, and I thought it would be a good idea to burn a kind of stuffed figure of old Stalin. That would show the Americans where we stood on Communism, wouldn't you think? But the people here absolutely put their foot down—head of a friendly nation and so on. So I agreed to drop it if they would stop pestering me about all the other things."

"Very adroit, sir."

"Well, now," said the Ambassador, "let's have a word about the other thing. I'm a bit out of my depth on it."

"I'm a bit out of my depth myself, sir. Hepworth said you'd explain."

The Ambassador leaned forward and detached the telephone from the outlet into which it was fitted. "We'd better follow the rules," he said. "Well, the whole thing turns on . . ."

He broke off, still looking at the telephone, and rose to his feet.

"Let's go for a walk and talk about it in the garden. It's easier there."

They walked together for a long time across the lawns, keeping away from the trees. Afterwards Ambrose went over to the Annex and wandered into several rooms, apparently in error, apologizing profusely to the occupants for his mistake.

The word had got round that he was back. When Ambrose returned to his room there was an urgent message from Walter Scott. Would he go with him to a cocktail party that evening at Edward Beauchamp's and have dinner afterwards?

Walter was a well-beloved friend from war days, too, a bachelor like Ambrose, but a scientist, one of those who knew what atomic energy was all about. He was from Aberdeen, and his tall, lean bones, and pink, well-scrubbed Scottish face always gave one a sense of ascetic but good-natured honesty. He shared one interest with Ambrose higher than his atomic physics, which he always professed to find a bore. The scientific philosophy of the ancient Greeks: the ultimate theory of scientific theorizing. That was worth discussing, and they had spent many hours discussing it.

Ambrose was to ring. Miss Hope-Little had gone. He put the call through himself.

"Scott here."

"And here"—in sepulchral tones—"is the Voice of The People!"

"Why Broz! You old Partisan!"

"And how is the Sage of Abbotsford?"

"Still grinding away at the Waverley novels, I regret to say. The rent is still not paid. You're coming with me to-night, aren't you?"

"I shall be delighted, delighted. But who is the estimable and hospitable Beauchamp?"

"Oh, he looks after South America. He gives good parties, with lots of native dancing-girls. I told him I would try to bring you and he said he would be delighted. He's 'heard of you', you know."

"I know, Walter. They've all heard, but they're all wrong. I shall be living here under false pretences. I am no longer the party butterfly, dazzling all with my gay flights. By a strange metamorphosis, I have become a grub again, living quietly off a leaf in St Mary's garden."

"Oh dear, is the food situation in England as bad as that? And I'm due to go home next week. Well, we'll try and feed you up to-night—lots of pretty flowers, if you can turn yourself into a honey-sucking bee. Always are at Edward's parties. Pick you up at six."

Edward Beauchamp, it transpired, had a large house set back in a pleasant garden on P Street. There was already a noisy crowd when they arrived, and, sure enough, their hats and coats were taken by two beautifully mannered peasant women in native costume—from Brazil, it seemed.

"Carrying realism a little far, don't you think?" murmured Ambrose. "I shall expect to find the Labour Attaché in corduroy trousers with a string around the knees."

"The only thing I promised you was beautiful peasant women," replied Walter, "and I have delivered. My heart bleeds for you, stuck away in the corner of an Oxford quadrangle. Ah, Edward. This is Mr Usher."

"I'm so glad you could come," said Beauchamp. "Can I introduce you to my wife? Pepita, this is Mr Usher."

Beauchamp was a small, florid-faced, meticulously dressed and unctuously spoken Englishman, the commuter from Surbiton, the timid bank-clerk type. What made these men marry Pepitas, and what happened to them when they did? Pepita was a highly rouged Spanish lady, somewhat attenuated, it was true, but still very dashing in her tight black dress, high at the neck and sparkling with ornaments. Her arms, too, tinkled with silver bangles. When she heard Ambrose's name, she uttered a shriek of excitement.

"It is so thrilling that you are here, Mr Usher. Everybody

26

tells us stories about you. You are a mystery man, are you not? We shall all try to solve the mystery this time."

"Dear lady, it is only the mystery of the dog in the night."

"The dog in the night? Edward, what is that?"

While Edward was explaining, a drink had been put into Ambrose's hand, and introductions were flying in all directions. He felt a gentle pressure behind him, and found that it was Walter, firmly propelling him through the room into a room beyond. "Come on through," said Walter. "It looks safer in here."

There was a group of four in the corner whom Walter seemed to be aiming for.

"Hullo, hullo," he said to them. "This is Mr Ambrose Usher, newly returned from Oxford. And this is Mrs Abbott-Hume, Mme Marot, Mr Hewitt, from the Embassy, and er . . ."

The fourth member of the group introduced himself. "Auguste Flantin, French Embassy."

They were a most agreeable group to look at, Ambrose thought, and having already had a drink or two, they seemed to exude a certain gaiety. Hewitt had apparently just told a joke at which they were all laughing, especially Mrs Abbott-Hume. She was English, young and pretty, the wife, he found, of Commander Abbott-Hume, special aide to the Ambassador. She was small, delicately formed, with a fresh pink-and-white complexion and a mass of golden hair. Her husband was not in evidence, but this did not seem to occasion Mr Hewitt much sorrow. He glanced at her rather frequently, and she looked back at him occasionally with what Ambrose thought was rather a direct regard. Hewitt, they told him, was an assistant to the Air Attaché. He was tall and dark, with a fine, lean face, softened, when he smiled, by a beguiling dimple. A strand of wavy hair fell over his brow, giving him a Byronic look.

"Didn't you pop your head through my door this afternoon?" he asked Ambrose.

"I think I did," said Ambrose, "but I was rather lost, and I can't quite remember. Things seem to have changed around a good deal since I left."

The talk was getting livelier. Flantin was a slightly built, beautifully mannered Frenchman, speaking, with infinite charm, the English of Charles Boyer. Mme Marot said little. Ambrose had difficulty in placing her. She knew them all, and Walter, it seemed, knew her well. She was not young— her hair was indeed iron grey—but she was slow and graceful, with an immense reserve. Her dark, languorous eyes turned on Ambrose now and then, not with a bold or inviting look but as from a great distance. She was dressed with exquisite simplicity.

"How I envy your life at Oxford," cried Flantin. "I was there for part of the war, after 1940. Wonderful place."

"Ah, I missed you then. I was away, having my finest hour. Did you teach?"

"No," said Flantin. "I was working with one of the de Gaulle groups there. Information and so on, you know."

"You must know a lot of the people there," said Ambrose politely.

"Oh yes, Meakers, Abbott, Hopkinson, and of course dear old Derzhinsky. Yes," he said reflectively, "I loved it. I had other interests too. I am an amateur of archaeology— I have dug in the Dordogne—and I knew Pulsifer at Oxford. You know Pulsifer's work?" He looked at Ambrose somewhat oddly.

"Certainly," said Ambrose. "He dines at St Mary's on the rare occasions when he is above ground. Great cave man, is he not?"

"Cave man? Yes, he has many interests. Ah, Oxford is so interesting," said Flantin. "Everything there is so interesting. Even your girl students with that horrible name

28

'undergraduettes'. I find them—I will not say beautiful, but there is some special quality about them. To me they are . . . what shall I say . . . unusual?"

"Ah, my dear sir," said Ambrose, "you should see a hundred of them, massed for attack, at one of my lectures. They are terrifying. First they get it all down in writing"— and as he spoke, he transformed himself into a note-taking undergraduette—"then comes the cross-examination." His voice suddenly acquired a high, ladylike precision. " 'Didn't you say last Wednesday, Mr Usher, that the good was a function of the useful? And to-day you have just said that the useful is a function of the good. Do you believe in interchangeable functions?' I am trapped and have to answer quickly. Risky subject! 'My dear young lady,' I say, 'how does one establish the point of departure? Is your wit a function of your charm, or your charm of your wit?' Then they all laugh and the bell goes, and I am saved."

His way of saying all this was so droll that they all laughed. Mrs Abbott-Hume said:

"I ought to be offended. I attended your lectures at Oxford for one term. But I will admit that I was not one of your questioners. The truth was that I couldn't understand anything you were talking about."

"I know, I know," cried Ambrose:

> *"Full of high sentence but a bit obtuse,*
> *At times indeed, almost ridiculous . . ."*

Hewitt carried on the verse, waving his glass cheerfully:

> *"I grow old, I grow old,*
> *I shall wear the bottom of my trousers rolled."*

"Quite, quite," said Ambrose. He turned to Mme Marot, feeling her eyes on him. "These are verses by an American, Mr Eliot, that we all have to learn at school now."

She smiled. "Yes, we know of him. Cultural Ambassador from the United States."

29

"Not quite that," said Ambrose. "Shall we say cultural *agent provocateur*. In the old days of the Entente Cordiale, the English sang 'Au clair de la lune'. Now they chant the love song of J. Alfred Prufrock."

How beautiful she is, he was thinking. Those lovely caressing deep eyes. And the grace of her neck turning so slowly. Where was she from? He had better find out. Walter seemed badly smitten, and that might not be good.

"I wonder how Eliot sounds translated into French," said Hewitt. "It must be wonderfully amusing. 'Shall I part my hair behind? Do I dare to eat a peach?' Est-ce que j'ose manger une pêche? To which, of course, there is only one reply: 'Oui, la pêche qui est dans le jardin de ma tante.' "

The tempo of the party was getting more and more shrill. New comers came into the group, introductions were exchanged, meetings half promised, but the six of them seemed to stay together. "Let's have dinner afterwards," said Hewitt. "I know a very nice place that Mr Usher will like," and it was agreed. A peasant girl had succeeded in pressing yet another round of drinks on them, fluttering her eyelashes submissively to the men as she served them. Ambrose found himself talking to Mme Marot. They were standing near the french window opening into the garden, and they wandered on to the porch, holding their glasses. Once again, looking at a Washington garden in the sudden stillness, he felt the immediate personal beauty of the scene. It was chilly, and Mme Marot seemed to shiver.

"Winter is coming," she said, "but I love the autumn best of all. Yet I don't know why. It threatens something. Verlaine. . . ."

"Yes," said Ambrose, "I remember:

'*Moi je t'aime, âpre automne, et te préfère à tous*
        Les minois d'innocents, d'anges,
    Courtisane cruelle aux prunelles étranges'."

He was standing close to her, and her fragrance was heady. As he murmured the last words of the verse, some odd association struggled in his mind. *Prunelles étranges— sloe-eyed?* Was it Medea who was sloe-eyed? Euripides called her a "black-lowering woman". It was near enough. This woman, too, had a dark look that could mean anything: *Courtisane cruelle aux prunelles étranges.* . . . Their hands touched, accidentally perhaps, on the porch rail.

Walter appeared at the door. "Party's breaking up," he said. "Are you two coming?" Is he annoyed, thought Ambrose? Did she come out here on purpose to annoy him? These Scotsmen always seem very much under control, but she would know the passion there.

As they came back through the door, the chatter and smoke enfolded them again, and Pepita swooped down on them. The party seemed far from over.

"Where have you been, Mr Usher?" cried Pepita shrilly. "We have been looking for you everywhere. We all want to ask you all kinds of questions. What are you doing here? Are you going to stay in Washington long?"

Oddly enough, no one had asked him that yet, not even the group he was with. Was it fancy that they seemed to listen rather closely now?

"I am turning historian," he said. "You see before you the Official Historian of the Economic Warfare Missions. Of course, I shall make it all up. We would never dare tell the true story of what we did here during the war."

"Will you tell me privately," said Pepita. "Edward and I missed it all. It is heart-breaking. We were buried in Stockholm."

"I will tell *you* anything," said Ambrose, bowing low to her.

"Aren't you going to give any lectures while you are here?" asked Mrs Abbott-Hume. "I would go to hear you just for old times' sake."

31

"Yes," said Ambrose. "I have been asked to give a lecture at Yale. Perhaps I could repeat it in the Embassy Cafeteria series."

There was a large group around Ambrose now. He was being forced to perform, he thought wearily.

"What are you lecturing on?" somebody asked. "Is it on philosophy?"

"Oh dear no," said Ambrose. "My lectures on philosophy are incomprehensible, as this dear lady will tell you. She is one of my victims. No, I think I shall lecture on American literature. Professor Hinchelwood knows my views. He wants me to flutter a few dovecotes. I believe, you see, that Americans have at last rediscovered the secret of what literature is really about. Shakespeare had a brief glimmering. But, for the rest, it is all rather weak tea since the Ancient Greeks. It's the same in science, of course. Walter will tell you that."

"Ancient Greeks?" said a learned-looking American lady. "You mean Eugene O'Neill?"

"No," said Ambrose. "I was thinking more of Mickey Spillane."

"Mickey Spillane!" cried Pepita. "He's adorable. We devour him. But do you read him at Oxford?"

"We read very little else," said Ambrose sententiously. "We find the secret of human existence in his work. Not the superficial decencies, of course, but the real driving force."

"You're not serious," cried Pepita. "Mr Usher, you are pulling our legs. What has Spillane to do with the Ancient Greeks?"

"Why, everything, dear lady," he replied. "Open Euripides. The *Medea*. Just the same, isn't it? Passage after passage of the same stuff. Try it."

"Oh, what a lovely game," shrieked Pepita. "Let's play. Edward. Do we have a translation of . . . what is it? The *Medea*?"

"Certainly, dear," said Edward meekly. He went to his neatly arranged book-shelves, and was back instantly with a volume which he put into Ambrose's unwilling hands.

They were enjoying it. But why did he have to start all this? However, he turned the pages, and found a passage.

"Well, how is this for Spillane?" he asked. "You remember the scene, or should I say: the set-up? Medea sends her rival a beautiful wedding-robe and crown, an irresistible creation. But they're both impregnated with a secret chemical that bursts into flame. The poor girl puts the things on and struts around, and then she suddenly gets what's coming. Isn't this right out of Spillane?

'The delicate robes
Had fangs to gnaw her delicate tortured flesh . . .
The gore
Dripped from her head's crown flecked with blended fire.
The flesh-flakes melted from her bones . . .'

Shall I go on? I don't think I can bear to."

"You're right," cried Pepita delightedly. "It's exactly the same. Here's something in *My Gun is Quick*. Listen! 'It was almost nice lying there. No pain now, just pressures and the feel of tearing flesh.' Ugh! Isn't it delightful?"

The American lady was excited too. "I remember that story," she cried. "It ends with an old man burning, like in *Medea*. Can I have the book? I'm sure I can find it." She turned the pages feverishly. "Oh, here it is: 'His hair smoked, puffed up in a ball of flame and he screamed again. . . . He was still screaming when I pulled the trigger.'"

Oh dear, thought Ambrose miserably. Let this be a lesson to me. I'll have them gouging each other's eyes out in a minute for a thrill. He waved his hands to the guests with a rather helpless expression.

"Well, now I have no need to give the lecture, except to

33

find out why they write that way. Ah, if one only knew. We must talk about it one day," he said, turning to Mrs Beauchamp. "Are your parties always as blood-thirsty? I must go and eat a very rare steak. Thank you so much for such a pleasant return to Washington."

The others, too, had gone to collect their things. As Ambrose walked down the hall, he saw Hewitt on the telephone, his back to the room, speaking quietly into the mouthpiece. In his awkward, rather bumbling way, Ambrose passed quite closely to him, but didn't catch any words. Just one phrase emerged. Hewitt was listening rather impatiently it seemed, with a slight frown on his handsome brow, and Ambrose, as he passed, heard him say softly: "I can't, Billy, not to-night."

Outside the house, Walter took Mme Marot's arm and guided her into his car. Flantin made his apologies. He had some work to do. Ambrose, waiting for the others, felt a question turning in his mind as he watched Flantin saunter off on his own. Something that had been said—or not said? It was intriguing. He could cable.

But now Hewitt and Mrs Abbot-Hume joined him on the pavement, and they all got into the car. "It's a little French place called *Fantaisie*," said Hewitt, and gave Walter instructions. Ambrose settled back for a little rest.

IV

They had only gone a few yards when Ambrose suddenly sat up and exclaimed: "My brief-case! I always do it. I left it at the Beauchamps'. My precious documents. Fate of a nation! Terribly sorry."

Walter slowed down and made a U-turn back to the house. Ambrose, still muttering apologies, struggled out of the car and returned a few minutes later with the case under his arm, a small brown case with a lock. "The party's still

34

going great guns," he said. "I suppose they'll be there all evening. All too strenuous for an old Oxford don."

He settled back gratefully again, and the car started. The night's magic had become deeper. The car moved silently through almost empty streets, fine houses fronted by gracious gardens, tall trees everywhere swaying gently in the slight breeze, and, above everything, a scudding moon flying through broken clouds. Inside the car, no one spoke for a time. It was as if they had all been playing a public game at the party, and were now released into their private worlds. In the close intimacy of the car, with each private world enfolding each individual, they were all suddenly strangers.

No, not strangers, thought Ambrose. In the car together, they shared the intimacy and hostility of allies. Each was guarding some position, each had some private arrangements, some special interests, and they would nurse them along, jockeying for place, while they spent a happy evening together. But what *were* the private arrangements? He was puzzled.

Mrs Abbot-Hume—Jill, they all called her—seemed clear enough. If she was holding something back, it was in one dimension. Her husband was away, she had no children. Hewitt was damned attractive. Did one need to look further. And Hewitt? All one could say was that he was not what he seemed—or perhaps, seeing that this was so obvious, one should say that he *was* what he seemed. What was Walter's position? Walter was the only one he knew, yet—perhaps because he had come so far in understanding him—Walter seemed to present the most concrete question. What was the most important thing about him? That he looked for absolutes behind the scientific process. He treated nothing lightly. Everything was worth following through slowly, almost relentlessly, to see where it led. Well, that could lead anywhere, and Walter, he knew, would stick by his own logic. That was where his Scottish birthright came in.

Had it led him to Thérèse Marot, and if so, where was he? Ambrose still knew nothing about her. She was French— no, he didn't even know that. It was just that she seemed an associate of Flantin. She obviously knew Walter well. Did she know Hewitt too? He had had no chance of finding out during the party whether they had just met for the first time; but in the small world of official Washington it was unlikely.

If anyone reserved her position, it was she. That passive, graceful self-assurance was just the opposite of Walter's stubborn conviction. Walter wanted everything to be logically worked out. But she waited for the truth to come to her. The odd thing was that the more cerebral a man was, the more he would seek the crown in just such instinctive confirmation. He would find no assurance, no security, until his doubts and logic were healed, or rather annealed, in just such a woman's confidence or love.

No man really trusted his cerebral processes, thought Ambrose. I don't myself. One knows how far they take one. One can prove anything. And at the end, one wants some evidence from the outside. What is it? Plain common sense, or something higher?

He was back now in his Oxford room, arguing this with his colleagues. This was what was really wrong with the phenomenalist position. It was not that their arguments were weak. They were damn strong. They could meet every criticism, provided you started out from what seemed obviously true, namely that sense-data were all that any observer could experience. Every proposition could be translated into sense-data language, provided you were willing to accept that when you said, "There is a book in the next room," it was the same as saying, "If I were in the next room (or if someone else were) I (or whoever was there) would see a book." But it isn't the same, thought Ambrose. It is no substitute for a categorical statement to translate it into a hypothetical one. Common sense refutes it, and common sense is right, damn it.

The car had now turned out of the quiet, stately residential streets of high-class Washington into a brightly lit road on which neon lights—mostly advertising restaurants and bars—cut through the mild air. As they approached a large restaurant at one corner, the doors were suddenly flung open and a man was literally thrown out into the street. They all sat forward in the car to look as the man slowly rose to his feet.

"What fun!" cried Jill. "I've always wanted to see that done."

"Is it anyone from the Embassy?" asked Ambrose hopefully. "There have been so many changes in the staff that I wouldn't know."

"Oh no," said Hewitt. "That's Joe's Grill, and the poor man is just another Late and Herkimer victim."

"What's that?" asked Ambrose, as the car moved on.

"Well, this is my theory," said Hewitt. "You wouldn't have heard, but two New York journalists called Late and Herkimer have written a book called *Secrets of Washington*, giving all the low-down on vice and graft. They've done a series. One on New York and one on Chicago. They name names, you know. Tell you where you can get girls, and dope—anything you like. Highly successful—all for 25 cents. Now my theory is that Joe's Grill must be one of the places where you can always get a girl. Just go up to Joe, according to the book, and say out of the side of your mouth: 'Hey, Joe, what about to-night?' and it's all fixed. Well, just imagine the stream of out-of-town drummers, arriving at Washington station, buying their copy of the book, and taking a cab out to Joe's Grill. At first Joe is amused. Good for business. But now he's had enough. So

37

when a stranger walks over to him at the bar and gives him that look, he and his chucker-out bounce the man out even before he can speak. All goes to show. People shouldn't read books."

"Mr Hewitt," said Ambrose gravely, "are you attempting to mislead me?"

"Good gracious no, Mr Spillane," said Hewitt in mock horror.

"I see, I see," said Ambrose. "Touché. But you will admit, I *had* to say something at the party. They expected it."

"Of course, if these chaps really wanted some fun," said Hewitt, "they should have come to me. I could have guided them to the real underworld."

"Such as the *Fantaisie?*" asked Jill.

"Well, wait till you see it. You'll have to agree that it *looks* mysterious, even if it isn't."

It did indeed. As they came through the door, a pall of darkness met them, pierced only by faint candle-light from the tables. Leaving their things with a dimly-smiling hat-check girl, they were taken in charge by the owner, whom Hewitt greeted as Paul, and groped their way, following him, to a large table in the corner.

"Shakespeare was wrong," said Ambrose. "How near that little candle throws its light! So shines a good deed in a naughty world."

"Perhaps this isn't a naughty world," said Jill, "though it certainly looks like one."

They took a long time ordering their dinner, and it took a longer time being served. When food began to arrive, Ambrose fell on his *filets de boeuf à la Carlsbad* with a moue of pleasure, and the burgundy was excellent. Food was the great leveller. For the moment he could forget the strangeness of his translation here, the wild hop across the Atlantic the day before, the unreality of the events and relationships around him, the quest for something elusive that, by its very nature, might be undiscoverable. They had filled his glass again, and he sipped the wine gratefully.

"How ironic it is," he said, "that the poor British, who never drank French wines before the war—at least *en masse* —*have* to drink them, bankrupt as they are, in order to sell their exports."

"How is that?" asked Mme Marot.

"Oh, I wish you hadn't asked me that," said Ambrose. "An economist explained it to me once, but I've forgotten. I think the idea is that the British sell cars to the Swiss who sell watches to the Swedes who sell ore to the Belgians who sell coal to the French who sell wines to the English. Unless we bought the wine from the French we couldn't sell the cars to the Swiss. It's called liberalization of trade."

Mme Marot smiled.

"How are things really in England!" she asked, in her soft voice. "We can't understand what has happened. During the war, England was so strong spiritually. To us in the Résistance, you were a symbol of something great—the power of an idea. One needs a symbol of this kind to give life a meaning. And then after the war, it is as if a decadence had set in. Do you feel it in England?"

"Not decadence," said Ambrose. "Impotence. You know, 'si vieillesse pouvait' . . ."

"Isn't there any solution?" asked Jill. "We're so tired of hearing about austerity."

"Of course there's a solution," said Walter suddenly and angrily. He looked so fierce that Ambrose wondered if the burgundy had gone to his head. "We're still living in the nineteenth century, on a coal economy. We should drop everything to do with coal and work for the real civilian use of atomic power."

"Like the Russians?" asked Ambrose softly.

"Yes, like the Russians—*with* the Russians, with anybody

39

and everybody," said Walter. "Oh, I know the Russians have made the bomb, but they've done other things too, or they say they have. Why don't we try to find out? How can we tell where the genius is going to be born who will do for atomic energy what Edison did for electricity? It may be some young Czech, or an Albanian." He looked down into his glass. "I tell you, Ambrose, I sometimes wonder what I'm doing here."

There was an uncomfortable silence for a moment. Out of the corner of his eye Ambrose saw Mme Marot lay her hand gently, comfortingly, on Walter's. Hewitt broke the silence with a cheerful laugh.

"Well, what are we all doing here?" he asked. "We are all students in one form or another. You are pursuing scientific knowledge. Ambrose here is collecting material for his lectures at Oxford. . . ."

"And you?" asked Ambrose.

"Oh, I am exploring the vagaries of human nature," laughed Hewitt. "I try out various hypotheses in various fields, looking for a common denominator. Quite pleasant, you know." He looked across at Jill, quizzically. "Great thing is not to be dogmatic. Life will catch up with you when you're not looking, whatever theories you hold."

Walter was still in an earnest mood. "You have to be dogmatic sometimes," he said, "no matter what happens."

"Why, Walter," cried Hewitt. "Them's dangerous thoughts. We'll have the F.B.I. on you in five minutes. Didn't you know that old Paul here is a secret agent?"

"No jokes about the F.B.I.," said Ambrose. "You are talking about the organization I love. What fun we had with them during the war! Dear old Tim," and he began to chuckle.

"Come on, Ambrose," said Hewitt. "Tim who? Do you mean our own Tim Sargent?"

"Yes, indeed, Sir Timothy himself," said Ambrose. "The

big white chief. Of course, he was only a First Secretary
here at that time. You know, people underestimate the
F.B.I. I remember getting a call from Grover one day—he
was my contact down there—asking me to come down as
quickly as I could to interrogate a music-hall acrobat they'd
picked up in suspicious circumstances, who said he was
British and claimed repatriation. Well, I rushed down
there. . . ." he began to wheeze again.

"You mean it was Tim Sargent," said Hewitt.

"Just the F.B.I. sense of humour," said Ambrose. "You
know Tim's little idiosyncrasy"—he turned to the others in
explanation—"he doesn't sit *on* a chair to dictate to his
secretary. He likes to sit on the back of the chair, with his
feet on the seat. And then he tips the chair back ever so
gently and balances himself on the two back legs of the
chair. He can keep up the position for hours. Well, he'd gone
there on business, and when it was over he'd persuaded
Grover to try his little trick—and it wasn't easy. Then a
police sergeant down there tried it and another officer who
dropped in, and when I arrived it was quite hilarious. Tim
was swaying backwards and forwards in triumph, one
policeman was on his back on the floor, roaring with
laughter, Grover was teetering a bit, shouting: 'Look, Ma,
no hands!' They just wouldn't let me take Tim home."

"I suppose you have to be at war to enjoy things,"
said Hewitt. "The cold war doesn't seem half such good
fun."

"Tim was always fun," said Ambrose. "He's in Rangoon
now, you know. I had a note from him just before I left."
He fished in his pocket and pulled out some letters,
extracting one and showing it to Hewitt. "Hasn't he got a
lovely hand?"

Hewitt took it and glanced at the handwriting. "Yes, very
attractive. A Winchester hand."

"Ah no," said Ambrose. "Much more. This is the hand

4I

of a man who can balance himself on two legs of a chair." He put the letter back in his pocket reverently.

They went on chatting for a little while. Hewitt disappeared for a few minutes, apparently to the men's room, and when he got back, Ambrose wandered off himself for a minute. He glanced into the cloakroom, where the coats and his brief-case had been left—there was no attendant in evidence—and then he stood thoughtfully for a moment in the shadows of the dimly lit restaurant, looking back to the table where the others sat, their faces glowing in the gentle candle-light. Standing there, at one side of the window, he was suddenly aware, in some instinctive way, that he was not the only observer of the table. Someone was looking in from outside the restaurant—a dark, bony face, not casual but intent. The face was there, and then it was gone. Ambrose moved quickly to the door. There was no one there at all.

He strolled back to the company, and they all began to get up to go home. Paul fussed around them. They picked up their belongings and were ready. Walter was to take Mme Marot home. Hewitt said he would drop Ambrose in a taxi and take Jill back. They agreed it had been a nice evening. Back at the door of the Shoreham, where he was staying, Ambrose waved to the departing taxi and ascended wearily to his room.

It was just midnight, he noticed, but he was very tired. Obviously, he wasn't yet in form for his normal Washington time-table. And there were still a few more things to do before he could relax.

He picked up his little brown brief-case, and, opening it, looked at the papers he had left in there. He saw something, and shook his head sadly. "Oh dear," he muttered, "just as I feared." Taking out some green papers from the bag with great care, he laid them on the table before him. He unlocked his suit-case, and took out a little bottle marked *headache powder.* Shaking the grey contents on the pages, he blew off the powder and saw the prints appear, two sets he noticed, as he looked at them closely with a glass. There was only one more test. He took out the envelope from Tim, and extracted the letter, laying it on the table too, with great care. Again he scattered the powder, and examined the prints under the magnifying glass.

"Oh dear," he thought. "What a nuisance it all is. What a misery."

There was nothing more he could do that night. He undressed and put on his old Oxford dressing-gown. From the bottom of his suitcase he picked out a small grey book, the miniature score of the Rasumovsky Quartets. He turned to the third, in C, and settled hopefully in the armchair. By the time he reached the slow movement, he had forgotten all his troubles.

v

He was awakened the next morning by the whine of the telephone, and as he picked up the receiver, aroused from the deepest oblivion of sleep, he felt in some half-conscious way that it had been ringing and ringing for a long time. Miss Hope-Little, at the other end of the wire, confirmed this.

"The Ambassador has been trying to get you for hours, Mr Usher. It's terribly important. Can you go round to him immediately?"

Ambrose was still only half-awake. "Slowly, please, Miss Hope-Little. Let me come down to earth first. Where am I? What time is it? What does the word important mean to-day?"

"It's nine o'clock."

"Nine o'clock! Oh, Miss Hope-Little, unkind, unkind."

"You *must* wake up, Mr Usher. I'm still at home myself. The Ambassador has been chasing you since eight this morning. Are you all right?"

Sleep seemed now to be draining off Ambrose most pleasantly, as when one rises dripping from a hot bath. The fatigue and the sudden transition of the day before were gone, and he felt suddenly very much alive.

"All right? I never felt better, Miss Hope-Little.

'*The force that through the green fuse drives
the flower . . .*'"

"Please, Mr Usher. Can you go over to the Embassy? What shall I tell them?"

"Half an hour. But suggest—let the intimation fall—that I will be helpless without a cup of coffee."

When Ambrose was shown up to the Ambassador's room he found a sideboard filled with chafing dishes of porridge, scrambled eggs, kidneys and others things, flanked by steaming pots of coffee and tea. But the Ambassador was in a grim mood. This was not the speed at which junior officers reported to the quarter-deck.

"You'll have to come and stay here. I can't chase you all over Washington. We're in trouble. Have some eggs. Do you know what's going on?"

"It's a little early yet, but I'm beginning to get some ideas. Shall I tell you how it is developing?"

"Oh, you mean what we talked about yesterday. That's not the trouble I mean. No, our trouble is that we're going to be picketed, whatever that means."

"Picketed? By a union?"

"Right."

"Good gracious! What have we done? Where's the Labour Attaché?"

"He's on leave in England. They told me you knew about these things. Can you do anything?"

"I doubt it. But what's our crime. Whom have we been unfair to?"

"It's the Guy Fawkes party to-night. I had to have stands

44

built for the display pieces, so we got a firm in Washington to put them up. . . ."

"And they are not union men?"

"They *are* union men, but the wrong union, apparently. It's all a lot of damn nonsense, but they say it will cause trouble. I believe it's blackmail. I know how I'd handle this if it happened on my ship."

"Quite, quite. Yes, I see the difference. Have you been told what the particular argument is?"

"Yes. The firm that built the stands are naturally construction people, and the men belong to—let me see, here's the name—the Construction Workers International, A.F. of L. Does that make sense to you?"

"Yes, indeed, entirely proper. And the rival union?"

"The other union claims that since the stands are to be used for fireworks, it should have been built by them. They are—here it is—The International Association of Signmakers, Display Fashioners . . ."

Ambrose broke in: "Convention Constructors, and Background Artificers, C.I.O. Isn't that it?"

"That's it. You know them."

"I know their President. Giuseppe Cantolli, a gentle old man. . . ."

"Gentle! They are threatening to march people up and down outside the Embassy with placards. . . ."

"Yes, I can see it. PASS THIS EMBASSY BY! GET YOUR COCKTAILS ELSEWHERE! UNFAIR TO AMERICAN LABOUR! Yes, very awkward, very awkward."

"I've been on to the police, and they won't help. I thought America was supposed to be a capitalist country! What kind of capitalism is this? It could never happen in England, and we're supposed to be a lot of Socialists! Can you suggest anything?"

"I might," said Ambrose slowly. "But it means a long argument over Croce." And he sighed heavily.

"Croce? Who's that? Some other labour leader?"

"No, he's an Italian philosopher. Cantolli is a great student of his work, and he loves to argue about him. . . ."

"You mean this labour leader is a philosopher?"

"Yes, a very ardent one, though limited in vision, I think. America is a strange country, is it not?"

The Admiral rose to his feet, muttering something under his breath, and walked over to the window. He seemed to forget his troubles for a moment, looking out with pride at the high stands in the garden, covered with wires and fireworks, and then suddenly to realize that all his beautiful plans might be disturbed.

"Well, get going, man, if you can do something. Ring him up from here."

"Wouldn't you rather I took the call outside? It may take a long time. . . ."

"No, let me hear this. And, in the meantime, you can tell me about the other thing."

The telephone operator reached Mr Cantolli's office in New York within two minutes, and Ambrose, taking the phone, asked the secretary to say that it was Mr Ambrose Usher of Oxford. In a second, an excited yelp from the phone caused Ambrose to shift it quickly away from his ear and leave it open to the room, where it acted almost like a loudspeaker.

"Ambrogio! This is a-wonnerful! How come-a you in Washington? I wanna see you a-very quick."

"I've just got here, Giuseppe. Of course, I will come and see you. Did you read Brinley's article on the 'Estetica' in the *American Journal of Philosophy*?"

"Dat sonnovabitch Brinley! He no unnerstand-a da first ting of Croce. He mix up *fantasia* and *immaginnazione*. Issa natural he getta confused. Issa crime he call-a himself philosopher."

"Of course, Giuseppe, but there is something I want to ask you."

46

"About Croce?"

"No, I know about Croce. It's . . ."

"I no sure, Ambrogio. You no seem a-sound to me on intuition. Why you no accept da full meaning? Wassa difference? So you intuit your own desires, so you intuit your own state of awareness. . . ."

"Oh, it's fine if you can swallow Berkeley."

"Wassa wrong with Berkeley? Issa very good philosopher."

"Giuseppe! Listen! I'm not calling about Berkeley *or* Croce. It's the union."

"The union? Why you no say so? Wassa wrong?"

"Oh, nothing really, Giuseppe, but there's been a little mistake that you can put right easily."

"Sure, sure. What is it?"

"We made a mistake here at the British Embassy in building something, and your Washington local wants to picket us."

"Ah. Dat's really interesting! Local 602. Luigi Castellano. Good boy! On his toes!"

"But it's all wrong, Giuseppe. It's a national holiday for us. We can't change it now. Next year we will do it with *your* union."

"National holiday? What is-a dis? July 4th suddenly?"

"No, no. We have an annual holiday on November 5th, a special one. As a matter of fact, it's kind of in memory of an Italian called Guido Fawkes, who lived in England three hundred years ago. We set off fireworks and things. And your union wants to stop it."

"In memory of an Italian, and dat stupid Castellano wanna stop it? He's a-crazy! You leave-a him to me!"

"You'll call him off, then?"

"Of course. In honour of an Italian! He certainly is one crazy guy that Castellano. I'm a-going to come down to Washington next week to see what else he's a-doing stupid."

47

"Giuseppe, I didn't really say in *honour* of an Italian. Croce would say it goes back much further—to some prehistoric fire-festival in the autumn. . . ."

"Ah, you see, Croce he unnerstand history! All experience, that's history! But you say this Guido, he was an Italian and he live-a in England three hunnered years ago. . . ?"

"That's right."

"Dat's enough. You have your holiday."

"Well, thanks, Giuseppe. Next year . . ."

"Next year! I wanna see you before next year. I come down to Washington next week. No, I come-a to-morrow. You have dinner with me. I have a new way I explain-a Croce's theory of communication. Listen! Suppose me, I'm a-looking at a tree in my garden, and my cousin in Italy he write-a me a letter describing exactly his a-sensations when he look at a tree . . ."

"Giuseppe, I can't discuss it now, but we'll certainly dine when you come down here."

"Good, good."

"And the picket line?"

"Don't a-worry about that. Dat-a crazy Castellano! In honour of an Italian. . . ."

Ambrose replaced the receiver, and turned to find the Admiral looking at him quizzically from a deep chair in the corner.

"I'm going to take up Croce," said Throttle. "Have another cup of coffee."

Ambrose smiled and turned to the sideboard, but as he prepared to pour out his cup, there was a knock at the door, and the Admiral's secretary came in.

"Johnson is here," she said.

"Oh, ask him to come in," the Admiral said to her. "He's the head guard," he explained to Ambrose, "and he's helping me with the fireworks. As a matter of fact,

48

he's a most unusual chap for a guard. I can't quite understand . . ."

Johnson walked in at that moment. He was ruggedly built and tall, with a dark, bony, and rather gloomy face—an obvious Scot, one would say; and, when he spoke, he had indeed a strong Scottish burr.

"I've brought along the preselector you asked me to repair, sir," he said to the Ambassador. "It's working all right now."

"Oh, show it to me," said Throttle eagerly. "Yes, that's right," he said, depressing the five buttons in turn and watching them spring back. "Fine. Let's go down there and fit it to the second stand."

Ambrose was looking at Johnson with some surprise. There could be no mistake. He was the man who had been looking in at the *Fantaisie* so curiously and so intently the night before.

VI

Ambrose swallowed his coffee and followed the Ambassador and the guard into the garden. Once out there, Throttle seemed a transformed man, back on his quarter-deck, and busily directing the operation. Close to, the stands were like the masts of some old-time schooner, and the Embassy servants—their arms full of fireworks—were the crew, scrambling up ladders, hammering in supports, splicing wires, bending frames to the right angles.

Johnson was helping, in charge of the others, but the Admiral had no patience even with his first assistant when things were not to his liking.

"No, dammit, Johnson! That's not for the rockets! I want my malachite specials in there! Bring those startlers more forward. Can't you understand? Pack six of the square trouncers—the delayed action ones—in each of the legs!"

Ambrose, watching from the terrace, suddenly saw the

scene in its true colours. It was *Mutiny in the Bounty*—one of his favourite old movies—Charles Laughton and the young Clark Gable—

"Send those men aloft, Mr Christian! Are they all asleep foretop?"
"Aye aye sir! Look alive, you lazy caterpillars!"

Or perhaps it was more like *Moby Dick*, thought Ambrose, as he watched the Admiral stride back and forth in the garden below. Oh, for the sinister tap of the wooden leg on the clean-scrubbed deck! Yes, the mate here was Starbuck as well as Christian, fixing the fireworks skilfully, obediently, yet resentfully, his will elsewhere; and the Admiral was Ahab, no doubt about it, with his White Whale fireworks—"and on that ribbed and dented brow the footprints of his one unsleeping, ever-pacing thought. . . ."

No, that's not it, thought Ambrose. It's Moby Dick all right, but for some other reason. It's Moby Dick with all of us Ahabs. He seemed to recall some statement of the problem that echoed to him out of the book and made itself tangible in the sharp November air; but for the moment it eluded him.

A tall, fair young man came up to the Admiral. Ambrose asked the secretary standing near him on the terrace who it was; and when she told him the name, he stayed for a moment before wandering off. So this was Jill's husband, Commander Dennis Abbot-Hume. He was as pretty as Jill. The perfect pair! What a golden aura of wealth, birth, and beauty these two must have generated walking out of St George's at Hanover Square, where they were undoubtedly married; or maybe it was in some village church, with the Commander's tenants, his friends and servants from boyhood, lining the approaches to the old Norman doorway, full of simple happiness at the fairy-book romance. But now? Ambrose thought of the glance that had crossed between

Jill and Maurice Hewitt the night before, and looking at the husband wondered—as he had wondered so often before—if it wasn't all written down in a book somewhere before they had started. They were as pretty together as a couple of moths, but perhaps there was no fusing-point in all that fair elegance, and each was left with the dark force unrealized. For Dennis Abbot-Hume it seemed to show up in sudden frowns that twitched across his forehead. There was a kind of restlessness there. Jill, fluttering round Hewitt's flame, had perhaps felt some other pull, and found it irresistible.

Abbot-Hume had apparently reminded the Admiral of an appointment. He looked at his watch impatiently and responded to the call of duty. With a last barked round of orders to Johnson, he turned and went indoors.

Ambrose went down the terrace steps towards Abbot-Hume and introduced himself. Abbot-Hume smiled at him, yet somehow in a rather distraught way, keeping his eye all the time on Johnson. Ambrose had the curious impression that he had been disturbed and had wanted to get hold of Johnson at that moment, with the Admiral out of the way.

When he spoke, there was a stammer in his voice. It was rather charming, and he was certainly polite enough.

"S-so sorry I m-missed you yesterday," he said. "I had a j-job to do for the Admiral. Q-quite a slave-driver, you know."

"So I see, so I see," said Ambrose cheerfully, waving his hand towards the busy scene before them in the garden.

Abbot-Hume smiled, and this time Ambrose got a new impression. Was he laughing at him, aware that he was being "inspected" by the visitor from home? Or was the flickering look in his face something that could not be interpreted so easily? Whatever it was, it shook Ambrose a little and forced him into a remark that he had not really intended to make.

"Your wife, I discover, is a disciple of mine," he said. "She confessed it yesterday. You mustn't blame me, though, if she holds the wrong philosophical views."

"I'm not aware that she h-holds any," said Abbot-Hume. "But now I have been w-warned, I will watch out." He looked across the garden to the stands, and broke off. "I m-must get on," he said. He flickered a smile, and left.

VII

Ambrose stood looking after him. I got off on the wrong foot, somehow, he thought. Was it something in me, or is there something peculiar in him that hasn't come out?

It's as if things are pulling him in different ways. Surely being attaché to Throttle isn't all that obsessive? Is it the Hewitt business cutting across it? But what part of the Hewitt business?

Hewitt. Odd, he thought, how much comes back to him. He must find the key to that young man. Surely it was not buried too deep. That easy-going façade let one imagine quite a lot behind it. There was passion, argument, conviction, disillusion—but how to smoke them out?

Ambrose wandered over to the Annexe and up the two flights, above the Library, to Hewitt's room.

"Mr Hewitt's out," said a girl in the next room as she saw him poke his head through the door. "He won't be back until after lunch. Can I help you? I'm his secretary."

There were two desks in the girl's room and two names on the door. Ambrose examined the names with care.

"My name is Usher," he said, "and yours? Don't tell me. Let me guess. Let me see—Miss Crumleigh or Miss Turenne. Oh, this is most dangerous. Yet somehow—no, you cannot be Miss Crumleigh. How do you do, Miss—er—Turenne?"

The girl laughed. "Yes, I'm Betty Turenne. But why shouldn't I have been Miss Crumleigh?"

Ambrose looked at her. "Because I like French names," he said gravely. "I suppose you are a Canadian."

"Yes, from a little village near Quebec, St Guillaume."

"Not one of Fletcher's Follies? Does it still go on?"

She laughed again. "Yes. Do you know Mr Fletcher?"

Fletcher was a blameless Canadian Government official of Ottawa who made the arrangements for Canadian girls who wanted to get a job at the British Embassy in Washington. Naturally they had to be skilful and reliable; but somehow the ones that came through had a tendency to be attractive.

"Only through his good works," said Ambrose. "Please don't tell me that he is a nice simple *bon père de famille*. I have always envisaged him as Adolphe Menjou, stroking a devilish moustache, and with a come-hither look in his eye penetrating to the remotest corners of Saskatchewan."

Miss Turenne was young, slight, and in colouring something of a red-head. Her features were not beautiful in a formal sense, but she had green-flecked eyes, and her whole being exuded something graceful and feminine. It seemed to be in the way she breathed and stood; and it made it easy for a man to talk to her.

"A cousin of mine, Marguerite Fougères, worked here during the war when you were here, Mr Usher. She has often told me about you. Do you remember her?"

"Yes, indeed. Miss Fougères. Charming girl. Worked in the Commercial Department. Yes, I remember her well. Where is she now?"

A shadow seemed to cross Miss Turenne's face. "She's married, and is living in Trois Rivières."

"Producing lots of children, no doubt."

"Yes, she has four already. She married an old school friend. . . ."

"And then, Washington, with all its excitement, ceased to exist."

She said slowly after him: "Yes, ceased to exist."

There was a slight pause. Ambrose felt that a certain sadness had come into her voice. Something deep had been stirred without her wishing to show it. How vulnerable we all are, he thought. A word of friendship, and our defences are down.

"Have you been here long?" he asked.

"Two years. And I have enjoyed it."

"St Guillaume and Washington," said Ambrose romantically. "What a wonderful life."

She smiled, but sadly. "Well, I *have* seen something else," she said. "I spent a year in Toronto, on my course."

Ambrose pulled a face. "Toronto! Not quite the same thing. Breaks the spell. You prefer Washington, I think."

"Oh yes, I love Washington."

"But one day—back to St Guillaume?" Ambrose asked softly. "Or will you never go back?"

"No, I'll never go back. But one day, one has to make a decision. There are changes. . . ."

It was odd to talk this way at such short acquaintance. Yet there was no forcing of confidence. A word of his had released something that troubled her, and he was touched at the naturalness of it all.

"Well, I must go," he said, and moved to the door with a friendly wave of his hand. "Tell Mr Hewitt that I visited him—*and found him out.*" He said the last words with mock seriousness, and left.

Walking slowly downstairs, he almost bumped into the guard Johnson on his way up. He stood aside to let Ambrose pass, but despite this polite gesture, he still looked as surly as before. Odd how he kept bumping into him. Looking up the stairs for a moment, he saw that Johnson seemed to have gone into Hewitt's room. Could this mean anything?

He resumed his way downstairs. As he passed the Library

door, the phrase that Miss Turenne had used was still in his head: *One has to make decisions.* How well it fitted his mood, the feeling that had pursued him since he had arrived. At some point a decision had to be taken—a deliberate act in which one took full part—not a careless act, not a conditioned act, but an act of choice. . . .

He felt himself groping for some words that he knew to express it. Once again it was *Moby Dick* that came to mind, as it had earlier while he watched the Admiral. He wandered into the Library to see if there was a copy on the shelves. There was; and opening the book almost at random, he found the words:

> All visible objects, man, are but as pasteboard masks. But in each event—in the living act, the undoubted deed —there, some unknown but still reasoning thing puts forth the mouldings of its features from behind the unreasoning mask. If man will strike, strike through the mask! How can the prisoner reach outside except by thrusting through the wall.

Yes, that's it, said Ambrose to himself. Somehow it helps to see the words in print. But who was it about? It was Miss Turenne who had started it with her sad little remark, but it wasn't really her. She was just being the Greek Chorus— and what a nice little chorus girl she was. . . .

Well, who then? Hewitt? Ambrose stopped for a moment to put his mind to it. Was this Hewitt? Yes, there was a secret life that he knew about, but he couldn't sense any struggle in it. When you met that gay nonchalance, you knew that he took life as he found it—enjoyed anything that lay before him—the mysteries and the fun—he carried it all off.

Then who was it about? Himself, perhaps? Come, come, he muttered as he wandered back to his room. Let's not get pretentious. . . .

Miss Hope-Little was waiting to receive him, guarding the red dispatch-box, and stroking a purring Palmerston. But she looked troubled.

"I've done your notes, Mr Usher," she said. "Will you need me now? I want to take Palmerston to the vet. I think he's been hurt."

"No, no, please take him, Miss Hope-Little." Ambrose bent down concernedly over their friend. "What has happened?"

"He seems to have a sore spot here, in his ribs," Her mouth set in a grim line. "I think someone has kicked him, and I think I know who did it."

"Oh, surely not," said Ambrose. "Why should any-one . . ."

"It's Johnson," she said.

"The guard?"

"Yes. I'm certain it's him. He hates Palmerston. Once Palmerston jumped on his shoulder and scratched him, and he threw him down, and Palmerston is always terrified when he is near. If he's hurt Palmerston, I'll . . ."

Her gaunt hands tightened, and her voice trembled. How very odd, thought Ambrose, looking at her with much sympathy as she gently picked up the soft creature and set out for the vet.

Left alone, he glanced through the papers in the dispatch-box, but found little to interest him. How willingly one shuffles off all this mumbo-jumbo, he thought—the démarche by Ankara, the fishing squabble off Heligoland, tariff concessions to Burma. . . . He flipped the papers over, but a name caught his eye, and he looked back at one of the papers. Funny coincidence. The telegram was about Professor Pulsifer, whom Flantin had mentioned to him the previous night. It was a cypher telegram, discussing arrangements to be made with Peru for an archaeological expedition going out there under Pulsifer to dig in the mountains in the south, where he thought there might be some undiscovered Inca remains. But why in cypher? Oh, yes, there was a cross-reference in it to a previous Secret telegram. Seemed a bit funny, but that's the way things always were. Hordes of clerks longing to classify quite un-secret papers.

He locked the dispatch-box and called for the messenger to take it away. Lying on his desk were the notes that Miss Hope-Little had typed out for the review of the existentialism book. He picked one piece of paper up—a rather long quote he wanted to use—and smiled to himself as he read it. The last sentence summed it up:

"Alors, d'un seul mouvement, ma volonté, fondant le contenu de l'acte, se légitime par lui."

Was he back again with *Moby Dick?* It might seem so, but what a difference there really was. Yes, it was a good point. He would use it in the review.

The real and the fictitious self. He felt almost inclined to sit down and start writing. But he was hungry. It was time he had some lunch. He slipped the notes into his pocket.

VIII

This was a day, he thought, to go off and lunch quietly by himself, and he picked up the telephone book to see if the little Greek restaurant in Georgetown that they had frequented in the old days was still in existence. It was. In ten minutes a cab had dropped him at the door. Entering, he saw Walter Scott and Mme Marot lunching tête-à-tête in a corner. Of course, he thought wryly. It had been a favourite of Walter's too. But it was too late to slip out: they had seen him. He joined them.

"How did you track us down?" asked Walter. "Your old

friends in the F.B.I. no doubt." He was unquestionably disconcerted, as one is on these occasions.

"Naturally," said Ambrose. "I needed your help, so I called them in to find you. They are super-efficient when anything less than the safety of the nation is at stake."

Mme Marot smiled at him quietly. "Why do you need our help?"

"I need to come down to earth," said Ambrose. "The more I deal with practical things, the more I am bothered by philosophical problems. Teaching at Oxford seems as practical as a factory compared with life at the Embassy."

"Well," said Walter, "describe your problem."

"Ah, if I could do that I should have the answer," said Ambrose, sipping gratefully at the cocktail that Xenophon had put before him. "Perhaps it's the problem of action and passion. Does one have to choose between them?"

"But passion *is* action," said Walter. "Do you mean action and passivity?"

"No," said Ambrose. "I mean 'action' as a deliberate external act which is aimed at rearranging the shape of things around you; and 'passion' as an internal state in which you are content to seize the meaning of what is going on, or should I say try to read some meaning into it—to let it make sense for you."

"I don't like your definition of passion," said Walter. "It sounds defeatist to me. You are content to examine what is around you. Don't we want to *change* the world, to make it a better place, to get rid of the evils around us?"

"Ah, Walter," said Ambrose. "Let me ask, in my best Socratic fashion, which of these objectives you attach the greater importance to, the positive one—'to make it a better place', or the negative—'to get rid of evils'?"

"I think I start with the second."

"Because you think you know what is evil and aren't sure what is good?"

"No, you tackle the evil, and when you've squelched it, you've created some good."

"Then to pursue the matter further, my dear Scoton, does the good seem to lie in a state of affairs you have created—which might, for example, be the achievement of something negative, like ridding a bed of fleas—or in your own satisfaction at having exercised your talent in a manner which you feel intuitively to be good?"

"I must say that it is the second, my dear Socrates."

"Then, may I ask, dear Scoton, whether you can ascribe some objective merit to an act as such, or whether you are not left with your own self-assessment—which I defined as passion—as the criterion of virtue?"

At this point, Xenophon's boy brought some food. Ambrose leaned towards Mme Marot as the food was served, and said with mock urgency, stroking his beard: "Please save me, Madame, before Walter demolishes my argument."

She smiled back at him, but Ambrose was not happy about the smile. He thought he saw a hard look in the corner of her eyes. He remembered his feeling of the night before—the "black-lowering" look of Medea which he had sensed as they stood looking out over the Beauchamp's garden.

"Are you sure that you want to be saved?" she said. "I have an idea that you shy away from solutions. You prefer the joys of uncertainty."

"Oh dear," Ambrose murmured. "You read my mind too well. Is it *all* solutions, I wonder, or just those we've been offered."

"Surely, Ambrose," said Walter, "you don't deny that reason, advanced far enough, can remove all doubts and get rid of the hatreds and inequalities that cause all the conflicts in the world to-day? Shouldn't we just work for that at any cost?"

"At any cost? That's my problem, I'm afraid, as this wise

lady sees so clearly. There *are* solutions that remove doubts, but they seem to remove other things too. I like reason to beckon me forward—the old goddess, you know, in a long white robe—saying: 'It's an awfully long road, and I don't know where it leads!' I'm suspicious when she says that we've arrived. I'm afraid she'll leave me—and I like her."

"You're afraid of the twentieth century," said Mme Marot.

"I'm afraid of some things in it," he sighed, bending over his stuffed vine-leaves.

"Do you want everything to stop where we are?" asked Walter.

"Just the opposite. I want to feel change in the air. I'm afraid that people are being conditioned to settle for too many ready-made solutions. Everything is becoming institutionalized:—even words—like 'institutionalized'."

"Only in America," said Walter. "Even science here has stopped being free enquiry. Everything now has to serve the great American myth. They talk about free enterprise, free enquiry, free beliefs—but it's all marshalled to defend big business. God, it makes you sick!"

"What do *you* think?" said Ambrose to Mme Marot. "Do you think America can be saved from itself?"

She shrugged her shoulders slightly, saying nothing. Ambrose felt a curious tension between her and himself, as if Walter were a stake they were playing for.

"You've been away too long, Walter," said Ambrose. "You think that mythology is peculiar to America. Every country has a mythology."

"Well, what is one supposed to do," said Walter. "Fight against it?"

"Not in itself," said Ambrose. "We live on myth. But I suppose we ought to make sure that it doesn't swallow up some of the old personal virtues. We may be pushed back to them."

"What do you call the personal virtues?" asked Mme Marot.

"Oh, the most old-fashioned ones that you can name. Things like patience, loyalty. . . ."

"I don't know," said Walter, looking down at the bread he was crumbling in his hand. "Perhaps you can take a nice relative attitude to everything, but it seems to me to be much worse here. It seems actually dangerous."

"Do you think so?" asked Ambrose. "Tell me some country whose citizens don't feel that their peculiar history and talents and situation have entitled them to some special place in the sun—that somebody else is trying to take away."

"Oh, I know," said Walter, "I'll never convince a historian about absolutes. But really, if you knew the scale of it here, the folklore that people are fed, the imaginary personalities that are created, the events that are blown up to the size of Greek legends. Someone ought to write a book on the American myth."

"A new Bulfinch. Do you know Bulfinch? There's a lovely passage on the American myth in him, as it happens?"

"What's Bulfinch?" asked Walter.

"Oh, it's the text they all use here on the legends of the ancient world. But there's a wonderful bit on America—I suppose it's unconscious—in a passage where he is discussing the Greek view of Elysium. Homer, he says, described Elysium as a happy land in the West where there is neither snow, nor cold, nor rain, and where everything is fanned by the delightful breezes of Zephyrus. Then he—that's Bulfinch—adds something like this: 'This happy land,' he says, 'may have been wholly imaginary. But it may possibly have sprung from the reports of some storm-driven mariners who had caught a glimpse of the coast of America.'"

"Good for Bulfinch," said Walter. "I couldn't have put it better myself."

On this pleasant note, lunch ended. Xenophon came up

and was blessed in appropriate terms. "We shall see you at our party to-night, no doubt," said Ambrose to Mme Marot as she prepared to leave.

"Ah yes, the Guy Fawkes party. What is it really for?"

"Oh, don't you know our rhyme," said Ambrose.

> *"Please to remember,*
> *The Fifth of November,*
> *Gunpowder, treason and plot."*

Mme Marot still seemed a little bewildered. "Gunpowder, treason and plot," she repeated slowly. "Seems a little ominous, doesn't it?" But she smiled happily at both of them as a cab came and she went off. Ambrose and Walter took another cab back to the Embassy.

There was a slight constraint for a moment when they settled back for the short journey, but then they both smiled at each other.

"Well?" said Walter.

"Well is right," said Ambrose. "As Mickey Spillane would say: Start talking!"

Walter lit a cigarette, and blew out a cloud of smoke before he spoke. "She is an attaché at the French Embassy," he said. "She deals with colonial affairs, or helps the man who does. She is a widow. She and her husband were both in the French Résistance, and he was caught and shot." He paused, and then added, "I like her."

Ambrose nodded. Then he said: "Have you known her long?"

"Yes, quite a time," said Walter, but he didn't seem to want to say more, and they finished the ride in silence.

IX

There was much to do that afternoon. But throughout it all Mme Marot's words kept coming back to Ambrose. Yes it *was* ominous. Once you heard the words that way, they could never sound innocent again.

He sat in his room reading reports and papers for a time, and then walked around talking to various people. It ended up, as it had to, in a long talk with Sir Hugh Eldridge, the Minister. Hugh had been a First Secretary at Washington in the early part of the war, but had risen since then with phenomenal speed. Now he was the professional in charge of everything. But he was still just as calm and unruffled in discussing these things as he would have been discussing exports—or Plato.

Finally Ambrose had a brief word with the Ambassador. He found him radiant with confidence. Nothing can go wrong, he told Ambrose. Everything has been thought of. Everything? Should one tempt fate with such confidence? This sounded really ominous.

X

At exactly 8.30 p.m. the two policemen on duty at the front entrance swung open the gates, and the cars began to arrive. Within a few minutes there was a steady line filling the drive to the covered entrance of the Embassy, and the guests were moving in a solid phalanx first towards the Admiral, resplendent in full-dress uniform, and then towards the huge open windows and the garden beyond.

It was a glorious evening. A slight warm wind ruffled the gaunt trees and stirred the myriad leaves underfoot. Flood-lights threw magic beams to the sky and turned the woods beyond into faery dells. In the grand reception room, hung with glittering chandeliers and flanked by the massive portraits of England's kings, the diplomats and their ladies examined each other, as they did at every Washington party, with frank recognition of their unique station in the chosen circle; and if there might have been, also, the usual note of suspicion and boredom, it seemed to be blown away this time by the pleasing tinkle of champagne glasses and the feeling that this was not an official party but a bit of fun.

In particular, there was something about the Admiral and his glittering medals that released a note of gaiety. No austerity for him: champagne and pretty ladies—and fireworks.

When a party starts off easily and happily in this way, without the shackles of duty to bind it too closely, it can generate a heady feeling of excitement.

Ambrose was aware of it as he walked through the french window, holding his champagne glass and chatting cheerfully to the protocol man, Matthews, whom he found standing, calm and immaculate, outside.

"Hampstead Heath on Bank Holiday, eh?" said Ambrose. "I miss the coconut shies, but apart from that . . ."

Matthews, who normally liked Embassy life to flow along accustomed channels, may perhaps have felt that the occasion was a little unusual. But he was incapable of an unkind remark. "God bless the Navy," he murmured to Ambrose. "What would we do without them?"

And now the talk was mounting in volume as the still-arriving guests poured out into the garden. All kinds of languages, and all kinds of faces to go with them, burgeoned into the night, as if performing in some crude but amusing school play—the turbaned Arabs, the jodhpured Indians, the bearded Sikhs, the slender French, the blond Scandinavians, the dangerous Latin-Americans, the safe New Zealanders.

"There's Lischev, the Russian Ambassador," said Matthews, pointing to a stocky man standing stiffly a few feet away and holding a frigid and watchful conversation with two very obvious satellites. "Do you know him?"

"No, I don't," said Ambrose, examining him with some

interest. "Who's the gent with the aureole? He doesn't seem very happy either."

Matthews was swept away before he could answer, and at that moment Ambrose heard a shriek behind him that made him turn round in startled fright. Pepita had just come through.

"Why, Mr Usher!" she cried. "How nice to see you again! Isn't it *fun*? Edward says it's all too wasteful, but he doesn't understand these things, do you, darling?"

Edward, behind her, cleared his throat a little nervously, but Pepita had seized Ambrose's arm and was pouring out more confidence in her penetrating falsetto.

"Do look at Paretscu, the Rumanian Minister, talking to Lischev! Don't you think he looks worried? They say he's going to bolt any day now."

"All Rumanians look worried," Ambrose assured her. "It comes from living so close to the Hungarians. Tell me. Do you know who that man is over there with the mop of wild hair?"

"Oh yes, that's Baron Ilano, he's on a mission from the Argentine. Isn't his hair cute? They call him *The Dervish* in the Argentine. We knew him well when we were at Buenos Aires. I'm surprised he's here, when he's come to Washington just to attack us."

Edward joined in pompously. "My dear Pepita! These feuds don't affect diplomatic receptions. It's their claim over the Falkland Islands," he explained to Ambrose. "Their Ambassador's gone back, and they've sent Ilano here on a special mission to get Washington support against us at the United Nations. And they've just sent us another threatening note."

"Oh dear," said Ambrose. "Is that still going on? I thought we'd given them the islands in exchange for a few shipments of meat."

"Oh no, never. We've just landed a party of Marines on

65

the islands, and they're threatening to bomb us if we don't remove them."

"Vincento!" Pepita had spotted a friend and dashed off to greet him in fluent Italian. "Why didn't you come to my party yesterday? You do not love me any more! Were you out with that Dutch girl again? She is not for you. Dutch girls have no temperament, have they?"

Ambrose moved on gratefully, stopping here and there to greet acquaintances or be introduced. Everybody was here. It was impossible to be surprised. But suddenly he caught a glimpse of Walter in close conversation with a strange-looking man, and whistled to himself softly. Sanati! What was *he* doing here? It was hard to think of him except as in the Physics Institute in Rome. What a strange man he was. That great, bald, bony head, that peculiar croaking voice, those piercing eyes—intellect incarnate, as you would expect from a really top-flight physicist—yes, but intellect with a question mark, intellect not quite human. Where did he stand now? Probably where he stood in those Rome days. The political winds had changed, but Sanati was not a type to tack very readily. . . .

For no reason that he could think of, he suddenly wondered if Mme Marot was there, and just then he saw her, reserved and distant as usual.

He moved across to her. "I enjoyed our lunch," he said.

"Yes," she replied, "it was pleasant."

He found himself becoming apologetic. "Too much talk, perhaps? We pursue the truth. . . ."

She looked at him very directly, as if she had decided to say something serious. "I think you pursue things too hard." What did she mean? He could not understand her tone. But she had turned round to greet someone else, and he felt dismissed.

There was a feeling now that the preliminaries were ending. An air of expectancy was growing. Ambrose glanced at his watch and saw that it was 9.30. The time had come.

At that moment, the lights in the house were dimmed, and all the main flood-lights in the garden lowered. In the half-gloom, a hush settled over the audience, and then polite applause broke out as spotlights suddenly picked out the Admiral, resplendent in his gold braid and medals, standing on a small platform near the fireworks. There was a microphone beside him, and he was clearly preparing to speak.

Ambrose heard a Frenchman near by mutter to his neighbour: "Cet Anglais a un aplomb étonnant! Chercher à obtenir les bonnes grâces des Américains par un tel spectacle, c'est un peu fort!"

"Vraiment, c'est contre tout protocole!" agreed the other. "Il nous faudrait en appeler au State Department."

"Your Excellencies, Ladies and Gentlemen," began the Admiral. "I will not make a speech, but I want to welcome you to our little party. As you know, the English are supposed to be a very dull race"—he paused to allow a little laughter to ripple round—"unlike our neighbours across the Channel"—the laughter was a little more sustained—"but on Guy Fawkes Day we let off steam a little, as our neighbours do on the 14th of July."

"Lui de comparer ceci au Quatorze Juillet," hissed the Frenchman, "c'est inadmissible!"

"C'est un affront!" agreed his companion. "Il faut bien en appeler au State Department."

The mild laughter subsided, and the Admiral proceeded. "On Guy Fawkes Day, we usually burn a guy—a stuffed guy of course"—more laughter—"but I thought that even that might be too primitive. To-night we shall do it in fireworks. I think we all like fireworks—perhaps we are still children at heart."

"Hypocrisie typique!" muttered the Frenchman. "Les Anglais prennent toujours l'air tellement innocent."

67

"Qui pensent-ils tromper?" said the other. "Je vous l'ai déjà dit, c'est un complot."

"The origins of this festival," continued the Admiral, "are buried in history. It goes way back beyond the recorded events which started it. Yet we can always find ways of re-interpreting the old legends in modern form, as I try to show in one of the set pieces here to-night."

"Voilà!" said the Frenchman. "Un complot politique!"

"I cannot guarantee that everything will go off as arranged," said the Admiral, "because I made the fireworks myself." A round of applause greeted this. "But let us hope for the best. Thank you."

The spotlights were abruptly switched off, and a few flashlights flickered in the darkness where the technicians were clearly preparing for the great moment. Ambrose had moved away from the Frenchmen and found himself standing behind Lischev. With the applause and the feeling of expectancy in the air, some lines of *Eugen Onegin* came into his head and he began to recite them softly in Russian:

"Theatre's packed—boxes resplendent—pit and stalls one big buzz—impatiently the gallery applauds . . ."

Lischev turned round to this voice from the semi-darkness. Unconsciously, almost, he continued the lines himself:

"and rustling the curtain swiftly rises."

He looked at Ambrose wonderingly. To hear Pushkin so far from home seemed to move him strangely. Was it the beard too? He looked as though he might have said more, when suddenly, with an almost human shriek of ecstasy, a mass of rockets—perhaps twelve or more—launched themselves into the air with one swoop from apparently every corner of the garden. It was an almost unbearable moment while everyone waited for the climactic height to be reached, then, all together, the sky was filled with myriads of coloured stars, and a great sigh of pleasure went up from the audience. Again a whoosh of rockets, and again the glorious release of dazzling light, this time with each rocket exploding a second time and a third as it floated slowly to earth. There was a pause, and then the rockets went up again, not silently this time but with a spluttering of light and fire in every direction. Great globules of light hung in the air and then seemed to raise themselves with inner energy to further soaring heights of grace and light before exploding into all the colours and stars that Heaven could dream of. They fell slowly to earth, and as they fell, the people below, their up-turned faces lit with the glowing warmth of the stars, broke spontaneously into applause.

There was a pause, and everyone turned to his neighbour to express his pleasure. Ambrose looked for Lischev, but he had disappeared. The flashlights were flickering near one of the big stands. Ah, here comes one of the set pieces, thought Ambrose. The Admiral was apparently supervising the last touches himself, and something was not quite right. They suddenly heard his voice barking out: "No, dammit, it's that switch on the left." The microphone was still alive, and he had spoken too near it. There was a delighted giggle of laughter in the audience, and then silence as the display began.

First, along the bottom of the huge stand, came long wavy lines of blue light. At first the audience was puzzled, and then all whispered at once: the sea. In the right-hand corner of the stand, a squat yellow shape began to appear, with white flashes bursting from it, and a tall tower becoming prominent: a submarine, they all saw. The yellow shape on the blue sea made a pretty picture. But now, in the centre and to the left of the stand a great green shape began to define itself—the hull and masts grew, and with the un-ceasing rattle of bangs and glorious red flashes the picture became unmistakable: a destroyer, with her guns raking the submarine. The yellow shape began to disintegrate, and suddenly it exploded with enormous flashes of white light rising and sinking into the blue. It all became clear to Ambrose. Of course, he thought, it's his V.C. episode, when the Falkland rammed the German submarine. . . . *"The Falkland?"* He suddenly exclaimed to himself. "Oh no!"

Oh yes. Remorselessly, the letters began to form on the green hull, not, of course, in the traditional spot, which would have been too small, but in red letters of fire right across the ship. FALKLAND. And then at the top left of the stand, the Union Jack began to wave in triumph. In bright, dazzling colour, the proud lines formed amid a thousand splutters and sparkles. The ship faded, and in a final burst of magic, the whole picture was released into a splurge of rockets, while the bold word and the flag remained as the Admiral's signature. The display died away, and there was a round of applause, which died away too. In the silence they all heard the human explosion from Baron Ilano. He was storming his way to the exit, his wild hair bristling with anger. "We will see," he was crying, "we will see if the Argentine Republic can be treated this way."

The only person oblivious to the incident was, apparently, the Admiral, who was delighted that everything had gone off so well, and now came to the microphone again. "Thank you, ladies and gentlemen," he said. "We now come to the final set piece in which I have used some experimental fireworks for which I crave your indulgence."

Again there was a burst of rockets and crackers, and then a very familiar shape began to trace itself at the left side of the stand in an outline of fire—Big Ben—clearly the Admiral's projection of the Houses of Parliament. As the clock appeared at the top, in beautifully clear red lines, there was a burst of clapping. Clearly the audience bore no grudge against the Admiral for having asserted himself on the Falkland Islands, even if the Argentine Republic did. Big Ben died away, and then in the centre of the stand, a monstrous figure began to emerge, fat legs, a fat body, fat outstretched arms, and then a great turnip head in green— Guy Fawkes himself. Below him, dazzling red fountains of light began to shoot out in rapid firing excitement, rising higher and higher—he was going to burn. It was delightful. But now the fire works began to lose a little of their clarity. The outstretched arms began to disintegrate in long white wiry puffs. And then the turnip head began to lose shape too. A great aureole seemed to ascend from the crown of the head. The effect was unmistakable. A great cry went up from the audience: Ilano! The flaming hair rose higher and higher. Above the cries came Pepita's shriek: "The Dervish!" Nothing now could be saved from the wreck. The guests dissolved helplessly into laughter, the tears streaming down their cheeks as the hair rose higher and higher and all the fireworks spluttered and sparkled into a mad confusion. This was Guy Fawkes, and he had undoubtedly burned.

The show was over. The floodlights were switched on, and the acrid air was seen to billow with smoke. Everything seemed suddenly flat and stale. The white light was cold and harsh after the myriad colours and sparkles they had seen. Gone was the magic of strontium sulphate and barium chloride—faded now the driving excitement of the Admiral's enthusiasm. The fireworks themselves had not quite given up hope. A few still spluttered ineffectually, and a couple of stray "salutes" rattled off, but nobody cared. The show was over.

It was time to go, and the guests began to move over to the Admiral to pay their respects. Eldridge walked up to the stand next to the Admiral, and Lischev was close by. Ambrose strolled across, waving to Mme Marot and Jill

Abbot-Hume, who were standing in a group behind. The three of them were talking together when an Embassy guard appeared on the fringe of the crowd, and pushed his way straight through to the Admiral. Ambrose saw, almost without surprise, that it was Johnson. The Admiral had turned to the guard impatiently. "What is it?"

"Sorry, sir," said Johnson. "There's been an accident. Someone's been killed."

A cold silence fell on the circle. Looking swiftly at the faces of the two women with him, Ambrose saw frozen horror there. He looked at Lischev and saw the Russian looking back at him—an inscrutable look.

"Who is it?" asked the Admiral sharply.

"It's Mr Hewitt, sir," said the guard. "We've just found him shot dead in the trees behind the Annex."

The Admiral stood motionless, then turned to Eldridge and whispered something urgently.

There was a sudden hissing sound. A rocket, delayed by a slow-burning fuse, shot into the air, and as it burst, the red glow of its stars seemed to tell of some agony unknown.

TWO

HAMLET: *. . . it might be the pate of a politician which this ass now o'er-reaches: one that would circumvent God, might it not?*

HORATIO: *It might, my Lord.*

HAMLET: *Or of a courtier, which could say, Good-morrow sweet Lord: how dost thou, good Lord? This might be my Lord such-a-one, that prais'd my Lord such-a-one's horse, when he meant to beg it; might it not?*

HORATIO: *Ay, my Lord.*

I

WHEN the call came through to his home, Captain Shaughnessy, of the Washington Homicide Squad, was watching *Crime Chief* on television, and he grumbled mightily when his wife called him to the phone. *Crime Chief* was not by any means the most popular police programme on TV; it had done little more than treble the sale of GLINT, the new shampoo, since it first came on the air a few months earlier; but at least it provided him, as all police programmes did, with the satisfying if somewhat surrealist experience of watching a crime being committed, discovered, investigated, and solved within thirty minutes, or, more correctly, allowing for the commercials, twenty-two minutes. It was somehow good for the soul of a policeman to see the police machine move at such speed. No sooner was the body on the floor than the siren was wailing through the busy streets. A girl-friend had only to be hinted at by the slovenly land-lady when a second later—or rather four minutes later, after the commercial—she was back at Headquarters in a low-cut gown, having been picked up singing the blues in a smoke-laden café-dive, and was giving out in her surly way the key information that would send a man to the chair, as sure as fate, within eleven and a half minutes. Yes, it was good for the soul of a policeman.

He was particularly sore to-night because it was Thursday, and it was barely an hour since he had been watching *Dragnet*. He was always sore for an hour or so, between 9.30 and 10.30 on Thursday nights, after *Dragnet* had closed. How was it that the police captain on *Dragnet* had a sergeant like Joe Friday, while *he* had to put up with people like Ferguson, Goldberg, and Reddin? With a man like Friday to call on, nothing could go wrong. Calm, tireless, ingenious, yet respectful—no wonder things went so smoothly. Why had *his* sergeants to be so unsatisfying? One was too smart, one too dumb, one was too soft, another too much of a bully. Sergeant Friday never seemed to worry about promotion. *His* men seemed to think of nothing else. It was most annoying.

As he barked "Yeah, what is it?" into the phone, he was all set to curse everyone for disturbing him, but when he heard the message his soreness vanished and a tone of something like satisfaction showed in his voice.

"At the British Embassy?" he growled, the Irish burr coming out rather strongly. "You don't say. I'll be there in ten minutes."

He was ringing off, when he suddenly called back the desk officer, "Who's going out for the Squad? . . . Oh, Goldberg. O.K. Has he gone yet? Let me speak to him."

Goldberg was on the phone in a second. "Oh, Mort," said Shaughnessy, "we'd better get the F.B.I. in right away. Maybe some funny business as it's an Embassy. Get on to McDonald in the Diplomatic Squad and tip him off. The Chief'll have to do it officially, but we'd better get them started quick. See you there in ten minutes."

Goldberg was good at that sort of thing, thought

Shaughnessy, as he put the receiver back. He'd really be O.K. if he wasn't always taking those crazy evening courses at Georgetown University. They always went to his head. Last year it was psychology and everything went back to Freud. This year it was anthropology, though God knows what that had to do with a policeman. Well, that could wait.

Mrs Shaughnessy was waiting to hear the news, and ran downstairs with him to get the car. "What is it, Don?" she asked. "Don't tell me someone's been murdered at the British Embassy."

"Yep," said Shaughnessy. "I'm going to have some fun at last. A British diplomat. Quite a story. First time I ever heard of this happening. I wonder how they'll take it? Probably insist on diplomatic rights to bump off anyone they like."

As his car sirened through the quiet streets, Shaughnessy turned over all the precedents he could think of. This was going to be a bit different from running into the negro quarters of Washington, where most of the murders took place, and barking orders at everyone until some sort of line emerged. The Embassy had invited them in: that was fine; but they'd probably stand on their dignity and try to hush everything up. Trust those Britishers. They would get out of everything. Well, not if Captain Shaughnessy had his way they wouldn't. This was going to be like any other investigation.

As he approached the Embassy, he saw the immense line of cars stretching down Massachusetts Avenue. He had known nothing of the fireworks party, but took the cars to be an ordinary reception. "Nice set-up for a murder," he said to himself. "Plenty of victims, and plenty of suspects." He double-parked near the gate, which was firmly closed, and leapt out. The policeman on duty began opening the door as he saw Shaughnessy coming.

"Who's here so far?" asked Shaughnessy.

"Only the Embassy doctor, Dr Carritt. No one else has gone through, coming or going. Here they come now." Sirens could be heard screeching up the avenue. They took their time notifying the police, Shaughnessy thought.

"Where do I go?"

"Right up to the main door, up there. The Ambassador is waiting."

By this time the other cars had arrived, and Shaughnessy waited for the passengers to get out. Goldberg was in the first car with the police doctor and photographer. Behind was the ambulance, and behind that two cars from which reporters tumbled out in happy anticipation of a Page One story. The sirens had already begun to attract a crowd, and cars had begun to stop, seeing that something startling had happened.

The two policemen on the gate were by now busily trying to move this crowd on, and the reporters, taking advantage of the break, pushed in with Shaughnessy. He recognized Jim Tillett of the *Post*, Jack Brommage of the *Washington Mirror*, and Slater, the *Mirror* photographer.

"What's the story, Don?" asked Brommage, as they walked up the drive.

"Story is that there probably ain't going to be a story for you boys," said Shaughnessy. "This is an embassy. They don't have to let *me* in, and they certainly don't have to let *you* in."

They were now at the door, and there stood the Admiral, tall, stern, and magnificent in his gold-braided uniform and decorations. Behind him, through the open door, they sensed the glitter and pageant of a great house. It was strangely silent, thought Shaughnessy, for all the people who must be in there.

Somehow the Admiral's uniform and bearing made him salute smartly as he gave his name. The Admiral nodded curtly and looked at the people with him.

"Only the police and the doctor will enter," he said sharply. "Everyone else will leave the grounds immediately."

Shaughnessy turned to the reporters, and they reluctantly began to move back. But in the meantime no one had seen the *Mirror* man get his camera up for a shot of the Admiral. There was the sharp flash of a bulb and they ran. With a shrug of disgust, the Admiral led the way inside.

"Who has been killed, sir?" asked Shaughnessy as they walked in.

"A member of my staff, Mr Hewitt. In the woods behind the Annex. He was shot in the head. Murdered."

"Any sign of a reason, sir?"

The Admiral's lips tightened. "You shall see things for yourself."

As they passed the main ballroom on the way to the garden, Shaughnessy saw the assembled guests, standing mostly and talking in hushed whispers.

"I've asked them all to wait," said the Admiral. "I can't keep them much longer, but I thought you would want to ask a few questions."

"Thank you, sir," said Shaughnessy. "I'd like a list too, but I can get it later."

By now they were in the garden. Shaughnessy's eyes opened wide as he saw the floodlights and the abandoned stands. The air was sulphurous after the show, and the Admiral felt called on to explain.

"We had a firework display earlier to-night," he said. It sounded a bit peculiar. Shaughnessy nodded.

"Who found the body?" he asked.

"Two of the Embassy guards and one of the chauffeurs. They heard the shot from the trees and ran in at once. But the murderer escaped. Here it is, just behind there."

They had passed the Annex, and could see a group of people some distance off standing in a circle in the trees, the scene lighted only by flashlights, eerily. In a minute they were standing with them, looking down at the body, sprawled grotesquely on the carpet of fallen leaves, with one leg bent as in a last despairing struggle for life.

"Take a couple, Joe, before we start," said Shaughnessy to the photographer.

No one spoke as the photographer moved round for his shots. In the half-light, hidden within the trees, it was like a grave-digging scene, or rather like some exhumation in the dead of night. Shaughnessy took a quick look at the circle of faces, trying to place them as his eyes got used to the light.

Standing next to the Admiral was an obvious top-drawer diplomat—beautifully tailored clothes, carefully trimmed moustache—another Anthony Eden was how Shaughnessy summed him up; he stood motionless, looking down at the body, without any recognizable expression in his handsome face. Near him stood another elegantly dressed man carrying a small leather bag—clearly the Embassy doctor. On the other side of the body were three members of another class—two Embassy guards and a man in chauffeur's uniform—obviously the people who had found the body. There were only two others there, and it was these two who interested Shaughnessy most.

The first was a very tall, fair young man with an expression on his face of what might be contempt, anger, or sheer fright. Every so often, as he looked down at the body, he drew a deep nervous breath, and his face seemed to twitch. Was this his usual look, or was it some special reaction to the murdered man?

The other was a squat little man with spectacles and a goatee beard who didn't seem to be looking at the body at all. Of all those there, he seemed most indifferent. His mind seemed elsewhere. If anything he seemed to be peering up into the trees, and at one point he did flash the electric torch he was carrying into the branches overhead.

Shaughnessy moved over towards him to try to see what he was looking at, but he had lowered the torch. Shaughnessy got a feeling that he had done it deliberately. He didn't like that. In fact, he didn't like the look of this man at all. Reminded him of a funny little man in the movies who was always behaving in a peculiar way. Peter Lorre, that was it. What was he doing here?

Shaughnessy was standing close to the two men, and caught a muttered word between them. The tall one had said something, shaking his head. The little man with the beard nodded. "Yes," he said, "how true, how true. Act Five. Scene One. Enter two clowns with spades. That skull had a tongue in it and could sing once. Yes, we knew him. Was he Yorick. . . ." His voice trailed away, and he seemed to be looking sharply, even penetratingly at the tall man, who turned his head away at the look.

What did it all mean? What was that about two clowns? Did he mean the police—himself and Goldberg, or perhaps the two doctors? Whatever it was supposed to mean, he didn't like it.

He saw the little man take off his glasses and pull a handkerchief out of his pocket to clean them, blinking round owlishly, and obviously lost without them. As his handkerchief came out, a piece of paper came out too and fell to the ground. It fluttered close to Shaughnessy's foot and on an impulse Shaughnessy put his foot over it. One never knew. Little pieces of paper might be quite useful when you were dealing with people who could fool you as easily as the British.

Shaughnessy's feeling about the British was perhaps inbred. As a boy in Donegal he had formulated the usual picture of the overlord people, but there was an additional reason why even now he found it hard to be objective about them. The fact was—and he could never forgive them for it—he owed his present position as police captain to the

British. As a young man he had served a short time as a London bobby, and on emigrating to the United States and joining the police force here, his pals had nicknamed him "the Englishman" because of his knowledge of English police practice. Whenever his superiors had praised him for something which he knew came from his London experience, he felt a particular irritation stir in him. It was so typical of the British to put their mark on you and never leave you alone. You had to watch them like a hawk if you didn't want to be fooled.

With considerable skill Shaughnessy, appearing to be examining the ground, had quietly transferred the small piece of paper to his pocket, and then he moved over to the body, which the police doctor was now turning over. A dark, handsome young man with a hole in the back of his head. It was clear even to Shaughnessy that he had been shot at the closest range. Almost like an execution.

"We have floodlights available," said the Admiral. "Shouldn't we bring some over here to make a search?"

It was an obviously excellent suggestion, and the gruesome scene around the body began to change in character immediately. The two guards went off with some of the policemen, who had now joined them, to bring the cable along. Goldberg and Shaughnessy began in the meantime to look around the area with torches for a sign of a struggle and the murder weapon, though there was little chance of spotting much in that light. The ground was inches thick with fallen leaves, and a search, even with floodlights, could be endless. Instead of the grim silence, there was now a busy, almost a cheerful air around the corpse. The crunch of heavy feet among the leaves, the shouts of interest or command between the different groups—the searchers, the floodlight squad, and the ambulance men—and finally, as from the eye of some great prehistoric animal, a huge beam of light sweeping the wood, turning everything before its arc either into dazzling white or—from behind—into black silhouettes.

Shaughnessy had left the search and gone to have a preliminary look at the contents of Hewitt's pockets, when he found the Admiral behind him. He felt the need to explain. "I'm going to have a look in his pockets," he said to the Admiral.

"I'll do it myself. You stand by."

Shaughnessy didn't like it, but he stood by. The Admiral produced Hewitt's wallet, with a fair amount of money, apparently untouched. There was a check-book, a small diary and a little notebook which the Admiral did not choose to open. A few letters in the jacket pocket, and a fairly large bunch of keys fastened by a chain to a trouser button completed the contents.

"Untouched, I would say," commented the Admiral. He made no move to hand over the articles to Shaughnessy. "Let's get him indoors."

The stretcher was laid on the leaves and the ambulance party lifted Hewitt gently on to it, covering him with a sheet and then carrying him slowly back past the Annex towards the Residence. In the cortege behind the body marched the Admiral, Shaughnessy, and the Embassy men. Gradually as they moved slowly on, the noise of the searchers died away, the floodlights ceased to illumine their path, and the procession took on an air of deep solemnity.

Once again, as Shaughnessy walked beside the Embassy men, he caught a few odd words exchanged between the two who interested him so much. They were not talking as much as murmuring things into the night air as they marched in the procession.

The tall fair man seemed to be bitter as he spoke. "We buried him d-darkly at dead of night," he muttered. "It all comes to the same, doesn't it?"

"I wonder," said the little man with the beard.

"Patriotism—in a foreign land? Yes. But y'know, Edith Cavell was right too. Patriotism is not enough. No hatred or bitterness to anyone. Wasn't that what she said?"

The tall man was silent. Shaughnessy felt the same irritation as before. Something was very wrong here. They knew things that they would keep to themselves. He would have to assert himself when they got inside and the real examination began.

Silently they reached the Residence. As the door opened, they heard a loud buzz of chatter which suddenly died down. The word had gone around that the body was there. The stretcher was laid carefully on the floor of the dining-room, and then the Admiral called Shaughnessy over to his group.

"I suggest that we ask the guests for information, if they have any, and then let them go," he said to him. "These gentlemen will help you in your enquiries. This is Sir Hugh Eldridge, the Minister"—this was the fashion-plate diplomat —"and this is my aide, Commander Abbot-Hume"—the tall nervous man. "Oh, and this is Mr Usher"—the small man with the beard. "He will help you a little later, as you will see."

As you will see? What *was* this? They seemed to have everything planned. However, there was nothing Shaughnessy could do. They moved into the ballroom, the Admiral leading the way, followed closely by Shaughnessy. Out of the corner of his eye he saw that Usher seemed to have disappeared.

The Admiral held up his hand, though there was no noise to interrupt, for the audience was deathly still. Shaughnessy, looking at these diplomats and their wives, their bright clothes and decorations glittering in the light of the gay chandeliers, felt more and more that this was something beyond him. How do you start finding a murderer in a crowd like this? You don't. You start by picking up bits of paper that funny little men drop. Much more profitable.

82

"Your excellencies, Ladies and Gentlemen," began the Admiral. "As you have heard, there has been a grave accident. I think we can say—a murder." At this expected but dread word, the hush seemed to get even deeper. "Mr Hewitt, whom many of you knew, has been killed. I have asked Captain Shaughnessy of the Washington Police to begin the investigation." (Asked? We'll see about that, thought Shaughnessy.) "I deeply regret that you have had to remain here so long, but it was, of course, essential. Captain Shaughnessy would like to know if any of you saw or heard anything that might have any bearing at all on this . . . on this crime. Anything at all that seemed unusual."

He paused. No one spoke, but all began looking at each other, questioning, hoping, wondering. Shaughnessy, at sea in this strange gathering, felt under-currents of feeling, but no one spoke. The Admiral waited, then resumed.

"I am sure everyone will wish to co-operate. It is possible that someone may wish to give some information to the police privately. Naturally I shall make facilities available. Captain Shaughnessy and I will wait in my study as you leave in case anyone wishes to speak to us privately."

At this, there was a slight hum of talk. The merest murmur. The Admiral had talked of leaving, and it had given the signal for normality. The shock was beginning to wear off. They could start being human. They were beginning to get ready to enjoy it.

"One final thing," said the Admiral. "This is a rather strange position from the diplomatic point of view, but I should like to ask for your indulgence. As you leave, Sir Hugh Eldridge and two other members of my staff will take your names—just for the record. I am sure you will co-operate."

Wow! Shaughnessy felt the shudder that ran through the guests at this. Their identity was to be checked. Righteous dignity struggled with reason. Each knew he was himself, but was there, standing next to him, some impostor? The murmur of talk now slowly expanded to an audible hum. The Admiral stood on one side, and as the guests, now thoroughly annoyed, began to move slowly towards the door, where Eldridge and two younger British diplomats stood waiting, with pads of notepaper, the hum expanded to a buzz.

The Admiral turned to Shaughnessy. "Come with me to my study," he said sharply. "Someone may want to speak to us there."

Shaughnessy followed him through the door, where the guests were already lining up, giving their names and being looked at discreetly by Eldridge and his helpers. He tried to find something to say that would take the ball from the Admiral, but couldn't. When they were alone again, the Admiral turned to him and said quietly:

"I have another reason for getting away. I've asked the F.B.I. to send someone over immediately. There are things I want to tell you."

Shaughnessy nodded. That was fair enough. Was it too fair? He would keep his eyes open.

They walked up the stairs and along the hall. Waiting for them in the study was a girl—clearly the Admiral's secretary—in a state of great alarm. "You're wanted urgently on an overseas telephone call," she began.

"I can't talk to anyone now," said the Admiral. "Tell them . . ."

"I think you will want to take the call, sir," she said, looking nervously from the Admiral to Shaughnessy. "Will you take it in my room?"

The Admiral looked at her. "Very well," he said. "Will you go down and find Mr Usher and ask him to come up here immediately? And ask the others to come up too, as soon as they can."

As the girl ran off downstairs, the Admiral disappeared

into the secretary's room. Keeping one eye on the door leading to the hall, Shaughnessy moved quickly and silently towards the secretary's door, his ear cocked for the Admiral's voice. All was fair in this sort of game. The Admiral had had too much advantage already.

There was not much need for precaution. The Admiral's voice came through the door as though he were on his own quarter-deck.

"They must be mad! Recalled? Do they really think I planned it this way? Anyone knows these things often go wrong."

Things certainly have gone wrong, thought Shaughnessy, as, hearing footsteps, he moved away from the door. I wonder now—if this is wrong, what was right? For the first time that evening he felt a little cheerful. Now we're getting somewhere, he said to himself.

II

Ambrose looked around the study, waiting for the Admiral to begin. How much would he say, and how much should he—Ambrose—say when his turn came? They would have to be told something of Hewitt, obviously, but how much—and what about the other things? How could he explain the way things had turned since he had arrived? If it all came out at this stage, it would just be asking for trouble. So he would tell them what would be useful to tell, and leave it at that.

The police wanted to find a murderer—solve the equation. Fair enough for them. But the truth was that that little equation didn't matter any more. By dying, Hewitt had ceased to be the centre of interest. What mattered now was what would happen to all the others—to those who had joked and those who were serious, to those who knew they were involved and those who were involved without being aware of it. Murder was only one form of violence. Catching a murderer was what the law demanded, but it was not the only way of getting the balance straight, and might not even be the best way.

Ambrose felt a pair of eyes on him: it was the Irish police captain, looking at him with a peculiar kind of suspicion. I suppose my beard looks funny to him, thought Ambrose, giving Shaughnessy a polite smile that seemed to annoy him all the more. The others had all settled down—Shaughnessy's assistant, a sergeant called Goldberg, sitting next to his chief, his dark intelligent head bent forward eagerly; two men from the F.B.I., McDonald and Erie, both square, solid men—no funny stuff; Matthews, keeping a sharp eye on protocol, no doubt; Eldridge, courteous and impassive. Only Abbot-Hume, completing the circle, seemed ill at ease, fingering his tie, his eyes darting round the room rapidly.

"What I have to tell you," said the Admiral looking round at the meeting, "may come as no surprise to the F.B.I. here. As a matter of fact it may not have anything to do with Hewitt's death, but then it may. No way of telling yet. But the police here have got to know, anyhow."

He cleared his throat and glanced at Ambrose as if for encouragement.

"The fact is," he continued, "Hewitt was not what he seemed. He was listed as an assistant Air Attaché. Actually he was a special agent. His job was to contact Communist groups here and see what he could find out—see how far they knew what *we* were doing. He'd had a special background that helped—at Oxford, you know, and in Bloomsbury. Writers and things. For some reason they're supposed to know what it is all about. Pretty tough job all the same, eh?" He looked over to the F.B.I. men. They said nothing The audience seemed to feel that there was more to come.

"Yes," said the Admiral, "there's more to it. Fact is, we

were not too happy about one or two things. Found out through other channels that they knew this and that. Shouldn't have. And Hewitt didn't seem to tell us until we knew. Well, you can guess. Put two and two together. Wondered if maybe Hewitt wasn't helping *them*. Can't tell in this sort of game, you know. Have to consider all possibilities. That's where our friend came in." The Admiral looked over to Ambrose, and they all followed his glance. Ambrose waited.

"The Foreign Office asked Mr Usher to come over," said the Admiral, "to see if he could sort things out. He's had a lot of experience at this. Did a job at Rome like it. But he's just had two days here. Don't really know what he found out. Perhaps we'd better ask him. Anything to tell us, Usher?"

Come on now, said Ambrose to himself. The truth, nothing but the truth, even if it isn't the whole truth. But can the truth ever be less than the whole truth? Ryle would say not. The part and the whole. Nice semantic problem. He launched into his usual rapid speech.

"I was beginning to think I had something to tell," he said, looking at the Admiral, "but now I am less sure. Lots of things, lots of facts—too many facts. That's what's wrong, I suppose. Everything can't be true. Life is selective. Like a tray of biscuit dough, you know. Need to stamp out the biscuits—or should I say cookies—and throw away what's left, but can't find the little round thing with crinkled edges to stamp them out with."

As he was speaking, a number of sharp images flicked through his mind. He saw the look in Jill Abbot-Hume's eyes as Hewitt turned towards her. He saw Miss Hope-Little stroking Palmerston, and Flantin waving his hand airily as he talked about Oxford. He heard the Admiral barking commands to Johnson as they worked on the fire-works. There was the pretty young Canadian girl sighing for the lost freedom of youth. Sanati—with his fine ugly old head—in close converse with Walter, and Mme Marot smiling at them all as from a distance. But it was Hewitt they wanted to know about. He went on talking.

"Yes, I found out quite a few facts," he said. "I discovered that Hewitt was a very intelligent man, and a very charming one too. They're facts, aren't they?" He smiled, but a little sadly. "For another thing: he went to some trouble to examine the contents of my brief-case when we were at dinner together. I gave him a chance, and he took it. Yes, he was rather keen about it all. It seemed as if he had a previous engagement, but he decided to dine with me instead. I heard him on the telephone cancelling an engagement—or should I say breaking a date. So it seemed anyhow. Someone called Billy. It certainly *sounded* as if it were a date." He sighed again. "I wonder where this all fits in. Is this any help, sir?" turning to the Admiral.

"You'd better give the police all the details," said the Admiral, "and of course the F.B.I. too. They'll want to find out who Billy is, I suppose. Shouldn't be too difficult. Was there anything else? Anything you can link directly to his murder?"

Ambrose hesitated. "How far back do we go?" he said finally. "*Of man's first disobedience?* Things go back, and I know so little. . . ."

There was an interruption. Abbot-Hume had got up in a jerky, clumsy way, made a gesture asking permission from the Ambassador to leave, and was quickly out of the room. The Ambassador apologized. "He has a job to do," he said in explanation.

It seemed odd, but no one said anything. "Well, there you have it," continued the Admiral cheerfully, turning to the F.B.I. men and the police. "No use theorizing any further. I wanted you to know about Hewitt's background. I suppose the odds are that this whole thing is connected with the

Communists . . . must be. But we'll have to dig up the connection—or rather *you* will. What's your plan?"

Captain Shaughnessy took over. "We'll have to search his home and his office," he said. "Then we'll want to examine all the people who knew him. We'll have to find out how he died, and look for the weapon. And of course the F.B.I. will have their own enquiries." It all sounded most thorough and efficient.

The Admiral stood up, and they all rose with him. Just then the buzzer rang, and he spoke to his secretary. "Bring them in," he said to her. "It's the doctors," he explained.

The doctors were an odd pair. Side by side with Carritt's professional elegance and distinguished calm, the police doctor, dressed in an old grey suit, with a shaggy mane of hair and a cigarette drooping out of the corner of his mouth, looked comically undistinguished. But it was he who gave the information.

"We've extracted the bullet. Just one shot in the back of his head. A Colt 38."

"That's fine," said Shaughnessy to him heavily. "Just about the commonest gun there is. Every bank dick in the United States has one. Well, let's start looking for it."

They all moved towards the door, but as they were going out, the F.B.I. men managed to get close to Ambrose. It was McDonald, the older one, who spoke.

"Excuse me, sir," he said quietly. "This Rome job that the Ambassador mentioned. Could you tell me when you did it?"

Ambrose turned a startled look on him. "Ah, *a grief ago, a grief ago*," he said sadly. "But that's not it, is it? You want the year and the month and the day. Let me see. . . ."

He walked through the door with him, giving him the facts. Behind he heard Shaughnessy, released from the constraint of the meeting, barking at Goldberg.

Throttle had motioned to Eldridge to stay behind, but before he spoke to him he buzzed his secretary. "Get hold of Johnson," he told her. "I want him immediately. And when he gets here, I don't want anyone to disturb us."

When the secretary had gone, he turned to Eldridge. "Have you spoken to London?" he asked. "What are they going to do?"

"Yes, I got through," said Eldridge. "They're sending some people out from Scotland Yard, from the Special Branch. It will be announced. The public counts on it," he added drily.

The Ambassador had mixed a Scotch and soda for Eldridge and was now mixing one for himself. From the way he dashed in the soda, it was clear that he was angry. "Who did you speak to there?"

"No one important," said Eldridge. "Botwood. Doesn't know about this side of things. Couldn't get hold of the Under-Secretary."

"You don't know about my call, then, eh?" asked Throttle.

Eldridge was clearly surprised. "No, what was that? Botwood didn't mention it."

"Hadn't come through, I suppose. Thought not, or I suppose you'd have said something. Well, I might as well tell you. They want to have me recalled. I got a call half an hour ago. Say I bungled things."

Eldridge looked into his glass. "Bungled things," he said slowly. "Do they mean . . ."

"Bungled. That's the word he used. Idiots. Do they think I planned it the way it happened. A thing can go wrong, can't it? Tell me. You know the rules about these things. I don't. I'm just a sailor. Can I be recalled?"

Eldridge still hesitated. "Well . . ." he began.

He was interrupted by a knock at the door. It was Johnson. The Ambassador jumped up energetically. "Let's leave it now, Hugh," he said. "We can discuss it in the morning. Just have a final look round, will you?"

Johnson stood impassively while Eldridge put down his drink and moved to the door. As he moved down the corridor, he heard the Ambassador say firmly to Johnson: "Well now, let's get down to it."

He walked slowly down the magnificent staircase, shaking his head at the royal portraits.

IV

Turning the door-lock to the empty house, Jill was suddenly overcome again with fear. Something new lurked there—not the loneliness that had so disturbed her before, but the feel of an uncertainty that cut like danger.

She had felt it ever since the moment in the Embassy garden when they had all waited for the name, and then heard that it was Maurice who had been killed.

At first she had been too bewildered to think of anything consecutive—just that he was dead. Then she had turned her head and seen Dennis looking at her, and suddenly a horrible fear had enveloped her.

The door slammed behind her, and she was all alone again. Unable to take her things off, she sat down on a chair in the hall and buried her head in her arms.

Had Dennis known all the time? And if he had, could he possibly. . . . She was afraid even to think of it.

She had never planned the affair, never even wanted it. What *had* she wanted? To break out, to assert herself, to grasp at the forbidden, to be reckless. Reckless, yes, that was it. Life had settled down too quickly, too securely.

What had Dennis done to deserve this? Nothing. He had

just seemed always to be away from her, the Dennis she had married. He was always going off on his own—speaking engagements, or obscure trips that he never even bothered to talk about. Why had he changed so much?

No, it wasn't true. He hadn't changed. It was she. She hadn't thought that anything was lacking, yet, when it had happened, it had seemed so natural, as though it filled a need.

And now Maurice was dead. He had been so gay, so impudent. That first day, when they had finished a tennis single and he had said: "Let's go and have a drink somewhere," he had seemed so casual, but they had both accepted it as a challenge. What was wrong with going off to have a drink? Nothing, and everything.

Two days later, with Dennis away again, they had gone for a drive and climbed to Sanctuary Ridge to get the view from the top. They had joked endlessly while they puffed up the slope, and it all still seemed fun until later when he kissed her. Just a kiss—but something had awakened in her.

It had made her bloom, somehow. People said how well she looked, but that wasn't it. Auguste Flantin had understood. At parties before, he had seemed to want to flirt with her, to win her confidence, but yesterday at the cocktail party he had looked at her quite differently. Yes, he'd understood.

How long ago was that? A day? An age. He was dead now.

But it wasn't only that. It was this other nameless fear. . . .

She forced herself to get up and go upstairs. Her bedroom was tidy and empty. No one telephoned. No one came. For long hours of the night, she lay awake, turning her grief over and over, and longing for the dawn.

THREE

"Say, first, of God above, or man below,
  What can we reason but from what we know?"
                                        POPE, Essay on Man

I

WHEN Ambrose woke the next morning, he felt a most extraordinary sense of well-being flowing through him. The nightmares of the previous night seemed to belong to some other existence. Throwing up his window to the keen autumn air, he stood there some minutes tingling with a kind of abstract pleasure, before he went into the bathroom to shave.

Even the slow careful business of shaving around his little beard seemed free of boredom that morning. As he pulled his cheek one way and another to meet the scratchy blade of his age-old razor, his mind seemed happily released. Consciously he thought of the work ahead that morning, and made plans; but in the middle of the planning he found himself occupied in trying to assess this irrational feeling of exhilaration into which he had woken up.

The only thing he could clearly recognize was the sensation that this day was, in some manner, a day of decision for him. Decision? About what? Hadn't the decisive act taken place? Wasn't the mission over? He had been sent out to see about Hewitt, and now—well, could he go back now and let the rest go on without him?

No, there was much more to come—the ripples were spreading—so many issues—and the police would get in the way. Well, he would just have to keep one stage ahead.

How ironic that Walter should be in this too, Walter, his friend. But he couldn't be mistaken. Of course there was no reason why Walter shouldn't have talked to Sanati while they waited in the ballroom. Every reason why they should. But it was the look in Walter's face that Ambrose didn't like. He had seen the same look of anguish and doubt flicker into his eyes while they had talked at lunch that day about secrecy and science, and the night before that at dinner. Mme Marot had laid her hand gently on Walter's arm and he had grown silent. Perhaps he was wrong. But he couldn't take the chance. He had to find out.

And if he had to act, there was only one way—to break into it directly. No time for careful probing. He would tackle it openly, whatever it did to their friendship. This was the hard thing. They would never be friends in the same way again. Friendship meant taking your friend for granted, no probe, no trick questions—just trust. He would have to ask Walter to expose himself. It was something new for Ambrose. He would have to come out of his shell. For once he would have to spell things out crudely.

This is what I should have done in Rome, he thought. I just let everything drift on, enjoying all the ironies, until they found poor old Whittaker's body in the Marshes. They said it couldn't be helped, but of course it could. Well, now I'm learning. He rubbed his palm over his cheek and decided that it could do with one more going over with the razor.

Picking up the shaving-brush, he spread a fresh, thick mound of soapsuds on his face, and somehow the act seemed to release a fresh evaluation of his whole position. It isn't only Walter, he said to himself. It's me. Something is going to happen to *me* to-day, something has been working up inside me, or outside me, and is coming to a head.

How can I know? Premonition? Well, why not? Suppose, in fact, I'm going to be knocked down by a car to-day, or hit on the head—could I know in advance? Of course I could, if I'm deliberately working towards it.

Well, am I, he asked himself, rubbing the soap brush

94

comfortingly under his jaw. Perhaps I am, he thought. Like Moby Dick yesterday. 'The living act, the undoubted deed.' He smiled to himself. He had only to frame the thought to know that it wasn't that kind of decisiveness that he felt this morning. It was as if decision meant this time letting go instead of taking hold.

He scraped at his neck carefully. Can surrender be a decisive act, he wondered. In painting, in music, you do it all the time, but in your own life? Suppose you fell in love, for example. Do you surrender yourself? Do you have to drown that precious ego, or does it just give up quietly?

He had finished his pseudo-shave now, doused his face in cold water, and was ready for breakfast. The phone rang. It was Miss Hope-Little, asking about his plans. He told her he would be going up to the Embassy, and asked if she would get some Embassy papers for him that he wanted to see. She sounded quite dejected, began to say something, and then rang off abruptly.

He caught something of her mood and felt sad too as he left the bedroom and walked down the hall. But as the doors of the lift closed and it dropped suddenly down the nineteen floors, the sense of excitement flowed through him again. It's like diving into a pool, he thought—and then he smiled to himself. Words again. Images. I've never dived in my life. I can swim, but I can't dive. Is that what's wrong with me?

All this was very good for the appetite. He felt cheerful as he sat down at the table, unfolded his spotless napkin, and contemplated the breakfast menu.

II

Shaughnessy had handled some interesting murders in his time. As far back as his London bobby days he had been caught up in a typically British *Jack the Ripper* murder with the culprit finally traced as a butcher, and thus caught, because he revealed a characteristic way of cutting up the body as if the parts were for sale. Washington murders had been fairly easy. They were mostly gang murders, and someone always talked—but there had been a few that brought innovations: the Senator's mistress, whose body had been taken away in a faked funeral car, with a crowd outside watching respectfully, and never seen again; or the Echo Park Gang, who had been the first to apply the classical phrase "take him for a ride" to an aeroplane, and had dumped the rebellious member of their gang, fully weighted, into the sea, ten miles out. By contrast, this British Embassy business was apparently straightforward, but it really gave you no chance. "With the others, at least," Shaughnessy told his wife while he dressed the next morning "you could see what sort of case you were dealing with, and you could tackle it your own way. Here I don't know where I am. Everyone's keeping things back. I don't even know where I am with the F.B.I. As for those British *diplomats*," he pronounced the word with heavy scorn—"God knows what game they're playing at, especially that Usher man."

It certainly was confusing. When he had gone to search Hewitt's office, Matthews, the protocol man from the Embassy, politely and firmly went along with him and examined the desk and filing-cabinet himself. As far as Shaughnessy and Goldberg could see, Matthews didn't take anything away. All the contents of the desk were laid out on top, but it was annoying none the less. Had the officials found anything they thought important they would have undoubtedly kept it back. Even at Hewitt's home they asserted diplomatic privilege, and did the search themselves. It was as if they were beginning to regret having called the police in at all.

Looking quickly through Hewitt's letters at home and at the office, with McDonald from the F.B.I. working with

96

them, they had seen nothing obviously suggestive, no secret papers or bundles tied up in ribbons. His private letters seemed to be about books and politics from friends in England, Paris and other places all over the globe—all in English. Of course, they would go over them more carefully and check the correspondents, but at first glance nothing had suggested itself.

Bleary-eyed from lack of sleep, Goldberg and Shaughnessy had gone home in the early hours without any lead, either from Hewitt's papers or from the search in the woods which had been pursued by their colleagues.

Perhaps only one thing had offered some hope. Hewitt's diary and little book of telephone numbers at home were far too innocent to be the whole thing. Checking the names with the State Department's Diplomatic Blue Book and with the Washington telephone book, they had not unearthed one telephone number that wasn't quite obvious. Well there was no doubt that in his secret job for the Embassy—or in his own private job—he had known names and telephone numbers that were not obvious. Unless he had some private system of recording or remembering them, there must be some other little book somewhere. But would they ever discover it?

What disturbed Shaughnessy was not the absence of a clear lead at first glance but the difficulty of penetrating the Embassy world in which these characters moved. They seemed to exist and speak not as individuals but with some higher identity. Who the hell did they think they were anyway? And how did they tick? He knew the motives that made ordinary people commit murder—greed, jealousy, passion, perversion—but he felt somehow that this wasn't the way it had worked here.

This Communist thing. Obviously it was the key. The F.B.I. took it all for granted. But what happened to these guys when they got mixed up in spying and counter-spying?

How far would they go? In a game like that, lying didn't count. Murder too, probably. It was like underground activity during the war—like the French underground. You just killed someone if they got in the way, even someone on your own side, if they looked as if they would talk, or break, and so give the game away.

He had seen lots of underground plays on TV. You had to act at a second's notice, and think afterwards. This is what had happened here, no doubt about it. But who was in danger? Who had had to bump Hewitt off?

The bell rang. It was Goldberg, come by arrangement to go with him to the Embassy in order to go over the ground in daylight. They had had only two hours' sleep, but a cold shower and a shave had refreshed them, and the smell of Mrs Shaughnessy's coffee and bacon and eggs from the kitchen was invigorating by itself. Goldberg had a bundle of newspapers under his arm. "Look at this one, Chief," he said holding up the *Washington Mirror*.

There, in full uniform, his face stern, his arm outstretched as if in accusation, was the Admiral—the whole of page one. It was the picture that Slater had shot at the door of the Embassy when the journalists had tried and failed to get in. An excellent picture. But it was the headlines that Goldberg had found so startling: ACCUSE SOVIETS IN EMBASSY SLAYING. *Exclusive.*

Shaughnessy turned quickly to page three, where the exclusive story proved to be by Marilyn Entwhistle, the Society hostess-journalist who attended every high social party in Washington, and had been there the previous night. It was a good story, worthy of Marilyn.

DIPLOMAT SLAIN AT THE BRITISH EMBASSY

"Work of Soviets," says British Ambassador

Political assassination, with far-reaching consequences, is thought to be the motive of the sensational murder last night in the grounds of the British Embassy.

I was standing immediately next to Admiral Throttle, British Ambassador, when the news was brought to him that 35-year-old Maurice Hewitt—a popular member of the British Embassy staff and a well-known figure in Washington society—had been found in the Embassy garden shot dead through the head.

I heard the Admiral say: "Look for Russia." Immediately afterwards an official ban prevented any member of the staff from commenting on this remark of the Admiral, but it is known that the police and the F.B.I. are actively at work on this angle of the crime. . . .

Shaughnessy threw the paper down in disgust. "Well, now, that's blown it all open," he said to Goldberg. "Why didn't he tell us he'd spoken out about it? Do the others have the same story?"

"Not yet," said Goldberg. "They will, when they get round to it. But Chief, don't you see what this means? He didn't mean the Russians. He meant that little Embassy man with the beard—Usher! 'Look for Usher!' He was taken off his guard, and he blurted it out. Later on he covered up; he didn't know they had heard him, probably. But this would make sense. Usher was brought over to do it. and bungled it by doing it in the garden. Probably it was some emergency . . . couldn't wait."

Shaughnessy whistled. "Mort, I think you're on to it. That's right. Adds up. They certainly bungled it. I heard him say it on the phone, on an overseas call, probably from London, that it hadn't gone according to plan. That's right. How did London know so quickly if it hadn't all been planned?"

Goldberg was delighted at this further evidence. "Of course. They admitted themselves they were suspicious of

99

Hewitt. Remember what Usher said about him examining his brief-case. 'Look for Usher.' Neat, isn't it?"

Shaughnessy had had enough. "O.K. It's neat. It's probably right, too. But how did you tie it on to them, and who did it, and where's the weapon? We haven't begun yet."

The bacon and eggs called them, followed by great mounds of pancakes swamped in maple syrup, and large cups of coffee. Shaughnessy said little as they drove off to the Embassy. It might well be that little man. He didn't like the way he talked or acted. On the other hand, Goldberg was always trying to be too smart. All those damned evening courses.

III

By nine, Ambrose was in a cab *en route* to the Embassy. He was still glowing with some of his early-morning excitement, but had somehow departmentalized it into the jobs that had to be done. An apperception to be tested on the big thing. A feeling to be explored on a small thing that might prove still bigger. And always—what was the motto for the day—oh yes: "One step ahead of the police."

At the gate of the Annex he got out of the cab, and asked it to wait. This thing mightn't take long. He looked round for Johnson and the other guards who had found Hewitt's body. Johnson was not there, but Wilmot, the little wizened old guard, was standing by, talking, as luck would have it, to a man in chauffeur's uniform, whom Ambrose saw was the chauffeur who had been in the search party.

Wilmot recognized Ambrose and saluted him.

"Good morning," Ambrose said to him. "Do you know where Johnson is?"

"He should be here soon," Wilmot answered in his cheerful cockney voice. "Can I help, sir?" He was clearly very proud of his new importance.

"Well, perhaps you can," said Ambrose. "Perhaps you can. I suppose you've told the police all you know."

"Oh yes," said Wilmot eagerly. "They were searching all last night."

"Then I won't ask you to tell me it all again. You must be tired of questions."

"Oh no, sir. Not a bit tired, are we, George?" He had turned to the chauffeur.

"Oh no, sir," said George. "Glad to oblige."

"Well, I just wanted to get the picture absolutely clear," said Ambrose reassuringly. "Let me see, now. You were standing with Johnson when you heard the shots in the wood."

"That's right, sir," said Wilmot in his eager, cockney voice. "We were at the bottom of the driveway, near the corner. We'd been watching the fireworks—you could see them very well from that corner."

"Had you been there all the evening?" asked Ambrose.

"Well, up and down, sir. We'd given a hand here and there. We each had various odd jobs to do, seeing to the cars and so on. But that's where we were standing just then, watching the fireworks go off, the big piece at the end."

"And then, when the fireworks were over, you heard the shots from the wood?"

"That's right, sir," said Wilmot.

"You both heard them quite clearly?"

"Oh yes, sir."

"How many shots did you hear?"

"We heard three shots, sir. Very clear."

"Now, Wilmot, think about this. There's been a lot of fireworks popping off that night. Did these shots sound very different?"

"Well, sir," said Wilmot slowly. "Fireworks do sound like shots, of course, but you couldn't possibly mistake these. These were gun shots."

"How did you know?"

Wilmot looked puzzled for a moment, and then his face brightened. "Well, partly from where the sound came from, sir. It was way behind us, and the fireworks were all in front of us. And there was something else, sir."

"Oh, what was that?"

"You could tell these were shots fired in a wood, sir. It was the kind of echo you always hear when a gun is fired in a wood, sir. A kind of deep sound. You know what I mean, sir?" he asked eagerly.

"Yes," said Ambrose, "I know what you mean. Well, that's very clear. It's lucky you've got such a good memory. You didn't have to say anything to each other when you heard the shots. You just ran towards them."

"That's right, sir," said Wilmot. "I don't really remember what we said. I believe Johnson may have said something like: 'Those were gun shots,' something like that. But there wasn't any doubt, sir. We saw that as soon as we found poor Mr Hewitt's body."

"Yes," said Ambrose. "It was all confirmed very quickly, wasn't it?" He turned to the chauffeur. "And you heard the shots too?"

"Yes, sir," said Watkins. "I was standing right about here, near the cars. I'd been looking at the fireworks—you could see quite a lot from this corner because of the rise— and then Johnson and Wilmot came running by."

"Had you wondered about the shots?"

"Wasn't much time to wonder, sir," said Watkins. "I'd heard them, and I just joined Johnson and Wilmot here, and we ran into the wood. I just stopped for a second to pick up a big flashlight I carry in the car, and overtook them. And there was Mr Hewitt lying there."

"Did you have to search much to find him?"

"Well, we were just lucky, sir," said Watkins. "We ran in, with our flashlights on. There's a kind of path leading to the clearing, and we ran along that path."

"Who led the way?"

Watkins turned to Wilmot. "I think it was Johnson, wasn't it, Joe? I would guess so."

Wilmot nodded. "That's right, George. We all ran together, but of course we had to be one behind the other in the wood."

"And you didn't touch anything when you found the body?"

"Oh no, sir," said Wilmot. "Johnson bent over the body and said: 'It's Mr Hewitt. He's been shot'—or something like that. And he felt his heart. Then he said: 'I'll go and get help. You stay here.' So we waited till everybody came."

"Well, that's all very clear," said Ambrose. "I can just picture it all now very clearly. Thank you very much . . . thank you. . . ." He smiled and moved on into the Annex.

Yes, he thought, I can picture it very clearly. I can see how, but I can't see why. I could prove it—or at least test it, but I daren't. Not till I know more.

He made his way to a phone in the outer office near the doorway. What is truth, he thought to himself heavily? I might be able to make a statement *x caused the death of y*, which would be a true statement, yet devoid of meaning. No, worse. It might destroy meaning—like pulling a card out of a card-castle and bringing everything down. Why won't they see that simple analytic propositions have no meaning except in relation to others?

He had asked the operator for the F.B.I., and then for Grover, his old friend there. Luck was with him. Grover was in and delighted to hear from him. "I'll be down in ten minutes," Ambrose told him.

Next, Miss Hope-Little. She was in too. He told her he would be back a little later as he was going down to the F.B.I. She still sounded curiously dejected, and he thought to ask her what was the matter, but she rang off.

Finally a call to Walter Scott. Not in yet, he was told, but coming in at ten. "Please tell him I want to see him," Ambrose told Walter's secretary. "At about eleven, if he can."

And now, his plans laid, Ambrose skipped back into his waiting cab, and settled back for the ride to the F.B.I. As he turned out of the gate, he passed a police car turning in with great dispatch, and caught a glimpse of Captain Shaughnessy, with Sergeant Goldberg at the wheel.

One step ahead, Ambrose murmured to himself, stroking his beard and chuckling at the thought. But then he sighed. What a pity it all is. I know what's going to happen. The police are going to plunge in—they'll uncover all kinds of things, follow all kind of trails—all part of the maize of truth—and perhaps we shall meet at the centre. What a bore it all is. But I must let them go their own way until I see: there's no alternative yet.

God knows what they'll uncover, he thought. Probably end up with me as the murderer. He was smiling to himself as the cab drew up at the F.B.I. offices.

FOUR

"'Tis like the howling of Irish wolves against the moon."
                                        As You Like It

I

B Y daylight the Embassy seemed much more normal to
Shaughnessy. The Ambassador and his decorations
and all the odd characters like Matthews and Usher who had
got in his way with their diplomatic rights and funny
remarks were mercifully elsewhere, probably conferring
with the State Department, where they belonged. Shaughnessy felt that he could start treating the case normally—
examining witnesses, looking for the weapon, and generally
smelling his way through the circumstances of the crime to
get a lead that would make sense.

He would have to start by making a real search for the
weapon. So far they had just looked through the woods.
But perhaps they could find out who had access to guns
here. The guards would know. They all carried guns, as he
had seen last night, and they might have some leads. He had
seen Wilmot, the little old guard, standing near the gate
as he drove through, and he wondered if the head guard,
Johnson, was around too. Johnson would be more useful.

Goldberg had swung the car round silently into a little
corner of the drive next to a low wall to park, and Shaughnessy, as he opened the door to climb out, heard a rather
unusual voice coming from the other side of the wall. He
looked—and then stopped. This was the sort of break he
was waiting for, catching the Embassy people off guard.
Johnson was standing there talking with Abbot-Hume, the
tall, fair, nervous-looking attaché of the Ambassador. It was
Abbot-Hume's voice that he heard, a rather high-pitched

voice, with a stammer. They were apparently deep in conversation, quite oblivious of the arrival of the car.

Motioning to Goldberg to be silent, Shaughnessy listened. Across the still morning air, he heard Abbot-Hume say: "We always give a t-test like this, but it isn't everything."

Shaughnessy couldn't catch Johnson's reply, but he heard Abbot-Hume continue: "N-no, it wasn't perfect, but it was good enough. You did the job and g-got away with it—that's what matters."

There was a pause; Johnson seemed somehow reluctant about something. Then he said: "So there's this, and my Toronto diploma." He sounded a bit sarcastic.

"N-No," said Abbot-Hume. "It's everything taken together. They'd be glad if you could fly over. There's a whole lot . . ." He was turning as he spoke, and Shaughnessy, seeing him turn, quickly slammed the door of the car to indicate that he had just arrived. "Good-morning, sir," he called out.

Abbot-Hume looked up. "Good-morning," he said. "B-Back on the job, I see." He walked over towards the police car, with Johnson following, and they both stepped over the wall.

"Yes," said Shaughnessy. "A bit easier in daylight. I wonder if you can help, sir. I need some information about guns here. We haven't found the murder weapon yet."

Abbot-Hume waved his hand airily towards Johnson. "Here's your man, Captain," he said. "Johnson's in charge of the guns." He smiled brightly. "N-no good dealing with amateurs when there are p-professionals around, eh? I must run. The Ambassador will be after my scalp." He turned quickly and left Johnson standing with Shaughnessy and Goldberg. The three of them strolled over towards the gate, where Wilmot joined them, eager to take part.

"Well, it's always good to deal with the experts," said

Shaughnessy. "Can you tell me who would have a Colt 38 at the Embassy? What guns do *you* use?"

Johnson pulled his own gun out of his holster. "We have Colt 38's. We all use them. There are quite a few at the Embassy."

"How many altogether? Who has them?"

"Well," said Johnson slowly, "as far as I know there are —let me see—yes, there are eight that we know of."

"Eight, eh? Where are they?"

"Well, there are these two that Wilmot and I have. We were carrying them last night, of course, when we found the body. Then Ponting, he's the third guard, he was on duty at the front gate—he has one. Then there's the one on the *Dove*. . . ."

"The *Dove*? What's that?"

"That's the Embassy plane. They always keep one there. Then there are four extra ones that are used by the Embassy Pistol Team. They're always kept down on the range."

"Who's in charge of them there?"

"They're always kept locked up in a steel chest. We have a key here, and of course the Captain of the Team has a key."

"Who's the Captain?"

Wilmot broke in at this point, with great eagerness. "Oh, that's Miss Hope-Little, sir. She's been Captain for years."

"A woman? Captain of the Pistol Team?"

Wilmot was clearly very proud of Miss Hope-Little, and somewhat surprised that Shaughnessy hadn't heard of her. "Oh, she's a Bisley Champion, sir. She won the Open Pistol Shot three times running in 1934, 1935 and 1936. Won the Cup outright she did. She's a wonderful shot, sir."

Johnson seemed considerably less interested in Miss Hope-Little's prowess. Shaughnessy turned to him. "Will you see if the key is there?"

Johnson disappeared for a moment into the room close

by, where, through the open door, Shaughnessy could see rows of keys arranged on the wall. He was back immediately with a small key, to which a tab was attached. "Here it is, in the usual place."

"Where's the range?" asked Shaughnessy.

Johnson pointed through the gate in the direction of the garden. "It's a way over there, beyond the swimming-pool."

Shaughnessy turned to Goldberg. "Go down there with one of the guards, Mort, and see if the four guns are there. Watch out for prints."

While Goldberg went off with Wilmot, Shaughnessy went round to the front gate to have a word with the policeman on duty there. It was one of the men who had been on duty the night before.

"Was the Embassy guard here all the time with you?" he asked.

"Yes, sir. None of us left the front gate at all. We were under orders."

Well, that's that, said Shaughnessy to himself. Let's see what happens at the range. He turned back, went to Hewitt's room, and stopped to speak to a girl who was sitting at a typewriter in a smaller room next door.

"Are you Mr Hewitt's secretary?" he asked her.

"No, sir," she said. "That's Betty Turenne. She hasn't come in yet."

"Will you get her on the phone if you can?" said Shaughnessy. "I want to see her as soon as possible."

About ten minutes later, Goldberg got back. Shaughnessy could see that something was afoot from the cheerful look on his face. He was carrying three guns, carefully supported on a large cloth.

"Here's three of them," he said. "And they've all been cleaned since they were last used. But the fourth one just ain't there. We've had a good look."

"Very nice," Shaughnessy said. "We'd better get hold of Annie Oakley—what's her name? Miss Hope-Little. God, they have the damnedest names."

Goldberg picked up the phone and asked the switchboard operator where he could find Miss Hope-Little. He listened, and then Shaughnessy heard him say: "Oh, is that so? Well, put her on." While he waited for the call to come through, he covered the receiver with his hand and whispered to Shaughnessy: "She's Usher's secretary. Ain't that something?" Then he spoke into the phone. "Hello, is this Miss Hope-Little? I'm speaking for Captain Shaughnessy, investigating the murder. Could you drop by to see the Captain? He wants to ask you something. He's in Mr Hewitt's room."

He listened to her reply and his friendly face changed a little. "But, Miss Hope-Little . . ." he began.

She was apparently not prepared to listen. Shaughnessy heard her voice through the phone, sharp and decisive, and then there was the unmistakable click as she replaced the receiver. Goldberg gave his chief a chastened look.

"Says she won't come over without asking Usher's permission. He's out somewhere. She's going to call him and get him to call us to find out what you want. I tried to argue, but . . ."

"Yeh, I heard. She certainly told *you* where to get off." Shaughnessy was quite amused.

"I didn't have a chance," Goldberg complained. "She just *told* me. Sounds like a very strange dame. Talks like a man. One of those dames, probably. That probably explains why she's such a good shot. She's really shooting at men when she shoots at the target."

Shaughnessy gave him a look. "Are you starting that stuff again, Mort? Thought you'd finished with psychology. Isn't it anthropology this year?"

Goldberg failed to see the sarcasm in the question and

took it as an invitation to explain something very important. "Oh, but you see, Don, it's really the same subject. She's like Hippolyta, Queen of the Amazons. You can't understand motivation without considering the cultural pattern. Take the Eskimos and sex. . . ."

"You take the Eskimos, I'll take the sex. Hey, what *is* this? Will you can it, Mort? We've got work to do." Shaughnessy shook his head sadly. The phone rang. He grabbed it quickly himself. "Captain Shaughnessy," he said smartly.

"Good-morning, Captain." It was Usher. He recognized that pesky cheerful voice instantly. "I gather you want to talk to Miss Hope-Little. She wants my consent, which of course I give willingly. Treat her kindly, of course. Simple questions. But wait a moment. Perhaps I am being too agreeable. What do you want to find out? Something about me? Miss Hope-Little is blameless, you know, quite blameless. It *must* be me—or perhaps you want to worm out some Embassy *secrets*." He rolled the last word annoyingly.

"It's quite simple, Mr Usher," said Shaughnessy, controlling his temper. "Just some questions about the gun. I gather she's an expert. But I do want to ask you some questions."

"I'm sure you do, highly advisable, very suspicious character." Usher sounded very pleased with himself for some reason.

Shaughnessy managed to stay calm. "Perhaps we can meet this morning. Where are you now?"

"Let me surprise you. At the F.B.I."

"The F.B.I.!"

"Yes, keeping one step ahead of you, eh?"

"One step ahead? What do you mean by that?" Shaughnessy asked sharply.

"Well, I assume you're coming down here soon to check up on me, are you not?"

"I am coming down, yes."

"Well I am one step ahead, am I not? All very innocent."

"Can I see you there, Mr Usher?"

"Ah, I fear not, alas. I have to leave in a moment. They have decided not to detain me this time."

"Are you coming up here to the Embassy?"

"It will depend. Do I sound evasive? I hope not."

Shaughnessy pursed his lips and said calmly: "Shall we arrange to meet later?"

"Of course, after lunch. Completely at your disposal. Where shall we meet?"

Shaughnessy suggested Police Headquarters at 2.30. "But that is splendid," said Usher happily. "You can really grill me there—much easier than the Embassy. Have you found the gun yet?" he added, very casually.

Shaughnessy smiled grimly, recognizing that Usher's interest was far from casual. "We're working on something," he said. "We have our ways, you know. We can discuss it all this afternoon."

As he replaced the receiver, there was a knock at the door. He called "Come in", and someone who was unmistakably Miss Hope-Little entered, tall, gaunt, and dressed in tweeds. She was as clumsy and brusque as she had sounded on the phone, yet somehow distraught, too.

Shaughnessy was very polite. "I've just spoken to Mr Usher," he said. "Very good of you to come. I wonder if you can help us. Mr Hewitt was killed with a Colt 38, and we're looking into all those we can find here. We were told that there were four down at the Embassy shooting-range, and we've only found three. We're having them tested, but in the meantime, do you know where the fourth one is?"

Miss Hope-Little hardly seemed to be listening. Her answer, in any case, was peculiarly off-hand. "Oh, isn't it there? It should be. I had it out with me the other day. I went over to shoot at the Centaur range, but I thought I'd put it back. Maybe it's still in my car."

Shaughnessy was appalled. "Miss Hope-Little. Is that how you deal with guns in your charge? Don't you know they're dangerous things?"

"Oh, don't be absurd, man." Miss Hope-Little clearly had no patience for such baby-talk. "I know about guns. If I have it, it's safe. I was sure, though, that I'd put it back. Perhaps some other member of the Team has it."

Shaughnessy found it difficult to maintain the calm that he thought was probably essential for dealing with these Embassy characters. Gritting his teeth slightly, he said: "Would you go and see if you can find it? You know there *has* been a murder here, with a Colt 38, and it would be quite useful to find the weapon."

"What makes you think it is this gun?" said Miss Hope-Little sharply. "It's a common type—commonest there is."

"Yes," said Shaughnessy patiently, "I know. Still, would you see if you can find this particular one?"

Miss Hope-Little seemed very weary about the whole thing. "Oh, yes, I'll have a look," she said, and started to get up. But she sighed deeply as she said it, and Shaughnessy sensing her unhappiness suddenly felt impelled to say to her: "Is anything the matter, Miss Hope-Little? I mean besides the murder?"

"Yes," she said. "It's Palmerston, my cat."

"Your cat?"

"Yes," she said slowly. "He was hurt yesterday, and I took him to the vet. Then I took him home with me to look after him." She stopped.

"Well?" asked Shaughnessy.

"He hasn't shown up this morning," she said, "and I'm sure something has happened to him." She almost burst into tears. "I'm absolutely sure. I feel it in my bones." She passed her hand distractedly through her gray close-clipped hair, and sighed deeply as she left the room.

Shaughnessy felt that things were beginning to move. They had hardly recovered from Miss Hope-Little when the next thing happened. This time it was a bit of luck, provided, ironically, by the Embassy's own machinery.

There was a knock at the door, and a small, nervous-looking man came in bearing a large Inter-Office envelope. He was clearly an Embassy messenger, and he was worried about something.

"This was for Mr Hewitt, sir," he said. "Miss Turenne isn't here. I thought I'd better bring it in."

"That's fine," said Shaughnessy quickly, stretching his hand out with authority to take the envelope. "You can leave it here."

"You see, it was delayed," said the messenger. This is what really seemed to be troubling him. "I don't know how it happened, but it should have been delivered yesterday." He seemed to want some reassurance.

"That's O.K." said Shaughnessy. "Perfectly O.K. You can leave it here now."

The messenger left with relief, and Shaughnessy untied the string fastening the envelope. Inside was a large sealed manilla envelope addressed to *Maurice Hewitt, Esq.*, and marked *Personal*, all in printed handwriting. There was no sender's name on it. After looking it over, Shaughnessy slit the envelope carefully, and found a smaller envelope inside, also sealed and marked *Personal*, but this time with Hewitt's name written.

"Well what do y'know?" said Shaughnessy. "Someone's making damn sure, eh?" With Goldberg bending over, he slit the smaller envelope carefully, and extracted its contents, a smaller piece of paper with two short verses typed on it. One could see instantly that the two verses had been typed on different machines, and by different people. The first verse was typed very unevenly, with a faded ribbon. It ran:

> *Jack and Jill*
> *Went up a hill*
> *To fetch a pail of laughter.*
> *If Jack falls down*
> *And breaks his crown,*
> *Will Jill come tumbling after?*

The second verse was well typed, and with a much blacker ribbon. It was obviously the reply:

> *Sceptre and crown*
> *Must tumble down,*
> *And in the dust both man and maid*
> *Will lie with the crooked scythe and spade.*

Shaughnessy read it aloud to Goldberg, and then read it again. "Well, what do you think?" he asked finally. "Isn't that the craziest bull you ever heard? Do you think it's supposed to be serious?"

Goldberg was thinking hard. "Well, the first part's easy. I suppose Hewitt is Jack, and we'll have to find out who Jill is. The second part—I seem to have heard it somewhere, or something like it, when we did literature two years ago."

"Your courses are a great help, Mort. Sure. I've heard it too—but what the hell. Who's Jill? That's what we want to know. Let's see if we can track down where it came from."

Goldberg went downstairs and asked the doorman to send for the messenger. When he got back, his chief was still looking at the verses.

"You know, I've been thinking," he said to Goldberg. "Scythe—that's the same as sickle, isn't it? And that's the Communist emblem, isn't it, something and sickle—

hammer and sickle, that's it. Then 'sceptre and crown tumbling down'—that's the same thing, eh? Getting rid of the royal family. Do you think this is some Communist message?"

"I don't know, Chief," said Goldberg. "Sounds more like a joke to me than a real message. I know I've heard something. . . ."

There was a knock at the door. It was the messenger.

"Come in," said Shaughnessy to the little man, who stood there, very worried at being recalled. "Just a little thing I meant to ask you. Do you know where this envelope you brought came from. Have you any way of telling?"

The messenger was greatly relieved that it was just as simple as that. "Oh yes," he said eagerly. "That came from the Private Office, from Mr. Abbot-Hume's room, sir. It was put in the box on Wednesday afternoon, late, and that's how it got delayed. It shouldn't have done, but it slipped to the bottom as it was late. Was there anything wrong, sir?"

"No, that's fine," said Shaughnessy. "That's all I wanted. Nobody knows, so nobody is hurt, eh?" he added significantly.

The messenger understood. "That's right, sir." He was clearly relieved that the incident was closed.

As the door closed, Shaughnessy was already going through the list of Embassy staff that had been given to him. There were three secretaries in the private Office.

"No one actually called Jill," he muttered, "but then he wasn't called Jack. So it's all a joke. Some joke! Look, Mort, will you get over there, wherever it is, and see what those girls look like. Try their machines, but don't let them know what you're looking for. There's got to be some Jill somewhere."

When Goldberg had left, Shaughnessy decided to go downstairs to see how the search for the weapon was getting on.

On the way down, he stopped at a bulletin board on which the Embassy advertisements and activities were displayed. It all looked so human and natural against the tragedy that had suddenly struck, lecture announcements, cars to be sold, houses to be sublet, hockey team fixtures. And in the middle of the sports activities there was the next engagement for the Pistol Team, shooting against the State Department team in three days' time. The notice was typed and signed, in minute handwriting, by Harriet Hope-Little. Now who would have thought that such a big woman would have such a small handwriting, Shaughnessy reflected. He looked at the typed names. There were four, including Miss Hope-Little; and the second on the list was Commander Abbot-Hume.

Something boiled up in Shaughnessy. He doesn't know about guns, he said to himself sarcastically—oh, no, I'm to get my information from Johnson. And what were those two talking about? Johnson—so Abbot-Hume had said—had "done the job and got away with it". Something smelt here.

He turned away in anger and walked round to the front gate to see if there was any news of the weapon being found. There was none. He walked back towards the Annex, and as he turned the corner he bumped into Goldberg, apparently on his way back, his mission fulfilled.

Goldberg was quite pleased with himself. "There's a Jill all right," he said, "and do you know who it is: it's Abbot-Hume's wife!"

Shaughnessy swallowed hard. Holding himself in, he said with unreal calmness: "Oh, I get it. Abbot-Hume's wife. How do you know she sent the note? Does she work there?"

"She doesn't, but she comes in and out. And on Wednesday . . ."

"She was there?"

"Yep. It was easy to check. Those Embassy secretaries are just as friendly as you could want. Jill came in Wednesday to go to a cocktail party with someone from the Embassy. Her husband was away. She waited in his room for a little while. Quite easy for her to type the note and slip it into an Inter-Office envelope. I checked the ribbon and the type. It fits."

"So she was just answering Mr Hewitt's poetry, eh? And her husband was away that day?" Shaughnessy was thinking aloud. "I wonder when he got back. Yeh," he muttered slowly, "it's building up. Y'see, Mort, he's on the Pistol Team too, like Miss Hope-Little, only he likes to pretend he doesn't know about guns. And his wife likes writing love letters to Hewitt. Yeh, let's get him in. No. Let's get her in first. Might be easier. Get her on the phone."

Goldberg found the number and dialled. He sat holding the phone for a long time while it rang and rang without a reply.

"O.K." said Shaughnessy. "Let's get her husband then. Can't afford to waste time." But they had no luck again. Goldberg rang the office, but was told he was out and not expected back until after lunch. Goldberg tried Jill's number again. Still no reply.

Shaughnessy was looking at him abstractedly as he put the receiver down. "Got an idea, Chief?" Goldberg asked him.

"Yeh, I think so," Shaughnessy said. "I've just been thinking about Abbot-Hume last night. He didn't say much, but he stuck pretty close to Usher. Heard them muttering something funny about two clowns. Y'know, I wouldn't be surprised if Usher isn't really behind all this. Don't forget what the Ambassador said."

The phone rang, and they both jumped. Shaughnessy yanked it up, and a happy smile spread over his face as he heard the message. He said: "O.K., I'll be there," and turned to Goldberg.

"It's the F.B.I.," he said cheerfully. "They want us to come down there. Got something interesting to tell us about Usher. Come on. Let's go."

They walked over quickly to their car. "Yeh," Shaughnessy muttered, as they got in. "Usher may not be as smart as he thinks. One step ahead of the police, eh? Well, we'll see."

III

At the F.B.I. office, McDonald was waiting for them. "Did you see Usher?" asked Shaughnessy.

"No, we didn't *see* him. We've got something on him though. Was he down here?"

"Oh yes, he was down here, or he said he was. I suppose he was talking to one of your big boys. What have you got?"

"It's a report from our man in Rome," said McDonald. "You heard what the Ambassador said last night, that Usher had done a job like this—looking for a double agent —in Rome. I asked Usher when it was, and cabled our man there to check on it. Want to read what he says?"

Shaughnessy read the brief report and smiled grimly. "Same thing, eh? Well, Mr Usher's got some explaining to do. What do you think?"

McDonald was unemotional. "Yes, we're looking into it. Can't go too fast. The report doesn't actually accuse him. Just that he went to Rome two years ago and three days later a British Embassy agent was found shot in a marsh near Rome. They don't really accuse him at all—just say that the murder was never solved. Of course, if the man who was shot was a double agent, anyone could have done it— the British, or the Communists, or the Italians themselves maybe—and of course it could have been just a non-political crime. They just don't know."

"Still," said Shaughnessy, "it's a funny coincidence. Usher just happened to be there, and he just happened to be here. Very funny. We'll see what he says this afternoon. Seeing him at 2.30."

"Have you any other leads?" asked McDonald.

Shaughnessy told him about the missing gun, and about Jill Abbot-Hume. McDonald made no comment on this, but said: "There's one other small thing that's come in that may lead somewhere on the Communist angle."

"Oh, what's that?"

"Well, we have some reports that mention Hewitt. We'd been told by British security that they were using him as an agent, and we allowed for that when we got reports in from *our* people. But naturally the British didn't tell us too much . . . don't really trust us, y'know, and, as a matter of fact, we don't really . . . well, enough of that. Anyhow, we had a few reports ourselves that mentioned him seeing various diplomatic people that we're watching, and there's one that we're particularly interested in for our own reasons. He's been seeing a lot recently of a woman called Thérèse Marot. She's at the French Embassy, and we have our eyes on her. Can't tell, of course, but we're pushing this a bit."

"Was she at the British Embassy party last night?" asked Shaughnessy.

"She was," said McDonald. "And she was also at a British cocktail party the night before, Wednesday. She went off to dinner afterwards with Hewitt, as it happens."

"With Hewitt? I thought he had dinner with Usher?"

"He did," said McDonald, "but Usher just didn't happen to mention that there were some others along too. She was there, and there was a man called Scott"—McDonald looked down his nose quizzically—"who happens to be scientific attaché at the British Embassy."

Shaughnessy looked at him "Scientific? You mean atomic energy and all that?"

"That's it," said McDonald. "And there was one more person in the party. Your friend Jill."

"She was? Very nice. And who took her home?"

"Hewitt," said McDonald quietly.

Shaughnessy was sarcastic. "Her husband was still away, I suppose."

"Got something on that too," said McDonald. "He may have been supposed to be out of town, but we've got a report here that puts him in town at 7 p.m. that night."

Shaughnessy looked at him with some admiration. "Don't miss much, do you? So he was back in town. Well, we'd better see him quickly. I think I'll get back to the Embassy. I want to see about those guns. Should have a report in by now."

He was silent as they drove back, but suddenly, as they turned a corner into Massachussetts Avenue, his hand slapped down on the wheel in excitement, sending out a piercing blast from his horn, which startled a timid pedestrian about to cross the road and caused him to dash back in alarm to the safety of the pavement, cursing all police cars.

Shaughnessy was exultant. "I completely forgot," he said to Goldberg. "I've got something direct on our friend Usher, a little gift that he doesn't know about. Got it right here." As he talked, he was delving into his coat pockets, first the left hand and then the right, from which he finally extracted the small piece of paper that Usher had dropped and he had picked up as they stood together looking down at Hewitt's body. He handed it to Goldberg. "I haven't even looked at it. What does it say?"

Goldberg looked at it carefully. "It's in French," he muttered. "A bit difficult to follow. Seems to be about interior movements . . . spontaneity, then there's something about my wish and the act . . . it's really a bit difficult. We can get someone to translate it," he concluded lamely.

Shaughnessy kept on driving, but managed to give him a scornful look out of the side of his eye. "All these evening courses, eh, and you can't translate a simple piece of French." I bet Sergeant Friday speaks fluent French, he thought to himself. "Why don't you take it up," he said with some sarcasm to Goldberg. "Quite useful, you know."

Sarcasm was always wasted on Goldberg. "I'm thinking of taking it next year," he said. "Ruth and I are planning to go to Canada for our vacation, and they speak French there, in Quebec."

"Yeh, I heard of it," said Shaughnessy. "Perhaps we should postpone the case till next year. Here, give it back to me," and he snatched the paper back and stuffed it into his pocket, his good humour over.

By this time they were turning into the Embassy gates. The policeman on duty had a note for Shaughnessy that had come up from the Police Station. They had examined the three Colts found in the range, and also recovered and tested the gun kept in the *Dove*. None of them had fired the bullet that had been found in Hewitt's head.

"Where's that female?" muttered Shaughnessy to Goldberg. "She'd better produce the other gun from the range."

They made their way up to Hewitt's office, which seemed to have become theirs by now. A pretty red-haired girl was sitting in the next room, and when Shaughnessy and Goldberg passed, she rose and said: "I'm Betty Turenne, Mr Hewitt's secretary. I think you wanted me." As Shaughnessy looked at her more closely, he saw that she was very distressed, her eyes swollen from weeping.

"Oh yes," he said to her kindly. "Are there any messages for me?"

"Just one," she said. "Miss Hope-Little phoned. She says that she doesn't have the other gun in her car. She says are you sure it isn't at the Annex, in the guards' room?"

Shaughnessy muttered to himself, and turned to Miss Turenne. "It's very sad about Mr Hewitt," he began. "You must feel it. Have you been with him long?"

Miss Turenne began to answer, but clearly found it too much, and burst into tears. It was most disturbing, the first time that Shaughnessy had felt the human side of the tragedy. He tried to help her by turning her mind to more practical things.

"Are you English?" he asked her.

She made a strong effort to pull herself together. "No," she said, gulping. "I'm Canadian."

"Oh, which part of Canada?" he asked.

"From St Guillaume. It's a little town near Quebec."

"I suppose you speak French as well as English," said Shaughnessy.

She smiled wanly. "Yes, I spoke French completely until I was twelve." She blew her nose with a tiny handkerchief, and tried to appear composed.

"I'd like to ask you a few things later," said Shaughnessy. "Is there anything that you can think of now that might help us to understand what has happened?"

Miss Turenne tried to speak. She seemed obviously trying to say no, but again the effort seemed to be too much.

"Now, now, don't worry," said Shaughnessy. "We'll leave it to later. But here, you can help me in one thing since you know French so well. Could you translate a few lines for me?" He pulled Usher's paper from his pocket, giving Goldberg a sly look of triumph.

"Oh yes, sir," said Miss Turenne gratefully. "I'll type it out."

She disappeared into her room, and for quite a time they heard her typing, at first hesitantly while she worked the thing out, and then quite regularly while she apparently typed out the final version.

"Nice girl," said Shaughnessy. "Quite useful knowing French, isn't it? You'll just have to take it up. Perhaps she'll teach you."

They joked for a few minutes until Miss Turenne appeared with the original paper and her English version in her hand. She gave it hesitantly to Shaughnessy saying: "It's rather difficult. I couldn't really understand it, so it isn't a very good translation," but then she appeared to be on the verge of tears again and left the room hurriedly. Shaughnessy and Goldberg bent over to read the lines:

> There is no point in my falling back on the interior process, which is anyhow devoid of any spontaneity. I must turn to concrete and specific activity, so that in aiming at an objective, spontaneous action has a chance to find expression. In having this objective, my spontaneity both establishes itself and is conscious of itself. Thus in one and the same process, my will determines the content of the act and finds its justification through it.

Shaughnessy looked at Goldberg. "What the hell is all this about? Does it make sense to you?"

To Shaughnessy's surprise, Goldberg seemed tremendously excited. "This is it, Chief," he said eagerly. "This is what you've been looking for."

"What I've been looking for?"

"It's Usher, isn't it? You want to tie him in. Can't see where he fits. Well this will show it."

"You mean this is evidence?" Shaughnessy looked at Goldberg incredulously.

"It's better than evidence. It's insight."

A policeman put his head round the door and came in, carrying a small package. "Oh, it's lunch," said Shaughnessy. "I asked them to bring something over from the Embassy canteen." There were sandwiches, pie and coffee. "O.K." he went on, picking up a sandwich. "It's insight. Let's have it."

Goldberg took a sandwich himself and held it in his hand rather nervously. "Well, it's just this," he began. "I think this note explains why Usher could have done it. It doesn't prove it, just shows the connection."

"Why is it in French?"

"Oh, that's easy. He was probably educated in France, or he thinks in French, or writes things down in French for privacy. That's quite easy with professors."

"Probably why he wears a beard, eh? O.K. So he writes in French. But what does it mean?"

Goldberg hesitated for a minute. "You'll probably get as sore as hell with me over this," he said finally, "but my idea is that maybe the clue to the whole thing lies—now for God's sake don't get mad at me—I think it lies in the cultural pattern behind this, and not so much in the ordinary evidence. Oh, I know how you feel about my anthropology courses, so I didn't want to say anything. But I thought this all along, even before you showed me the paper from Usher. Now that I've seen it I'm convinced this is the right approach."

Shaughnessy said nothing. Perhaps he groaned slightly. Goldberg looked at him nervously. "Well you do agree, Chief, that the message on the paper doesn't make any sense by itself."

"Oh, I agree with that," said Shaughnessy. "Go ahead, Mort. Who knows? You may have this whole thing wrapped up in anthropology. No, it's O.K. Go ahead."

"Well," said Goldberg, greatly encouraged, "what are the alternatives? Either we can start off with the ordinary clues, like the gun, or the Communist business, or that Jack and Jill business, and look on this Usher paper as a sideshow, or we could start with the Usher paper, see where that leads, and then bring in the ordinary evidence."

"Well, where the hell does it lead?" asked Shaughnessy irritably. "What the hell does it mean?"

"I think I know," said Goldberg, "but of course I can't prove anything. It's one of those cases where you have to use intuition. I felt this from the beginning."

"*What* did you feel?"

"I felt that this wasn't an ordinary killing, not a crime of passion, nothing related to a rational object. For some reason—perhaps because of all these crazy diplomats—I got the feeling that it was more like a philosophical murder—and then Usher's paper came along to back it up."

"Mort, I'm listening to you, I'm being patient, but I swear I haven't the first idea what you're talking about."

"Well, let me put it this way, Chief. We think of murder as someone called x being killed by someone called y. Everything centres round the death of x. Why did he have to be killed? But suppose the emphasis is on y. The question then becomes: 'Why did y feel the need to kill?'"

"Oh, you mean you look for a crazy guy who likes killing, so he killed the first person he meets without any reason, or he has some crazy reason, like he thinks he's been insulted. . . ."

"Oh no, he has a good reason for killing, otherwise it would be Gide's gratuitous act."

"Gide's what?"

"Sorry, Chief. Skip that. It's something we were doing last year. I shouldn't have mentioned it. No, there *is* a reason, but it's the same thing as when a hunter kills an animal. He needs it for food, but the act of killing is more significant than getting hold of food. It has importance in itself. Like the Zuni. . . ."

"The Zuni? Listen, Mort. . . ."

"Well, the Zuni Indians—we were studying them just

last week—they're not violent for the sake of violence. They're nice, gentle people. They accept death as being inevitable, and if someone dies, his close relatives have to sit quietly by themselves for some days because they, as much as the dead man, have been brought directly into the mystery of life and death for a short while. The point is, though, that even if someone kills someone else, it's still the *living* man, the murderer, they're sympathetic to. They feel that he's been touched—almost sanctified—by the mystery of death, so he has to go away for a while. When he comes back they look on him with increased respect."

"And you think we've got a tame Zuni running around here?"

"No, Chief, what I tried to explain was that if you were looking at a death among the Zunis . . ."

"Mort, will you come to the point?"

"But, Chief, this *is* the point. If you were dealing with the Zunis, the cultural pattern would show not a different motivation for killing but a different attitude *towards* killing when it happens. Well, here we're dealing with a different attitude too, and it may show us who did it. I think Usher's paper *does* show it."

"How? It seemed to me just a lot of words."

"Exactly. The Zunis couldn't explain in words. Words aren't their medium of expression. But this man Usher is in a word culture—that's Oxford—and he has to put things down in words before he does anything significant."

"You mean this paper says he was going to do a murder."

"Not a murder—an *act*—an external act. He says in his paper that his moral conscience requires him to find something external, something specific to do. It's got to have a desired objective, but Usher is more interested in the effect on himself than in the act's content. Or rather it's both: the content of the act and the satisfaction of looking at it and realizing that he, as an individual, has acted. Here,

Chief," he said, handing Shaughnessy the paper. "Read it again and see if it doesn't make sense."

Shaughnessy read the few sentences slowly and tilted his chair back. For once he was quite impressed by his sergeant. "You mean that if he felt Hewitt really deserved to die—suppose he were found out to have been a traitor—Usher would actually want to perform the act himself."

"I'm not sure if he would actually do it himself. He might. But it might be enough just to plan it—to be directly involved in it."

"So it might be anyone—Abbot-Hume, or Usher's secretary—what's her name—Hope-Little—or Johnson—no, it couldn't be him—but somehow Usher's involved!"

"Exactly," said Goldberg eagerly. "The key thing is that he needs something external—he says so clearly in the note —something positive, violent. The more violent the better. A killing would be ideal from his point of view."

"Would he admit this? Is that part of the act?"

"Oh no," said Goldberg. "Just to admit it and go to the electric chair would be a negation of life. He wants to live. He intends to. You can see that by what he writes. No, he won't admit anything. If he did it himself, or if they did it between them, their tracks will be completely covered. You'll have to get them with black-and-white evidence—ordinary evidence. But if I'm right, we know where to look, and we won't be fooled by clues that point elsewhere."

"Do you think he would manufacture those sort of clues himself?"

"Oh yes, if he thought they would take. I shouldn't think he wants anyone else to be actually executed. But we can certainly expect all kinds of false leads."

"So the best thing to do is to sit tight, and watch him, and watch all of them."

"That's what I think. With luck, something will go wrong for them. They're smart, but they're only human.

Something unexpected will happen if we wait for it and watch them."

"Y'know, Mort," said Shaughnessy, "I probably ought to have my head examined, but for the first time I think you may have something. Let's get the Boss in on this."

He picked up the phone and in a moment was talking to Rawlins, the Assistant Commissioner responsible for this section of police work.

"It's the British Embassy business, Chief," he said. "I've got a man coming down to Headquarters at 2.30. I don't want to say anything—I'm at the Embassy now—but could you put your head in for a moment while he is there? I'll tell you all about it when I get down." Rawlins agreed, and Shaughnessy replaced the receiver.

At that moment there was a knock, and a policeman from the gate came in. He looked rather mournful. "We've found something new, Captain," he said.

"You've found the gun?"

"No, it's a cat, a Siamese cat, in the wood, shot dead."

"Shot?"

"Yeh, neat little hole. Wandered around bleeding for quite a time. Not very pretty."

Shaughnessy and Goldberg looked at each other. "Hope-Little's cat," muttered Shaughnessy. "She thought something had happened. Where about in the wood did you find it?"

"Oh, a way out at the other end. We've brought it in. He's downstairs, in the guards' room."

"I'll come down in a minute," said Shaughnessy. "Want to make a phone call first."

The man went off, and Goldberg tried again to reach Jill. There was still no reply. "We'll have to send someone out there," he said. "Maybe she's just not answering the phone. Come on, let's go down and see the cat."

They went down together and saw the fine sleek animal

128

lying in the majesty of death, with the policeman bending over, trying to extract the bullet with a small knife.

"Send the bullet down, and let me know what you find," said Shaughnessy after a little while. "We're going down to Headquarters. Oh yes," he added. "I want one of you to go out to this address and see if you can get hold of Mrs Abbot-Hume." He gave them Jill's address, and left with Goldberg.

Their car was in the Annex parking-lot. As they got in, Shaughnessy said to Goldberg. "You know, your theory about Usher's fine, but I'm still interested in a few simple things, like the gun, and Miss Jill and her husband. I'd like to lay my hands on them. I'd know where I was."

He started the car and drove towards the main road. Just as he was turning out of the drive, a little British car—an Austin—darted round sharply and almost took off one of his fenders. Shaughnessy swore as he swerved to avoid the car.

"Woman driver," he muttered. He had had time to notice that the driver was a pretty young girl.

In the little Austin, Jill, sitting nervously at the wheel, sighed with relief at the narrow shave, stretching out her left hand to make sure that the gun, hidden under maps and papers, was still safe on the little shelf in front of her.

FIVE

"Secrets with girls, like loaded guns with boys,
Are never valued till they make a noise."
                              CRABBE, The Maid's Story

I

SHE had been awakened that morning by Dennis coming into their room. She blinked her eyes for a moment in the bright sunlight. He stood there, fresh from his shave, tall, slender, quiet.

He heard her move and came over to the bed. "Oh, Dennis," she said. "Did it really happen?"

He sat down on the side of the bed and took her hand. "Yes," he said, "it happened." She held on to his hand, and it seemed to give her strength.

"Dennis, I must tell you . . ." she began haltingly.

"About Maurice?" he asked quietly.

"Yes, about Maurice. Did you know . . ."

"Do you really want to talk about it now, Jill?" he said. "Shouldn't we wait?"

She could say nothing, but simply held his hand tighter, feeling his strength flowing into her. In a moment he left her, softly, and went downstairs to drink a cup of coffee and drive off to the Embassy.

How am I going to get through the day, she thought, and all the days to come? She got up painfully and stood staring out of the window for a long time without seeing anything.

Dennis must have known all the time, she said to herself. It must have been obvious. That night a week ago when he was so quiet and withdrawn. Was he planning to kill Maurice then? No, no, he could never *plan* a thing like that.

It must have been some sudden fight. No, even that was impossible. The whole thing was impossible. This kind of thing only happened to other people. It had not been Dennis at all. Someone else—a hold-up man—some private enemy. Yes, but if it were Dennis. . . .

She had nothing to do that morning. That was what had been wrong with life in Washington. Dennis went out to his job full of purpose. Usually all she had to do was to give the maid instructions, and then if she wanted she was free. Free for what? In the old life there had always been things to do, activities that led somewhere. At school, at Oxford, there had been so much going on of which she was the centre. In London even more, there was the flat to furnish and take care of, shopping, seeing old friends, week-ends in the country, odd trips to Paris—life seemed to bounce along cheerfully all day. And when the moment finally arrived for the evening glass of sherry before dinner, she and Dennis had sipped it quietly together in happy enjoyment of each other.

How different it all was from the round of cocktail parties that saluted the evening in Washington. She had enjoyed these cocktail parties so much at first, they were so lavish, so easy . . . in a few minutes one moved so deliciously to a lighter plane of existence. In a way they seemed to provide the release she needed here. With the pattern of life set so securely during the day, the second cocktail brought a reminder to one of powers unrealized. With the third cocktail one began to feel the horizons lifting—one talked with so much more freedom about oneself, one's friends—anything. Life ceased to be a dull road that one could see ahead, and became a mysterious path that could lead anywhere, with all kinds of adventures on the way. She had had so much fun with Maurice at these parties—he had seemed part of the mystery and excitement. And now he was dead and the whole cocktail business seemed dry and rotten.

She wandered slowly round the kitchen—it was the maid's day off—putting things away. She glanced at the papers and read the details of the murder without taking much in. The phone rang. She listened to the ringing for a moment, almost afraid to answer. Then she picked up the receiver. It was Flantin, sad and sympathetic. He said almost nothing, just seemed to want to show that he was there, and understood. Was that all? There was something rather odd in the way he always seemed to be around—as if he were waiting for her, somehow.

She went upstairs and wandered aimlessly into her bedroom, picking things up and putting them down. Coming to Dennis' dressing-room, she sat down looking at the neatly-arranged toilet articles on his chest of drawers, at the closets full of carefully hung clothes. It was his world—she rarely came in here—but to-day she opened a closet door, and aimlessly pushed the hangers along the rail, straightening them mechanically as she did so. One hanger, on which there was an old sports jacket, seemed to hang rather crookedly. Lifting it, she felt a heavy weight in one pocket, and she put her hand inside to see what it was. Her fingers closed round the handle of a revolver. She pulled it out miserably. It was a Colt 38, the gun of the murder according to the papers. She broke it open. There were three bullets in it.

II

And now she felt real despair come over her. She must do something. It looked like the guns that they practised with at the range. That was where he had got it, no doubt. Could she return it there without being seen? She dressed quickly, with the gun lying before her on her dressing-table urging her on. She would drive there immediately.

But suddenly a new thought crossed her mind. What if she were seen? And yes. If she returned it there, they could still connect Dennis with it. He was up at the range constantly. It was a mania of his.

No, she thought. I must get rid of it quickly. Into the river. That's the safest place. She was ready now. Picking up a small handbag, and at the last minute snatching a raincoat to cover the gun, she ran into the garage to get the little Austin she used. She opened the garage doors, and was just backing out with the gun and her bag beside her on the seat when a voice hailed her.

"Hallo, Jill. Coming to fetch me?"

Jill was so startled that for a moment she didn't recognize who had spoken. Then she saw. It was Lady Eldridge, the Minister's wife. Coming to fetch her? Oh God, she had completely forgotten. The Bazaar that the Embassy wives were arranging to raise funds for the Daughters of the British Empire Society. Oh, surely she didn't have to go through with this, not to-day!

"I'm so glad we have this to do," said Lady Eldridge, opening the door of the car and settling herself comfortably in the seat next to Jill. "It will take our minds off this terrible thing. Isn't it awful? Poor Maurice. Hugh is absolutely baffled. What does Dennis think?"

As Lady Eldridge opened the car door, Jill had just managed to push the gun into the little shelf in front of the driving-wheel. She hardly knew what she replied. It made no difference to Lady Eldridge, who had no real interest in what either Jill or her husband thought. A murder to her was, in a sense, something that didn't belong to an Embassy or its activities, even if a genuine Foreign Office character happened to be the victim. Lady Eldridge was a tall, stately woman, shedding around herself, though no longer young, the still effulgent rays of a fine pre-Raphaelite beauty. The Worcestershire vicarage in which she had been nurtured remained her spiritual home, whether she served in Oslo or Tibet, with rummage sales and other good works her daily

133

meat. A true Daughter of the British Empire, her mind was full of the Bazaar they were working on, and a murder was not likely to upset her schedule.

"I'm a bit worried about some of the helpers," she confided to Jill as they drove up Wisconsin Avenue towards the Parish House of St Sebastian's Church in which the Bazaar was to be held. "They don't all seem to be pulling their weight. I wonder if you could keep an eye on the Lucky Dip Section this morning. I don't quite know why we left it to Mrs Childs. She tries very hard, of course, but she doesn't quite seem . . . well, you know what I mean."

Jill knew. Mrs Childs was a dreamy kind of girl, without that kind of discipline, developed in a good English school, that could apply itself to good works, at a moment's notice, in any foreign land. Lucky Dips included a Riddle-Me-Ree Section for which individual Quizzes had to be made up. This had all been allotted to Mrs Childs automatically because her husband was the Educational Attaché; but somehow it wasn't working. It was a compliment to Jill that she should be asked by the Minister's wife to act as her Lieutenant, but it was also an order.

There was no time to do anything about the gun after they arrived. Jill locked the car and went in, dazed, with Lady Eldridge. The Embassy wives were all waiting in the Parish House, buzzing with talk of the murder, but in a moment Lady Eldridge had rallied them to the tasks in hand. Cast-off clothes were being sorted and priced, cakes and cookies baked in their homes by the good ladies were being packed into Huntley and Palmer biscuit tins in preparation for the day, a special curtained-off stand was being assembled for Pepita Beauchamp, who had undertaken to read palms, and over· all, perched on high ladders, the more agile ladies, neatly clad in their regulation uniforms— tailored suits and little cloche hats—were spreading flags, paper streamers and other decorations.

Jill found herself working in one corner with the flustered Mrs Childs. There was much to do, and it was impossible to leave. At around twelve-thirty some of the workers managed to excuse themselves in order to go home and take lunch with their families, but Jill had agreed to lunch with Lady Eldridge. Could she get away?

"Should we skip lunch?" she suggested timidly to Lady Eldridge. "I want to go up to the Embassy to see Dennis, and you probably have lots to do."

"Nonsense, dear," said Lady Eldridge. "You've been such a help. I want to give you a very nice lunch. You don't eat enough—you're all bones—and if you go up there, Dennis will give you a sandwich in that horrible canteen. You come with me, and you can take me back to the Embassy right after lunch. I have to see Hugh."

Jill took a frightened look at the shelf when they entered the car, but the gun seemed well enough hidden by the maps and other papers there. At lunch she took an old-fashioned to steady her nerves, and managed to get through the meal without trouble.

They drove up together to the Embassy after lunch. Jill was so nervous as she turned into the drive that she almost hit a big black car that was swinging out. It was a narrow shave. She sighed with relief. Her ordeal was almost over. She stopped in the car-park and was standing there saying good-bye when suddenly Lady Eldridge had a bright idea.

"You'll be with Dennis for a little while, I suppose," she asked Jill.

"Just a little while," said Jill, thinking quickly. "He wants me to go over a list of guests for a cocktail party we're giving next Thursday. I hope you'll come."

"Love to," said Lady Eldridge heartily. "You and Dennis give such nice parties. So many young people. But I wonder, dear, if you could do me a favour. I want to run home to get a book I promised to give to Hugh, for the Ambassador. I meant to bring it with me, but I forgot. Could I borrow your car for ten minutes?"

"Oh, I'll run you back," said Jill eagerly.

"Nonsense, dear," said Lady Eldridge. "You have to go and see Dennis. Besides, I love driving these little toys. I wish we didn't have to run the Bentley. These little things are so much more fun." She took hold of the door handle firmly and was about to enter.

Panic seized Jill. Quickly, she bent into the car ahead of Lady Eldridge and snatched at the gun and her coat, muffling them together. "I'll take my coat," she said lamely. "It looks like rain."

"Do you think so?" said Lady Eldridge, settling herself comfortably into the seat. "Looks fine to me. Well, see you in about quarter of an hour."

Jill was left standing miserably holding the coat, the gun, and her bag. "I'll get a taxi,' she thought, and was turning to leave, when out of the corner of her eye she saw that the Ambassador had turned through the gate and was bearing down on her. She was standing in the parking-lot next to an open car, an old vintage model. Quickly she slipped the gun into the car. There was a wide pocket in the door, and the gun slid in there easily.

Yes, the Ambassador was coming straight to her. "Good-afternoon," he said genially. "Isn't it a lovely day? I'm just going for a little walk in the garden. Why don't you come with me?"

She could hardly refuse. It was clear that he wanted to talk to somebody. "How tragic about Hewitt," he said. "Very tragic."

Jill tried to reply suitably. "Yes," she said, "and it was such a perfect evening before it all happened."

The Ambassador brightened. "You did like the fire-works," he said. "It was sad it all ended that way, but it wasn't a bad show before that, was it?" Yes, he wanted to talk about the fireworks. They walked around the garden for about twenty minutes until finally Jill was free.

As calmly as she could, she strolled back to the parking-lot to retrieve the gun. She looked around her speechlessly. The old car was gone.

Behind her, there was a joyful tooting. She turned. Her little Austin was bouncing up through the gate. "Thank you so much, dear," said Lady Eldridge, getting out of the car, with a large book in her hand. "Such fun to drive. Have you finished the list already? Well, I must go and see Hugh. Good-bye, dear. I'll come for you to-morrow at eleven. We've a lot to do yet for the Bazaar."

SIX

*"Is it I who draw the bow, or does the bow
draw me, into tension?"*

Zen and the Art of Archery

I

Now why on earth did I have to adopt that tone to that poor, harmless policeman, thought Ambrose, replacing the receiver in the little room outside Grover's office. I suppose it's the atmosphere down here. The F.B.I. never seem quite real—like the Holy Roman Empire. Perhaps coming down here has taken me back to the old days. I was young then, and we joked about everything.

It was good to see Grover. He had always liked him— a Harvard man and a Rhodes Scholar. He was one of the anonymous people of the F.B.I. The public never heard his name. He had worked on security questions then. Now he was on different work—drugs. He had put on a lot of weight but he was the same Grover. He was delighted to see Ambrose.

"I'll never forget the night we had Tim Sargent down here," he chuckled. "Do you remember? We all tried to do his trick of rocking on the back of a chair. Do you know, I can still do it." He climbed up on to his chair, pushed it gently off the perpendicular, and teetered cheerfully back and forth. "Or do you think I'm too old now for this sort of stuff?"

"Oh no," said Ambrose, *"Donec virenti canities . . ."*

"Abest morosa," Grover chimed in. "Do you remember anything else? I've forgotten all my Latin except dear old Horace."

"Ah, but I'm paid to remember it all," said Ambrose. "However . . ."

"However, you haven't come to talk about Horace, I know." Grover climbed down carefully. "I suppose it's the murder. McDonald is working on it."

"Yes," said Ambrose. "I met him last night. Very solid Scot. But no, there's something else I want to ask you. What do you know about Sanati?"

"Sanati? Do you mean Vittorio Sanati, the Neapolitan dope agent. Runs a ring through Jamaica. Yes, we know a lot about him."

"No, I mean Emilio Sanati, the physicist."

"Oh, he's beyond me."

"Well, he's over here at the moment from Italy. Could you find out?"

"Subito, signor," said Grover. He disappeared and was back in a few minutes with a quiet, almost meek-looking F.B.I. man whom he introduced as Gustafson.

"I've told Gustafson about you," he said. "He knows all about your Sanati."

"Sanati is over here to give three lectures at Columbia University," Gustafson told them. "And he was one of the speakers at a meeting here this week of the K.F.W.F. group. . . ."

"K.F.W.F.?" repeated Ambrose.

"Oh, that's *Keep the Free World Free*—strong anti-Communist organization. They had a big rally the other night at Constitution Hall."

"Ah, that's interesting, very. Must have been a heavy cultural gathering to use Sanati. Pretty solid stuff, his physics."

"Oh, he didn't talk about physics. They had a lot of scientists and writers on the platform. The meeting was organized by Hubert Ross, the ex-Communist. He got people there from all over the world."

139

"Hubert Ross? Otherwise Umberto Rossi—Umberto Angelo Rossi, I think it is. Ah yes. We all know dear Umberto. Second only to Whitaker Chambers. He's really a good boy now, is he? Public figure, eh? Organizes meetings: *Why I left Communism*. Made a good thing out of it, no doubt . . . $50 a day retainer . . . lives at the Mayflower with a bevy of beauties. . . ."

"Oh no," said Gustafson. "Nothing like that. He lives all alone in a little house in Bethesda. Devotes himself to the cause. Does splendid work."

Ambrose dropped his head apologetically. "Sorry, forgive me. Mustn't joke. So he arranged the meeting at which Sanati spoke about the dangers of Communism?"

"He didn't really make a speech. Just got up for a minute. But he's got a big name, they say, and that was important."

"Yes, indeed. And now tell me, if I do not shock you, have you kept an eye on Sanati while he's been in Washington? Perhaps you know what he's been doing during the last couple of days?"

Gustafson looked at Grover, who nodded. "Yes, sir. We've looked after him." He opened a notebook that he had with him. "He was the guest of honour at a dinner at the Italian Embassy on Wednesday night. On Thursday morning he stayed in his hotel, the Century, and then in the afternoon he visited the British Embassy"—he looked up and smiled at Ambrose—"but I don't know who he saw there. Later on he was visited by Ross, then he dined with some Italians from their Embassy, and after dinner he went out to your Embassy again, to the reception, the fireworks party, with them. I suppose you may have seen him there. Excuse me, sir, but could you tell me . . ."

It was at this point that Grover's secretary had come into the room and said that Ambrose was wanted on the phone. He took it in a little room outside. It was Miss Hope-Little, sounding very perturbed. A police captain up at the

Embassy wanted her to go and talk to him. Should she go?

"Why, certainly," Ambrose had told her. "Tell them all. I'll ring up and see what it's all about. Must give them a helping hand, you know."

He phoned Shaughnessy, and then, back in Grover's room, made his apologies and prepared to go.

Gustafson still pressed for an answer. "Is there anything you can tell us, sir, about Sanati?" he asked.

"Nothing much to tell yet, Mr Gustafson. But there may be. And you are helping, yes, very much." He looked at his watch. "Oh, I really must run. Thank you all so much." He quickly made his adieus, caught a taxi at the door, and was off up Massachusetts Avenue.

II

He felt that something was emerging. It might be true, or it might not. But he could visualize it as truth, and if it were, there was no time to be lost. Arrived at the Embassy, he ran up the stairs to Scott's room, closed the door carefully, and said: "Walter, can we talk? I don't want to waste any time."

Walter looked at him in obvious surprise. The usual flippant greeting was arrested by this very odd approach.

"Can I pull this out?" asked Ambrose, detaching the telephone from its outlet. Scott waited, silent.

"Walter, how well do you know Sanati?"

Walter lifted his head in amazement at the question. He seemed absolutely dumbfounded: speech had been taken from him. Then he said slowly: "I know him: he's quite a well-known physicist, you know."

"Walter, don't let's waste time," said Ambrose. "I may be a hundred per cent. wrong, but I've got to ask you. Did he come to see you yesterday afternoon?"

"Yes," said Walter quietly.

Ambrose steadied himself for the real question. "And did

141

you decide to show him some of your work, your secret work?"

It was out in the open. The pain between the two friends filled the small, bare room. Scott said nothing for a moment. Some awful torment seemed to be passing through his mind, and then it was as if he had come through to calm water.

"I've been crazy, Ambrose. I don't know how you guessed. I need some advice. I've been an absolute idiot."

"Tell me just what happened."

Scott lit a cigarette to give himself a moment, and then spoke quite calmly. "It's funny. I think our talk at lunch yesterday must have pushed me into it. You remember. We talked about scientists being cut off by all the suspicion and cold war—*I* talked anyhow—and when I got back here, Sanati came—it had been arranged some days ago—routine diplomatic channels—but we talked, and he's a great physicist and I suddenly felt: to hell with all this secrecy. He didn't really press me to find out what we've been doing. It was I who felt that I wanted to assert the principle. . . . Oh, it's been building up in me for some time. I've hated the whole business of secret government work, but yesterday, it seemed to hit me. . . . He was sitting there, one of the great minds of our time, just where you're sitting, and there behind, in that steel cabinet, I had some papers I was working on, and I asked him if he'd like to see them. . . ."

"There was no suggestion at all from him?"

"Well, yes. I think somehow the conversation got round that way . . . perhaps he steered it . . . I don't know. If he did, I was ready for it. I said I wanted to give him some of our work on a purely personal basis, to assert the principle. After all, he's a great physicist, nothing political in it, and he said he'd be very interested."

"And did you give it to him?"

"No, I said I'd get it ready. I've been working on . . ."

' Don't tell me what the subject is. I don't want to know."

"Well I told him I'd make an abstract of some really interesting stuff that we've developed. It really derives from some published work of his. I thought that he *should* see it. I wanted to take any technical stuff out of the papers . . . application and so on. . . . I just wanted him to see the theoretical stuff. I said I'd have it ready for him by this afternoon."

"Have you got it ready?"

"Well, almost. I worked late yesterday. It's there in my cabinet."

"Does he know it's ready?"

"Yes, I told him last night at the party that it was pretty well finished."

"But you've given him nothing so far?"

"No." Suddenly Scott broke down from his calm. "Oh, Ambrose. What an idiot I am. How could I have been so stupid? If you hadn't come in now and asked me. . . . But what was wrong? I know that there's something wrong, and yet I was acting from the best of motives. There was nothing personal, no personal profit—it was to ease my mind, my conscience . . . and yet . . ."

Ambrose smiled at him. "Yes, now we can talk about it. What *was* wrong? Why shouldn't an individual act as an individual, freely? Well, for one thing, there are situations in which we aren't individuals. If that weren't so, how can you explain a thing like trust? Why does it mean so much? I suppose we know that a thing like that is just as important as the assertion of individuality. If we betray it, we betray ourselves. . . ."

"Yes," said Scott slowly. "I lived with this for a night and a day. It was horrible."

"And for another thing," Ambrose smiled wryly at him, "what makes you think that this was one scientist talking to another? Well, perhaps it was, at one level, but at another level . . ."

143

"You don't mean . . ."

"Yes, indeed, I *do* mean. Signor Sanati is not quite as pure a scientist as you thought. Or let me be fair to him. He has his own set of loyalties. . . ."

"Good God!" The whole thing suddenly became clear to Scott. "Good God, man. Is that it? Yes, I think you're right. Some things he said. . . . Oh, my God."

"Well, it's all over now," said Ambrose, "and you're going back to England next week, so it won't come up again."

"Yes, thank God. I've had enough of Government work. I'm not really fitted to do it. I'll be back at the university teaching. What a relief. But do you think . . . ?"

"Don't worry about it. I don't think you will hear any more of it. When do you actually leave?"

"I'm supposed to fly to Toronto this afternoon to deliver a lecture at the University. I am staying at the Royal York. Be there for two days. Then I come back here, and sail for England on Monday. Should I still go to Toronto?" Scott looked at Ambrose humbly and sadly.

"Why not? Very good thing for you to go, precisely now. You'll have to forget all this . . . well, you can't forget it: just add it to your experience. It cost you a lot. Don't throw it away. But before you go, there's one thing you have to do."

"Phone Sanati?"

"Yes. Don't tell him you've changed your mind. Tell him the papers aren't quite ready yet. We will want to give him a little rope."

Scott connected the phone and put the call through. When he spoke to Sanati, he tried to be at ease, wrapping up the message in a little polite verbiage; but to Ambrose his voice sounded stilted and unnatural. However, the message was given. Scott was to telephone him again in two days time on returning from Toronto.

The call over, they sat looking at each other silently for a moment. Then Ambrose said: "There's just one more thing I'd like to ask you. What about Mme Marot?"

"What about her?" Scott asked gruffly.

"Has she been an influence one way or another in this thing?"

Scott looked down at his desk. "I've never talked to her openly about it, but somehow she seemed to sense what was going on in my mind. We talked many times around the subject. I wasn't sure what she meant. She disliked the whole Iron Curtain business, secrecy, hate—everything, and yet . . ."

"Yes?"

"It's as if she didn't want to press me into anything. She wanted me to find out things for myself, to be at ease with myself. It's as if she wanted the truth to come to me, what I was, what I really believed in. . . ."

The phone rang. It was someone from the Supply Mission down town who wanted Scott to go down and talk to them about details connected with the handing over of his post. There was an official car at the door, as it happened, and Scott hurried off to catch it. Ambrose waved good-bye. Walter looked sad and lonely as the car carried him away.

III

Now for a little homework, thought Ambrose, as he strolled over to his office on the Chancery side. Miss Hope-Little was out. There was a brief note from her on his desk saying simply that Palmerston was lost and that she had gone off to try and find him. There was also a separate message saying that Sir Hugh Eldridge had the file with the papers that he had asked about that morning.

Ambrose telephoned Eldridge's secretary, and she brought the file over, waiting while he read it. When she had left, he sat for a few minutes thinking over what he had read. So that was why the cable about Pulsifer's trip was marked Secret. There would be some other people on Pulsifer's team when he went to Peru to dig for Inca treasure. *Prolifium.* Fifty times as fissile as uranium. It might show up. This was their chance. And Flantin just happened to mention Pulsifer the other night. He thought a little longer and put in a call to the French Embassy for Mme Marot.

She seemed quite unsurprised at his call. Yes, she was free for lunch. They agreed to meet at one o'clock at a little restaurant behind the Mayflower: *Aux Quatre Saisons.*

Is it too soon to talk to Throttle about everything, Ambrose asked himself. Perhaps I should make myself available at least. He may expect it. He walked up the stairs and along the corridor towards the Private Office. As he got to the door, it opened, and Johnson, the guard, came out, surly, rather threatening—or perhaps threatened. . . . Yes, that might be more like it. But after all, thought Ambrose, it's the same thing. My instinct might be right, if only there were a connection.

Their looks had crossed, as if there were an unspoken question between them. I had better say something, thought Ambrose. Anything will do.

"Still working on the fireworks?" he found himself saying.

Johnson smiled constrainedly. "Yes, sir," he said. "The Ambassador is trying to find out what went wrong last night."

"What went wrong? Ah yes. Fascinating. So many possibilities. . . ."

Johnson looked at him, his eyes narrowing. Then he seemed to pull himself together, turned, and went off down the corridor.

Ambrose stood still for a moment looking after him. Then

he opened the door of the Ambassador's office and put his head inside.

"Anyone signalling for me?" he asked the secretary. "Should I go aboard?"

She was a little uncertain. "Is it very urgent?" she asked. "He's just gone downstairs into his lab, and once he's there, he hates to be disturbed if it can wait."

Ambrose was greatly relieved. "Oh, it's far from important. Just the future of the British Empire. Say I was here." He beamed at her and left.

Glancing at his watch, he saw that he still had a little time to spare, and thought he would look in at the Embassy library to see the newspapers. He was glancing through the morning papers, now rather crumpled, when the messenger came in with a batch of the early afternoon papers, fresh and enticing. Ambrose seized them eagerly. I really love newspapers, he thought to himself. What a pity I shan't be here to see how Scripps and Hearst handle the Day of Judgment.

The morning papers had seemed full of the murder, but nothing compared with the afternoon papers, for they had had a chance by now to start looking for new angles, and also to report the British reaction. The American reporters all seemed intrigued by the idea of tying up the murder, somehow, with the fireworks, and there was a special aspect of this which excited them—the insult to the Argentine. Ilano had, apparently, been as good as his word. In the name of his Government, he had handed a formal protest to the State Department that morning, demanding Admiral Throttle's ouster on the grounds that he had deliberately staged the fireworks party to insult the Argentine people in general and the Special Mission in particular.

Now let's see how the Communists arranged all this, thought Ambrose, turning to the *Eagle*, the real anti-Communist Washington paper; and sure enough, here was the link. Senator McGrowle's Committee had exposed an interesting Communist angle within one hour, following up the story that had appeared in all the morning papers that the Ambassador made his own fireworks. An *Eagle* reporter had discovered that the Ambassador bought his materials from a certain chemical firm in Perryville, Pennsylvania. Senator McGrowle had immediately let it be known to the Press that this particular firm happened to be on the list for investigation by his Committee. The reason? It was handling secret defence orders, and yet it had a number of Reds working there. Herbert Ross, the Committee's star ex-Communist witness, had the proof of this, and he was never wrong.

The Press had asked the Senator if he thought there was any connection between the fireworks, the Reds, and the murder. He had replied, according to the *Eagle*: "Everything is connected. The Communist plot is a razor poised at the jugular vein of the American people." "What about the Argentine link?" he was asked. That could be connected too, he had replied. The Reds were trying to get a foothold in South America. It would all come out at the hearings of his Committee.

Tom O'Connell, the *Eagle's* star columnist, took it all a stage further. Picking up the Senator's hint, he explained that the murder itself had probably been instigated by the late President Roosevelt for his own purposes.

The British newspapers had another approach, Ambrose saw, looking down the page. They were all, apparently, boiling mad with the Americans over the murder. It was all due, they said, to "hysterical American anti-Communism". On this occasion, however, the American sabre-rattlers and Senator McGrowle had over-reached themselves. The British people would not stand for British citizens being murdered abroad, even if they were only Foreign Office officials. The London *Evening Mirror*, bringing in the Argentine story, expressed the whole position by saying ominously:

Was it the long arm of coincidence, or the long arm of American imperialism, that brought the protest from the Argentine so rapidly after the murder?

Good Lord, I'm late for lunch, thought Ambrose suddenly, throwing down the papers in alarm, and sprinting towards the front gate. Fortune favoured him. At the gate he found Eldridge just about to drive down to the Metropolitan Club for lunch. A lift was offered and accepted. As the Bentley sped silently down-town, Ambrose asked Hugh what he made of the Argentine protest.

Hugh laughed. "I shouldn't worry too much."

"Won't even dismiss him 'pour encourager les autres'?"

"Like the other Admiral? I doubt it. As a matter of fact," he told Ambrose, "I got this all wrong the first time I heard of it. He had a direct call from our Ambassador at Buenos Aires last night, warning him that this was coming. They used the word 'bungled', which annoyed him, and rather misled me. I thought he was referring to something quite different. No, he'd never be recalled on the Argentine business. In fact, I'm not at all sure that it wasn't all rather useful. Something rather funny going on down there. Expect to hear something to-day or to-morrow."

It was very restful and reassuring to talk to Eldridge.

IV

Mme Marot was waiting for him at the restaurant, but with no sign of impatience. That seemed to be her character. Nothing pressed on her or disturbed her. She was willing to let things spin on, while she waited for the moment. Not that she was not involved in what was going on; but she could sit, gracefully, remotely, and let things come to her in their due time.

Ambrose felt himself slowing down a little as he talked

149

to her. There was no need to talk too much. They sipped a sherry slowly while their *sole lyonnaise* was being prepared.

They had begun, inevitably, by talking of Hewitt's death, and then, as if they had both expected it, they talked of Walter. With all his senses alert, Ambrose still found it hard to decide what she felt. There was some deep personal attachment—that he was sure of. But what weight did she give to personal things?

Certainly she was very concerned over Walter. "He has seemed so unhappy recently," she said. "At war with himself."

"Aren't we all?" said Ambrose very obviously.

"Not always," she replied. "Sometimes the self gets out of the way—things fall into place."

"When one has some coherent philosophy—Buddhism, Marxism?"

"No, I was thinking more of when one is concentrating on some immediate limited objective."

"Like running for a bus?"

"Possibly. It would depend on why you were running for the bus. I was thinking of how satisfying it is to have some job to do that one accepts for its own sake. It may be part of a cause, but there is no visible connection. One is simply carrying out orders."

"Like in the Résistance?"

They were well into lunch now. The mood between them was relaxed. She had given up some of her remoteness. The sherry, and the white wine which followed, were doing their work. Surely she was talking quite sincerely, with no arrière-pensée.

"Yes," she said, "in the Résistance one lost a sense of one's own identity. There were jobs to be done. You had to get an R.A.F. flyer from the North to the South through innumerable barriers, or you had to steal a paper from the office of the local German chief, or plant a paper there—you concentrated all your existence on the task—you risked everything, yet at the same time you were fulfilled as an individual. Your personal life, your personal relations, were *more* intense, not less."

Ambrose had heard other Résistance workers talk this way. But how far was it still her way of life?

"And now you live a very peaceful existence," he said to her as they stood up ready to go.

"Peaceful? Well, yes. No adventures. All my training wasted. Do you know," she said with a smile. "I could once open any lock with a piece of wire. I seem to have a gift for it. But now I don't have any locks to open."

"There are many kinds of locks that have to be opened," said Ambrose sententiously.

She looked at him. "I'm not too good at the other kind of lock," she said. "It isn't really half as easy."

"So I may ask you for help only when I lose my latch-key," said Ambrose. "So be it. That will be very frequent. I am always losing my key."

As they were getting their coats from the cloakroom, she asked him if she could give him a lift. She had her car there, she said. Ambrose accepted quickly. There was still one subject that he had to explore.

They wormed their way into a tiny Renault that stood outside and drove to Police Headquarters. It was quite a short drive. Almost before they had settled down they were there. They sat still for a moment, as if there was still much to say, though neither could begin.

Finally she thanked him for the lunch, and he stirred himself to go. Then she said: "If you need me for anything, will you call me? I may be able to help." Was she serious? He wrote down her home telephone number in his little black book.

Feeling rather baffled, he stood on the sidewalk outside

the police building watching her drive away. It was odd: he had not felt able to ask her anything about Flantin.

V

"Good of you to come down, Mr Usher," said Shaughnessy, as Ambrose was shown in. "There are a few points we'd like your help on."

The transition was a little too swift. They would want to talk of Hewitt, and his mind was full of the other things. He had tried to come down to earth as he was led by the uniformed policeman along the busy corridors into the quiet, well-furnished room where Shaughnessy and Goldberg awaited him. "I hope I can help," he said. "Have you made any progress so far?"

"Oh, I think we have quite a lot," said Shaughnessy. He seemed to bear no resentment at Ambrose's levity on the phone that morning. "Things are coming through. It's on the background that we need help. It's a little unusual for us."

"Ah, there I can help you," said Ambrose brightly. "I'm essentially a background man."

"Well, tell us more about Mr Hewitt's background. How did he come to choose this sort of work?"

"Did he choose it?" asked Ambrose, "or did it choose him? *Do I draw the bow or does it draw me?* Do any of us choose? He was born into an age, a position, it sent him back and forth, first the Party engulfed him, then another kind of awareness. . . ."

"Oh, he was a Communist once, was he?"

"He was and he wasn't. I think perhaps he used Communism as a working hypothesis."

"Then he knew what it was all about?"

"Oh yes, he knew, he knew."

"So, if he was working *with* them now, it wasn't a

152

temporary switch, but it meant that he'd deliberately deceived the Foreign Office right from the beginning?"

"Yes, I think so," said Ambrose reflectively. "But even that is perhaps too decisive an approach. I didn't feel when I met him that he had made up his mind about everything. He was still experimenting. Life seemed to him a constant experiment, I would say."

Shaughnessy changed tack. "You can't remember anything more about the appointment he cancelled on Wednesday night? Nothing that would indicate who it might have been with?"

Ambrose shook his head. "No. He stood at the telephone rather impatiently, I would say. His eyes wandered to the ceiling and around the room while he was listening. But all I heard him actually say was one sentence: 'I'm sorry, Billy, I can't, not to-night.'"

"Do you think the murder could have been an act of vengeance by the Communists if they thought he was double-crossing them?"

"Oh, I hardly think so," said Ambrose, smiling at Shaughnessy. "Communists don't go in for vengeance for its own sake, you know. Thoroughly bourgeois idea. Far too sentimental. Of course, if they have some concrete objective to gain, that's another story. Never shirk a disagreeable job, if it's to achieve something practical."

"They wouldn't remove him for having given away their secrets?"

"Oh no, not if it was all over. They're very realistic. They know their secrets are always coming out. No, when I said practical, I meant something really specific, such as to stop him exposing someone they're keeping under cover— something like that might make it worthwhile, I would say. But after all, who knows? A Communist might do a murder for a non-Communist reason, you know. That would really fool us, wouldn't it? Wouldn't know where we were."

Ambrose saw that Goldberg was impatient to take up the questioning, and that Shaughnessy gave him a slight nod of approval.

"What about the British viewpoint, Mr Usher?" Goldberg asked. "If he had been double-crossing the Foreign Office, there was nothing you could have done legally to punish him, was there?"

"Oh yes, he would have paid the supreme penalty—dismissal from the Foreign Service."

"Just dismissal. Yet it would be equivalent to treason, and if you were at war it would be punishable by death."

"Ah, you are looking for the moral crime. Yes, nothing to choose. The law doesn't really take care of things, does it? Lucky there are other ways."

"What do you mean by that?" Shaughnessy broke in sharply.

"Oh, life has a way of catching up with these anomalies, don't you think?" Ambrose turned to him smiling.

"You mean everyone gets the right punishment in the end?"

"Ah, to say that I would have to know what the *right* punishment is. No, I mean that an act and its sequence form a whole. Must wait to the end before you can decide how things work out. Providence has many instruments, you know. The police . . ." he bowed to Shaughnessy, "they are one. But there are others. Wouldn't you say that usually the act—the original crime, I mean—has a way of bringing along the second part inevitably. The police are just there to tidy up. I hope this doesn't offend you," he added anxiously.

"Now, just a minute," said Shaughnessy. "Are you saying that a traitor of this kind might be punished outside the law?"

"Oh dear," said Ambrose, "you still talk of punishment. I prefer to think that something he did would catch up with him in one way or another."

"You mean it could be accidental?"

"Oh no, there are no accidents. Everyone is involved, don't you know? The unconscious agent, *B*, impinging on *A*, is also being impinged on by *C*. All highly involved."

Goldberg broke in. "You mean," he said to Ambrose, "that this agent *C*, as you call him, would have his own motivation outside this particular event?"

"Why, yes, I think that puts it admirably," cried Ambrose. "But aren't we getting a long way from our particular murder? I thought we would be discussing clues. Have detectives given up clues?"

"Yes, we have clues," said Shaughnessy, "lots of clues. But we're interested in this too, very interested. You see, we rarely get a chance to talk about philosophy with an expert. At least *I* don't. Of course, Goldberg does. He takes evening courses at the university—in anthropology. Supposed to be useful too."

"I'm sure it is," said Ambrose, "most useful. Many a murder must be fundamentally ritualistic—like the disposal of the Priest-King in primitive society. How advanced Americans are! They—shall I make up a word—they de-compartmentalize knowledge. Excellent."

Goldberg pressed to speak, but Shaughnessy seemed to have had enough. "There's just one other thing, Mr Usher," he said. "Are there any other people at the British Embassy who might have been involved in this Communist business? It would be important, don't you think. Suppose they are trying to get at your scientific discoveries. Who would be the key-man on that?"

"Atomic energy and all that? Yes, we have the appropriate wizard. His name is Walter Scott. They call him scientific attaché."

"Well, do you think he could be a Communist?" persisted Shaughnessy.

"Oh, I don't think so," said Ambrose. "He could do all kinds of other things, but he could never be an actual Communist."

"You sound very sure. Why?"

"Because he believes in free enquiry. And do you know, that's no fun either. Can get a man into plenty of trouble too, you know."

"Well, there are other key-men, I suppose. You don't mind our asking you all this, do you?"

"Far from it," Ambrose reassured him with a wave of his hand. "Most interesting approach. Most stimulating."

"Well, who stands closest to the Ambassador? What about the man we met last night, Commander Abbot-Hume? Could he be one, secretly, and you would never have known?"

Ambrose was a little startled. "Abbot-Hume?" he repeated. "Now that's a strange question."

"Well, what do you think?"

Ambrose thought for a minute. "I'm trying to envisage the thing. Of course, I assume he's not. *Theoretically* he could or he couldn't. Nothing to determine it that I know of."

"Oh, you think these things are determined? What about you? Anything to determine it in *your* case?"

Ambrose slapped his thigh, apparently delighted at the question. "Captain, I believe you've been working up to this all the time. Is this the third degree? No, of course not. Far too pleasant. It must be the nth degree. Yes, at last I meet the nth degree. But how shall I answer? If I *were* a secret Communist, I would say 'No' anyhow, so any answer I make must be meaningless. Suppose I just refuse to answer—stand on the 5th Amendment. That's it. I've always wanted to know what it felt like. Do you now cite me for contempt of police force?"

At that moment the door opened, and a tall, burly,

grizzled-haired man stood there. "Oh, I see you're busy, Don," he said.

Shaughnessy and Goldberg had risen to their feet, and Ambrose followed them. "Oh, no, Commissioner," said Shaughnessy. "Come in. I'd like you to meet Mr Usher of the British Embassy. We've been going over some points about the murder there. This is Assistant Commissioner Rawlins," he added to Ambrose.

Rawlins shook hands with Ambrose and looked at him shrewdly. "What a terrible business it is," he said. "I hope you can help us. I gather this is a bit of a change for you, coming from Oxford into all this."

"Oh, not a bit," said Ambrose brightly, "no change at all. We've been talking about philosophy all afternoon. Quite an agreeable experience."

Rawlins looked at Shaughnessy. "Philosophy? I didn't know you were interested, Don. Is that your subject at the university, Mr Usher?"

"I'm *its* subject. We all are. It rules us. Especially the Captain. I'd like him in my class. And it's not far off from the murder, you know—motive, psychological approach—we've been exploring the whole field. Fascinating."

"Well, I shall look forward to hearing about it," said Rawlins, a little grimly, Ambrose thought. "Come and see me later, Don. Good-bye, Mr Usher."

They remained standing after he had left, and it seemed to Ambrose that the interview was now over. Shaughnessy confirmed this: "If you think of anything more," he said, "will you give me a call? Any time. You can reach me at home. I'll give you my home address and telephone number."

Ambrose took his little black book out of his pocket to write it down. "This is my Christmas Card book," he said. "Once you are in here, you receive a card from me for the rest of time." He was turning the pages as he spoke, to get the right initial. "Now let me see: I must get it right. S-h-a-u-g-h-n-e-s-s-y." He spelt it out, while he wrote. "Captain Don—Don for Donald, I suppose."

Shaughnessy smiled at him. "No, it's Don for Donegal. That's where I come from. It's a nickname that stuck. My real name is Patrick."

"Ah, that explains everything," said Ambrose. "Patrick. That's better. Somehow you never looked like a Donald to me." He took the address and telephone number and turned to leave.

"Oh, there's one bit of news that just came in," said Shaughnessy to him as they stood near the door. "Your secretary's cat has been found shot."

Ambrose stopped and turned a startled face to Shaughnessy. "Palmerston! Shot! Where? In the wood?"

"Yes, but not where Hewitt was killed. A long way off. But he might have been shot in the same place. Could have dragged himself a long way before he died."

"Oh, my poor Hope-Little! She will be heart-broken. Have you told her?"

"I should think they have by now. What do you think? Could there be any connection with the murder?"

Ambrose sighed. "It was his home. He loved that spot. He was the witness. I must go and comfort her." He left, shaking his head sadly.

VI

Yes, Palmerston was the witness, Ambrose said to himself as he stood waving to a cab outside the police building. And now—poor Palmerston, *"you cannot witness for me being slain."*

Telling the driver to take him to the Embassy, he settled back for a few minutes of rest. On the whole it had been quite an interesting interview. He liked young Goldberg, the policeman who wanted to be an anthropologist, and Shaughnessy wasn't as bad as he seemed. . . . Captain Don of Donegal. Quite a character.

Donegal! Suddenly he sat upright. Oh, my goodness, he said to himself. Is *that* it? Don of Donegal, Tex of Texas. . . . Was it as simple as that? He began to feel a sparkle of excitement. By itself it meant nothing very much, but given one more connection, one more link, the chain would be complete, with everything in place. Everything? Well, everything of that particular chain. How could he find out? Maybe the personnel files would help. A little research.

He was still turning the thing over in his mind as the cab came near to the Embassy. The traffic was heavy, and while the taxi-driver was waiting to make the turn across the road, Ambrose decided to get out and walk across to have a few more minutes of thought.

It was getting dark as he passed the Annex parking-lot, wrapped up in this new idea. A man was standing by an open car in the lot, apparently looking for something. Ambrose was walking by casually when the man, suddenly hearing his approach, started furtively and slipped away. As he turned, Ambrose recognized him. It was Abbot-Hume. What an odd thing! Could this be connected too?

It would have to wait. First things first. He had better get across to Chancery to have a look at the personnel files. He began to walk down the Annex path towards Chancery, but as he passed the Annex door another idea came to him. I must try some shock tactics, he thought. It's the only way I'll ever know.

Johnson, standing at the door, saluted him, and Ambrose walked upstairs to Hewitt's room. The door was locked. In the next room a young girl sat typing. It was not Hewitt's secretary whom he had talked to the previous day. It must be the other one, with the English name, Miss Crumleigh. She saw him looking at the locked door, and said to him:

"The police have locked it and taken the keys."

"I suppose Mr Hewitt's papers are all locked up in there?"

"I suppose so," said the girl. "Miss Turenne would know. She's Mr Hewitt's secretary—or she was," she added lamely. "But she's gone home. She didn't feel well."

"It's of no matter," said Ambrose. "I can come back later." He went down, slowly, and was about to go through the door when he suddenly stopped. "Is there a telephone here I can use?" he asked the guard.

"Yes, sir. You can use the one in Miss Proudfoot's room." He showed Ambrose into a neat little room next to the entrance, the sanctum of the invaluable member of the Embassy staff who handled diplomatic liquor. In an extension off the room, Ambrose could see rows and rows of Scotch and other beverages. It was a thirsty sight.

He waited until Johnson had closed the door and then he called Mrs Bristol in the Registry. She was an old friend of war days, and he knew he could count on her.

"Oh, I'm glad to have found you in," he said to her when she answered the phone. "Is it too late, or can I come over and look at a few files, some personnel files?"

"Why, of course," she said. "It's not too late at all. Who is it you want to look up?"

"You *will* get them yourself, won't you," said Ambrose. "I'd like to see the files on some of the secretaries—Mr Hewitt's, Mr Scott's, Mathiesson, Burbank, Garrywood"— they all worked in the Annex—"Oh yes, and I'd like to see the files on the guards. Could you get them ready for me?"

"I'll have them ready in a few minutes," she said.

Before placing the receiver, Ambrose listened very carefully for a moment. It seemed to him that he heard a very faint sound. He had thought he might.

Emerging from Miss Proudfoot's room, he went over to

Chancery and spent about half an hour there with the files. He looked into his own office, but Miss Hope-Little was not there. She must have taken Palmerston away, he thought. Poor Hope-Little. He read for a little while, and through his window saw the night settling peacefully and beautifully over the roofs and trees. Was it all coming to an end? He had an impulse to reach out again for the beginning, retracing his steps of the first day in the clearing of the wood, when poor old Palmerston had leapt down to greet him.

VII

It was very peaceful in the wood. The police had all gone. There was no trace of the grim events of the night before. The tall oak, Palmerston's home, had gathered up its secret. Man had staged a flurry of excitement, a momentary ruffle of Nature's ineffable calm, but now man had gone. The trees and the leaves rustled softly in the dusk.

As he stood there, a sense of foreboding came over Ambrose. He thought he heard steps in the fallen leaves. He stood still and listened. Was it a footstep? Was it a squirrel, or a stoat? He listened again.

There was no sound now, but Ambrose felt danger in the air. Looking quickly around him, he suddenly recalled the scene at the opening of *The Golden Bough*. Here he was, at the oak of the sacred grove. Somewhere in the shadows a grim figure prowled, in his hand a drawn sword—the Priest-King, himself a murderer, waiting for his successor to leap on him. Ambrose waited and then smiled. There was not a sound except his own breathing. So much for premonition.

But he was keen nevertheless to get back to his hotel. He knew something, and needed a little time to tackle it. And somehow he felt saddened at the whole thing—so much human folly amid so much beauty.

He had thought to call a taxi at the Annex door, but it was locked. It seemed a little odd. There should have been a guard there. Presumably he had gone off for a moment and locked the door. Perhaps it was just as well. He would walk to the Avenue—perhaps he would walk home, across Rock Creek Park. A walk would do him good.

The Avenue was bright with the stream of headlights, and he crossed it with care. In a moment it was dark and peaceful again in the Park's shadows. He strolled along slowly and thoughtfully, feeling far from the turbulence that had encompassed him. So much turbulence where there could be so much peace.

Walking along the path, he felt a little earth slip into his shoe and stopped to work it out with his finger. As he bent down, he heard footsteps behind him. His heart thumping, he looked round, but there was nothing to be seen in the dark, and nothing to be heard. He walked on for a moment and then stopped suddenly. Again there was a rustle behind him, unmistakable this time.

So now the moment had come. He sensed it in every fibre. This is what he had expected all day. There was nothing to do except to walk on firmly, and to be ready.

When the first blow fell, he wheeled around, and it lost its full force. Instantly he leaped on the dark figure behind him. A fist crashed into his mouth, but he had found the man's neck and was squeezing it with a mad rage. The man shook him off and crashed another blow into his head, striking him behind the ear. Instinctively Ambrose knew he must stay close. He jumped at the man again and found his arm, which he twisted with all his might, kicking at his stomach. The man wrestled to free his arm, punching with his other fist. Ambrose loosened one arm himself and punched at the man's face, feeling the bone and flesh under his fist. They struggled in the dark, breathing heavily. Ambrose could feel the blood streaming down his face and

162

every bone in his face and shoulders ached with a terrible intensity. He put all his force into a desperate lunge, falling heavily on the man, but at that moment, he felt a great, unutterably painful blow on his head, and all his senses left him.

SEVEN

"O What men dare do! What men may do!
What men daily do, not knowing what they do!"
Much Ado About Nothing

I

AT first he lay without any consciousness of being. Who and where he was, what sounds he heard, what living itself meant were all obscured in a fog of oblivion. His only sensation was of being far off—suspended somehow in time—a warm, grateful feeling. There was a soft hissing sound, which spread into a murmur and slowly clarified into words.

"How come she suddenly found it?"

"Yeh, two of 'em. Dropping from heaven."

"It's the time of life. What with having a mania for it anyhow. . . ."

"Look, he's coming round."

The words stopped, and some dark shapes were before him.

"Mr Usher, are you feeling better?"

Slowly he was descending. The fog around him began to disappear. He felt that his head lay on a wide, cool pillow. He was ready to take in the world, but no words came out of him.

"Take it easy, Mr Usher. You're all right now. You're going to be fine."

In a vague way he may have smiled. He was in no hurry to get back to life. It was so comfortable to let life come creeping back slowly, first the yielding comfort of the pillow under his head, then the delicious sense of being extended on a soft bed, the warm glow of shaded lights, and his own senses coming back to him one by one, his legs, his arms, his fingers—and the memory, slowly slipping back.

It was Shaughnessy standing over him, his knobbly Irish voice steeped in unwonted friendship and anxiety.

"Can you talk, Mr Usher? There's no hurry. We'd just like to know what happened."

There was Goldberg too. Nice to see them again. He just wanted to take it in nicely and slowly.

Shaughnessy leaned over him again, despite the nurse's frown. "Can you understand if I talk, Mr Usher?"

Ambrose smiled back. He could understand perfectly. Just felt a little remote. They got the idea.

"A whole lot has been happening, Mr Usher. If I tell you, perhaps it will help to get us going on whoever attacked you."

Ambrose nodded. Shaughnessy continued.

"It's all happened at once. The worst thing is that the head guard at the Embassy—Johnson—has been shot, killed. Just in the same place as Hewitt."

Ambrose felt his lips moving, but as yet it was a bit hard to talk. "Johnson," he managed to murmur. He felt himself smiling slightly. It was really too ironic. "What does the Ambassador say?"

"Frankly, the Ambassador's fit to be tied," said Shaughnessy. "Blames it all on us. Thought we had policemen on duty. *We* thought we weren't allowed to patrol diplomatic property. It's all blowing up now, this diplomatic business. The Ambassador wants to talk to you, by the way, as soon as you're able to talk."

Ambrose showed his desire to postpone that pleasure for the moment. "What else? You said this was the worst."

"They broke into the Embassy—don't know who— could be the people who killed Johnson, but we're not sure —opened several filing-cabinets on the third floor of the Annex. Don't know what's stolen yet."

"The burglars . . . why don't you think. . . ."

"That's the hard part," said Shaughnessy. "You see, there's something else." He looked at Ambrose anxiously. "It's your secretary, Miss Hope-Little. Something seems to have happened to her. We found her shooting away with two guns up at the Embassy. She says she was shooting at the burglars. But she's rather incoherent. Her clothes are torn. Her hands are badly scratched. Seems to have had a sort of breakdown."

"Hope-Little! Poor Hope-Little!"

"Yeh, its not good. But what about you? Do you feel better?"

"Strangest thing." Ambrose began to find speech getting easier. "Do you know, I feel fine. I can hardly believe it. As if I've woken up after a long sleep."

"You nearly didn't wake up," said Shaughnessy grimly. "The doctor's done a nice job on your head."

Ambrose stretched his hand and found that his head was covered in a bandage. He touched it gingerly. It didn't seem too tender.

"Do you know who attacked you?" asked Shaughnessy.

"It was a man," said Ambrose. "I never saw him. It was dark. But what you tell me seems much more important. So Johnson has been shot. Tell me again about the burglars. Did they break into the safes, and did they rifle the filing cabinets?"

"The burglars, eh? Yes, they seem to have grabbed some things. We haven't been able to check yet. They seem to have worked through about five rooms on that floor, including Mr Scott's room, by the way." Shaughnessy looked at Ambrose closely to see how he was taking it.

"And Miss Hope-Little says she was just there and shot at them?"

Shaughnessy looked grim. "Yeh. Very funny story. Says she found a gun in her car, and saw them coming out and shot at them. Then, while they were running away, she says they dropped a gun and she picked it up and went on shooting. We're checking on both guns to see if one of them was the gun that killed Mr Hewitt. Y'see, they're both Colt 38's."

"And how is she?"

"She's not good. Hasn't been good since she heard about her cat being shot, and now this on top of it. We took her home, and we've got a nurse looking after her there."

"So she's all right for the time being. Talking of the time being, what time is it, by the way?"

"It's just after one a.m.," Shaughnessy told him. "We picked you up at 11.30 last night, just an hour after we got the news about the Embassy business. A young couple who'd gone into Rock Creek Park for their own business found you and gave the alarm. Quite a busy night. But you should get some sleep. We can get on with this in the morning."

Ambrose closed his eyes gratefully. "Yes, I think I'll rest a little," he said. "Nice comfortable room. Where am I, by the way?"

"Oh, this is the Charlbury Nursing Home at I and 18th Street. The Embassy insisted on you being brought here. It's a place they use. Nice and private."

"Fine. Now I can really rest, safe in the arms of the Embassy—and the police. Let's talk in the morning."

Shaughnessy and Goldberg left him. The nurse smoothed his pillow, smiled, and left, too.

Now he could think. This was serious. The burglars. Was there anything he could do?

Mentally, he felt marvellously clear. He tried, carefully, to raise himself on one elbow to see if his strength was back. There was a slight ache in his head, but surprisingly he felt strong and refreshed. He touched his head at the bandage. Yes, it was a bit tender. Well, he would have to watch it.

But if he did anything, he had to do it quickly. There was one possibility, and he could check it.

There was a phone at the bedside. Lifting it, he heard a gentle voice answer immediately: "Can I help you?"

Ambrose took a chance that the night operator had no idea whether this or that patient was supposed to be resting. "Yes, indeed, miss," he replied brightly. "I just can't sleep, so I thought I would make a telephone call. It won't disturb anyone, will it. I will whisper. And it will give you something to do, eh? Must be very boring for you all night."

"Oh, it's perfectly all right, sir," the girl replied. "What number do you want?"

"Could you get me the Royal York Hotel in Toronto?"

"Certainly, sir. Will you hold on? Then I won't have to ring your room."

In half a minute, it seemed, he heard a crisp Canadian voice answer, and ten seconds later he was talking to Scott.

"Walter, it's Ambrose. Something has happened here. Don't be alarmed. Probably perfectly all right. Just one question. You remember you had some papers in your filing cabinet yesterday afternoon? Did you leave them there, or lock them up in the safe?"

Scott gasped. "Oh, my God. I forgot. We talked, and then we left together. They're still there? Has anything happened?"

"It may have done, my boy. It may, but we can't tell yet. When are you due back?"

"Sunday morning, but I could come earlier. Should I take the first plane in the morning?" Scott's voice was full of anxiety.

"Just wait," said Ambrose. "I'll telephone again. Maybe it won't be necessary. Don't worry too much. I'll telephone you. Good-bye."

So that *was* it. Ambrose replaced the receiver, and lay back, letting his strength flow into him. They had banked on a chance, and it had come off. Very smart. But perhaps he was still one play ahead.

Ross must be the key. Sanati could not take any direct part in all this. But suppose he'd reported that Scott seemed to have cold feet. Would they have decided on a long shot? Sanati would have said that the papers were probably ready —and in the filing-cabinet—Walter might well have made some remark about the cabinet, perhaps looked at it, when Sanati visited him the day before. So there was a chance that they could get at them while Scott was away. Very smart. And now what?

Ambrose lay completely relaxed for a few minutes, and then again tried his strength. He sat up in bed. His head throbbed a little, but felt good. He put his feet on the floor and sat on the side of the bed. Yes, he was ready.

Next to the phone was the Washington and district telephone directory. R for Ross. Yes, there it was. Right. Next step.

There was a little white closet in the far corner. His clothes were probably there. He stood up, and walked slowly across. Yes, they were there. He took his little black book out of his coat pocket and walked gently back to the bed. It was worth trying.

He picked up the phone again. "It was such fun telephoning," he told the girl. "I think I'll have another call." He gave her the number.

He heard her dial, and a moment later Mme Marot's voice was on the phone.

"It's me, Ambrose." He waited for the operator to put her receiver down. "Can I speak to you?"

"Of course," she said. "Has something happened?"

Ambrose felt happy to hear her slow, warm voice. "I have to ask you one thing first," he said. "I can't help this. Are you alone?"

It was the first time he had heard her laugh so freely. How

funny that it should happen under such circumstances. "Yes, I'm alone."

"Then here it is," said Ambrose. "I have to do something for Walter. Will you help?"

"Yes."

"Your car, is it available?"

"It's parked outside my apartment."

"Can you meet me with it?"

"When?"

"Now. In half an hour."

"Where shall I meet you?" She was so easy to talk to. No explanation demanded.

"Corner of I and 17th. And by the way, do you have any brandy?"

"I have."

"Please bring some with you. And one more thing."

"Yes?"

"Some wire."

"Wire?"

"Do you remember our conversation at lunch yesterday?"

"Oh, wire. Well, I suppose the less I say, the better."

"You have some?"

She thought for a minute. "Yes," she said finally. "I have something I could use."

"Then I will see you in half an hour."

He put the receiver down and lay back again to store up some strength. He decided that he felt fine, especially with the thought of what lay ahead. For a moment, as he lay back, he felt himself about to question his motives. Was there any chance that it could come off? Had he some other reason? But then he shook off his doubts, and climbed out of bed.

He dressed quickly, and then, moving as silently as he could, opened the window to see what floor he was on and whether he could get out. It was the fourth floor, but there, before him, was a fire escape. It was a dark night. Everything was in his favour. He began climbing down. The steps were steep, but it was not too difficult. *Facilis descensus Averni*, he chanted to himself. There was a faint clanging sound from each step. Now he was level with the second floor and there was a swing ladder for the final descent. He tried it. It swung down easily. He was on the ground, a little breathless with the excitement.

He waited for a moment in the shadows, and then walked quietly over to the corner of the next street to wait. There was not a sound in the air. Even the trees had rested from their autumnal sighing. In the far distance he heard the sound of a car. It came nearer. Suddenly the little black Renault slipped round the corner. He went across to it and got in quickly. "Just drive on towards Wisconsin Avenue," he said, "we're going to Bethesda."

She set off without a word. After a couple of blocks, she turned her head and had a look at him. Seeing his bandaged head seemed to remind her of something. "Do you want some brandy?"

"Oh, good." He took the little flask that she offered him and gulped a good quantity down.

Keeping her eye on the road, she drove on quietly and Ambrose began to talk. When he had finished, she said: "Yes, I think it's worth trying." And then for the first time she relaxed, and gave him a nice, friendly smile.

II

Along Wisconsin Avenue, a main road out of Washington, there was a stream of cars going back and forth, despite the hour. Ambrose and Thérèse stopped for a minute to consult a street map which she had in the car. Then they drove straight on for about two miles, slowed down at a

171

crossing, and turned off the main road into a very quiet area, with few houses and some large open spaces. With Ambrose holding the map on his knee and watching it with a torch, they made several turns and were soon in a tree-shaded street with one small house standing apparently alone at the bottom of the road. "This is it," said Ambrose. "Go straight past without stopping. It's not a cul-de-sac."

She drove by the house, turned right, left, and right again, and was back surprisingly quickly into the bright lights of the main Bethesda road.

Almost at the corner was a large all-night garage. "I'll do the call from here," said Ambrose. "Drive by." She drove past, turned the corner, stopped the car and turned off the lights. Ambrose got out and walked back to the garage. The man on duty came forward.

"Can I use your phone?" asked Ambrose.

"Sure thing," the man replied. Nothing surprises Americans, thought Ambrose. Stranger walks in at two in the morning to use the phone. Perfectly normal. He went into the telephone box and closed the door firmly.

Here it comes, he thought. Easy enough to be a mimic at Oxford parties. How would it work here?

He dialled. The phone rang for quite some time, and then a sleepy voice answered very guardedly: "Yeh? Who is it?"

It wasn't enough to speak the part. Ambrose found himself suddenly crouching over the phone, whispering urgently into it in Italian, in Sanati's famous croaking voice that he recalled from the Rome days.

"This is Sanati. It is urgent. Are you alone? Can you speak?"

Ross replied instantly in Italian. "What has happened? You are crazy to call me!"

"It is necessary," croaked Ambrose. "You must come here quickly. Immediately."

"With the papers?"

172

"No. Leave them. Are they safe?"

Ross seemed to snigger a little. "Yes. Quite safe. I'll come immediately."

Ambrose put down the phone and straightened up. He found that he was sweating profusely. How absurd, he thought. There had been no danger. But I was afraid all the same. He walked quickly round the corner to Thérèse. "It worked," he whispered to her. "He has the papers. And he's going. Wait."

They waited, saying nothing. Five minutes later, they saw a car turn out of the side road near Ross's house, and go speeding down Bethesda Avenue in the direction of Washington.

"Right," said Ambrose. "Here we go." Thérèse started the car, and drove it down the side road, parking a little above Ross's house. Each carrying a torch, they ran quietly towards the garden gate. It was a very large garden, with a small old-fashioned cottage at the bottom of the path. Thérèse got her wire out, and began working quietly at the door lock of the cottage. It yielded in a few minutes and they were inside.

Flashing the torch on the ground, they saw a desk in the corner. It was locked. "They won't be there," whispered Ambrose, "but we'd better try." While Thérèse worked on the desk lock, he went into the bedroom. It took a minute to work through the chest of drawers, the closets, the seats of the chairs, the bed mattress. Nothing there. The desk was now open. They went through it quickly. Nothing there. The kitchen, the refrigerator, the gas stove, the back of the pictures—it was all hopeless. No safe, no secret places that they could spot. Yet the papers *had* to be there.

As they stood wondering where to look next, they heard a car in the distance. "Oh lordie," muttered Ambrose. "He's coming back. Probably smelt a rat." They quickly moved to the door and began racing down the path. But there was the car, with lights blazing, turning the corner towards the house. "Quick, this way," said Ambrose. He had seen a small shed in a corner of the garden. They got in and crouched on the floor. Through the tiny window they saw the car lights continue down the road and heard it disappear into the distance. False alarm.

Ambrose cautiously flashed the torch around the shed. It was carefully arranged for fruit and vegetable storage. "Keen gardener, our friend Umberto," he whispered appreciatively. "Quite self-sustaining apparently." There were trays of apples and pears, piles of celery and beets, a large barrel of potatoes, and a row of huge pumpkins.

"Pumpkins!" exclaimed Ambrose. "Pumpkins! My God! You don't think that he could possibly . . ." They pounced on the pumpkins, fine massive specimens, proud and golden along the shed floor.

It was in the fourth pumpkin. The top came off. The inside was scooped out, and there, in the hole, were the papers. Ambrose and Thérèse looked at each other, dumb-struck but half hysterical with suppressed laughter. Then quickly they were out of the shed towards the gate and racing towards their car. They jumped in. Thérèse bent over the ignition with her key.

As he sat waiting, Ambrose had a sudden and horrible premonition of fear. There was someone in the back seat of the car—waiting. . . .

III

He had felt the man's presence in the split second before he heard the coarse, sneering voice.

"Think you can get away with it?" At the sound of the words, Ambrose felt himself shiver. His skin prickled with fear. Thérèse had frozen too, bent over the ignition. Neither of them dared turn their heads.

"Well, perhaps you can after all," said the voice, but somehow it had changed. "Let's get going." Oh, that new voice! That lovely Irish brogue. That heavenly darlint tongue.

"God bless you, Shaughnessy," said Ambrose. "But how *could* you?"

"How could *I*, the man asks? How could *I*? Now, really. . . . But come on, miss," he said to Thérèse. "We've no time."

Thérèse started the engine. "This is Captain Shaughnessy," Ambrose said to her. "He's investigating the murder of Mr Hewitt. And this lady is Mme Marot," he said to Shaughnessy, "my assistant in crime. But how he got here . . ."

They had turned into the Bethesda road, and were rolling comfortably along, Ambrose holding firmly to the package of papers.

"Now, really, Mr Usher," said Shaughnessy. "You didn't think I could leave you alone to do a job like this. Have to keep an eye on you, you know."

"But do you mean you've been following me the whole evening?"

"Well, let's say we were a little curious. Wondered about all that telephoning at the Nursing Home. Quite interesting, you know, listening in. How do you feel, by the way?"

"I feel wonderful," said Ambrose. "Just madly exhausted, and faintly amused. Otherwise perfectly normal. By the way, where is your own car. I assume you have a car."

"Oh, behind us somewhere," said Shaughnessy airily. "I will say one thing for Goldberg. He can keep out of sight."

Ambrose sighed. "I'll never trust a policeman again. Do you mean that when I was crawling down that fire escape . . ."

"That's right. We were watching. You took it too

quickly, you know. Nearly tripped at one point. You need a little practice. And by the way, I don't suppose you feel like telling me what this is all about. Or are you too tired?" he added with heavy sarcasm.

Thérèse was driving on steadily without a word. "It's not difficult to explain," said Ambrose. "You heard me telephone to Walter Scott in Toronto—you must have understood. I'm a friend of his, and so is Mme Marot. We wanted to help him. He made a bad mistake—fault in security. I had a hunch when you told me about the Annex being broken into. I wondered if there was a chance of getting the papers back, and I played a long shot, and it came off. And here they are!" He held up the little package of papers triumphantly. "But what about you?" he added a little lamely. "Isn't it a little unusual for the police . . ."

Shaughnessy smiled grimly. "We decided to give you a bit of rope. And that seems to have worked, too. You wanted something out of that house—that's fine. *We* can't break in without a warrant. *You* can break in and be arrested afterwards. So now I'd better arrest you, I suppose. By the way, you wouldn't like to tell me whose house you were burgling, would you, or is that an Embassy secret?"

"That was Ross's house, Hubert Ross, famous Communist, famous ex-Communist, and now famous anti-Communist. And perhaps you'd like to know where we found the papers? In a pumpkin. So unoriginal. Poor Umberto. How could anyone be such a copy-cat?"

"Can you go a bit more slowly," said Shaughnessy. "Where does Ross come in?"

"Oh, it's all open and above board," said Ambrose cheerfully. "If I can stay awake, I can explain it quite easily. I told the F.B.I. about it this morning—well, yesterday morning—Gustafson, he'll tell you. It's all to do with Sanati, the Italian physicist. It seemed a bit odd to me to find him teamed up here with an anti-Communist like Ross, so I worried about it. I wondered if Ross was quite so anti-Communist as he pretended to be."

"So Ross broke in to steal the papers—and shot Johnson? Is that your theory?"

"I don't know," said Ambrose. "I wouldn't think he did it himself. Far too close for him. No, I would guess that if he wanted to break in, he'd hire the appropriate thugs to do the job. Do you remember Ross when he was Rossi? Before he was a Communist? Had a nice little career as a gangster, I seem to recall. One doesn't forget one's way around. I don't think he'd have any difficulty in laying his hands on suitable burglars, day or night."

"Well, at least we know who burgled *Ross's* house" said Shaughnessy. "This is going to make a very nice item in the papers to-morrow. Mme Marot and Mr Usher. French and British Embassies. Courses in burglary. Very nice."

Ambrose and Thérèse exchanged a look. There was something in Shaughnessy's tone to indicate that they were going to be let off for the moment. They were in Washington now, in the bright lights of Wisconsin Avenue. Ambrose passed his hand over his eyes. He suddenly felt completely exhausted.

"Oh dear, I'm so tired," he said. "I'm going to need a lot of sleep. Got to look after these," he added, clutching the papers.

"I'll take them for you if you like," said Thérèse. "I have a little safe in my apartment."

It was the first thing Thérèse had said. She stretched out her right hand casually for the papers, keeping her eye on the road.

"Oh, I think we ought to turn in the swag to the police, don't you?" said Ambrose. "Do you mind taking care of them?" he said to Shaughnessy. "You can seal them up in an envelope, and sort it out with me to-morrow, if I'm not in jail."

Shaughnessy took the papers. Thérèse said nothing.

Somehow Ambrose's act seemed to restore Shaughnessy's good humour completely.

"Well, this looks like the end of Mr Ross," he said cheerfully. "Seems to have had a nice little racket."

Ambrose felt himself falling asleep. "Yes," he murmured, "sceptre and crown must tumble down. . . ."

Shaughnessy sat forward, startled. "What's that?" he said sharply.

"Yes," murmured Ambrose. "I suppose this is the end for him."

"No, what did you say before?" asked Shaughnessy. "About sceptre and crown?"

"Did I say anything?" Ambrose could hardly keep his eyes open. "Just an old verse—Shirley, isn't it?—

> *And in the dust be equal made*
> *With the poor crooked scythe and spade.*"

"Just an old verse?" asked Shaughnessy.

"Oh dear, I'm so tired," said Ambrose. He let his head fall back, and was instantly asleep. Vaguely he was aware of the car stopping not long after and of being lifted up bodily and carried through some doorways. But the rest was oblivion.

IV

"No, sir, I haven't brought a message," said old Needham. "I just came to see you."

"I couldn't be more pleased," said Ambrose. "The ideal visitor. You can tell me all the news. It all comes past you in a narrow stream, through the Embassy door. *It matters not how strait the gate*, or rather it matters very much."

Ambrose had found the Embassy head porter sitting quietly at his bedside when he awoke. Looking at his watch, he saw that it was just noon. Nice and restful to look at the old man, his white hair and drooping moustaches gleaming softly, his wise old eyes warm and friendly. Yet odd that he should be there of all people. He had thought at first that the Embassy must have sent him up there to keep a watch on him, but Needham, he now saw, had some other purpose. Outwardly he looked at ease, but there was anxiety as well as friendship showing in the creases of his eyes.

"I believe they are not supposed to admit visitors to you," he said blandly, "but they know me rather well. We have often sent patients here." *We. Often.* There was a calm assumption with everything old Needham said that the individual and the immediate events of the day were not the final issues. You had to take a very long view, and perhaps an unconventional one, too, by ordinary standards.

"Well, I'm delighted," said Ambrose. "Tell me what is going on before the watchdogs get at me."

"I was very concerned about the attack on you, sir," said Needham gravely. "I hope the effects have not been serious."

"Let us hope so," said Ambrose. "Yet, it was a wild night. Far too much blood and thunder. I suppose the doctor will come and tell me soon if I am going to live."

"They told me he was due to come in at twelve, sir. I think I hear him now."

It was indeed the doctor, accompanied by the nurse wheeling a trolly containing bandages and medicaments. He looked at Ambrose grimly as he stuck the thermometer into his mouth and reached for his pulse.

"I gather that you don't like staying in bed," he said. "Well, we'll let you go as quickly as we can get rid of you. Don't like keeping people here against their will."

Ambrose could say nothing for once. With the thermometer in his mouth, he could only grimace and raise his eyebrows in what he hoped was an expression of both gratitude and humility. The rest of the examination was conducted in silence. When it came to looking at Ambrose's head wounds, the doctor grunted with satisfaction, and replaced the large bandage by some small adhesive coverings. "You'll be all right," he said reluctantly, as he turned to leave. "You can get up later if you want to."

Needham had stood looking out of the window during the examination, and now turned back.

"Apparently I am as healthy as I feel," Ambrose told him. "It's probably frightfully good for me. Now, where do we stand?" He settled back comfortably in the bed to listen.

"I don't know how much you have been told, sir," said Needham. "You know that Johnson was found shot dead, and thieves broke into the Annex." Ambrose nodded. "And you know about Miss Hope-Little?"

"Only the vaguest outline," said Ambrose anxiously. "Please tell me more."

"It was Miss Hope-Little that gave the alarm about the thieves," said Needham. "No one knows exactly what happened, but they heard a number of shots and ran over from the Residence. They found her with two guns firing away, and the thieves disappeared. And they found Johnson's body. She's had a collapse, and they're looking after her at her home."

"Well, of course she loves guns," said Ambrose ruminatively, "but this is perhaps carrying things too far. What did she say?"

"She was very disturbed, sir. She has been very disturbed since they found poor Palmerston's body yesterday. She told the police that she found one gun in her car and fired at the thieves with it, and that they dropped the other gun and she picked it up while chasing them and fired with it too."

"What a strange story. I suppose she can't prove anything."

"No, sir. But"—Needham paused, with an odd glint in his eye—"neither can the police. And that's what I have come to ask for advice about."

"To ask *me?*" Ambrose sat up and looked at Needham. "Do you mean you know something more?"

"Oh yes. I've seen one or two things in the last few days. And I need advice on how much to tell the police. After all, it is *within* the Embassy. I know the police have been invited in by the Ambassador, but that was not strictly necessary."

Ambrose continued to look at him rather blankly. "But, Needham, this is all rather serious, you know."

"It is indeed, sir, most serious, and I am puzzled to know whom I could ask. Normally I should have gone to the Ambassador. I remember I did that in 1912 when young Lord Briscombe seemed likely to get into trouble over the body of that gambler they found in Arlington. But in this case—well, perhaps you understand, sir. I hope I can speak frankly. The Ambassador is rather new to Embassy practice. I don't think he should have called the police in at all. We have diplomatic immunity. I am sure that Lord Bryce would not have done so, or even a modern Ambassador like Lord Halifax. And so I have come to you Mr Usher, since you came out specially from the Foreign Office on this subject."

He gave Ambrose the warmest smile.

"Well, that's very nice," said Ambrose. "And what's the problem?"

"It's Miss Hope-Little, sir," said Needham. "You see, I happen to know that her story that she found the gun in her car is correct. It's a big old-fashioned open car. I saw the gun being put there. Or rather I saw something being put there during the afternoon, and when I checked up I found it was a gun."

Ambrose looked at him with astonishment. "But you did nothing?"

"No, sir. It's not my business to interfere with these things. I have seen many things in my time. I do just try to keep an eye on everything."

"Well, now, at least you can tell the police that her story is true."

"That's just it, sir. I need your advice on how much we *should* tell them."

"But we have to tell them everything. They want to get at the truth about all these murders, and all the business behind it. Why do you think we should hold things back?"

"If Miss Hope-Little will not suffer—if they can't prove anything against her, might it not be better to leave it at that? It might save a lot of trouble."

"But who put the gun in her car?"

"That's just it, sir. Mrs Abbot-Hume."

"Mrs Abbot-Hume?"

"I rather think she may have been doing it for her husband."

Ambrose gazed at Needham with increasing astonishment. "And what was *he* doing with a gun?"

Needham smiled with something like deprecation. "Oh, Commander Abbot-Hume is on the Pistol Team, sir. Very good shot."

Ambrose was still spluttering. "But in that case, it is Commander Abbot-Hume's gun. . . ."

"That's where I need your advice, sir," said Needham calmly. "It goes back to Mr Hewitt's death. If this were the gun, it might bring a lot out."

"It might indeed," said Ambrose. "Do you think Commander Abbot-Hume killed Mr Hewitt?"

"The police think it possible."

"With what motive?"

"Oh, I believe they are thinking it might have been jealousy. Mr Hewitt was very attentive to Mrs Abbot-

Hume, you know. Of course, it *may* have been. But then—
well, it may have been something else."

Needham looked at Ambrose again as if he expected him
to add something. Ambrose waited.

"Yes," said Needham. "The police would like to connect
Commander Abbot-Hume with the murder of Mr Hewitt.
It would just fit in with a little theory they hold."

"And what's that?"

"Oh, you must surely know, sir. They think *you* arranged
the murder."

"Me?"

"Oh yes. They . . . er . . . they have an idea about Mr
Hewitt's real work—I suppose you told them—and they
think you may have had him removed for one reason or
another."

"Needham, let's take this slowly. First, what do *you*
know about Mr Hewitt's work."

"Oh, one somehow gets to know things, sir, when one
has been here as long as I have."

"And my part?"

"Well, I take it you came to see what was happening, and
you may have been disappointed in Mr Hewitt."

"Disappointed? Lovely word. So I arranged for him to
be eliminated?"

"They wouldn't think it impossible."

"I didn't do it myself?"

"Oh yes, they have thought of that, too. But Commander
Abbot-Hume is so much more experienced with fire-arms."

"But you haven't told them yet that Mrs Abbot-Hume
put the gun in Miss Hope-Little's car?"

"Why, no, sir. That's what I came to ask your advice on.
If Miss Hope-Little cannot be connected in any other way
with the murder, it might perhaps be just as well to leave
the matter of the guns a mystery. After all, this *is* an
Embassy matter."

Ambrose finally grasped it. "Needham, do you mean that you think that perhaps I *did* organize it with Commander Abbot-Hume?"

Needham raised his eyebrows slightly, clearly rather surprised at Ambrose's tone. "Well, we have often had to take difficult decisions, sir. I know that. I am sure that if anything was decided, there were good reasons for it."

"Good reasons?"

"Sometimes it is the only way. I remember in my first post, before I came to Washington. It was in Carácas. We had a very difficult decision to take there. A matter of blackmail."

"But of course we never let the Venezuelan police into the Embassy?"

"Why, no, sir. Sir Nicholas—he was a great believer in diplomatic rights. And I do believe it pays to be strict. How much simpler it would have been if the Admiral hadn't called the police in here."

Ambrose tried to speak quite calmly. "But you think we might still get away with it, if we don't mention about Mrs Abbot-Hume's putting the gun in Miss Hope-Little's car?"

"I would think so, sir, unless you advise to the contrary. I don't know all about the details—I don't want to know, sir—but, of course, Commander Abbot-Hume . . ." he paused slightly, apparently again expecting a response from Ambrose. "Well, anyhow," he resumed, "it seemed to me simpler to tell you and let you decide." He got up, ready to go.

"I wonder, Needham. Is there anything that goes on at the Embassy that you don't see?" Ambrose asked.

"Oh, it's just part of my job, sir," said Needham modestly. "I just sit there and watch things go by."

How funny, thought Ambrose. It's a real philosophy. If you sit still, instead of rushing around, everything comes to you—if you sit in the right place, of course, and have eyes like Needham. No, it's no mystery that he picks up so much. People walk by him without noticing him, or without being on guard—their character, their plans show in the way they walk, the way they look, the things they carry. And there he sits, ethically neutral—watching, absorbing, assessing. It's how we look to God, I suppose.

"Good-bye," he said to Needham. "Let me think it all out. You can leave it to me."

The old man took his leave gratefully. This was the way things ought to be done in the Foreign Service. You did your duty, and left the decisions to the right people. It was all just another little link in the great chain of Foreign Office history. "Good-bye, sir," he said to Ambrose. "I hope your wounds will soon heal."

My wounds, thought Ambrose. The word made him feel very stricken. Yes, my wounds, he thought. All our wounds.

v

For a few minutes after Needham had gone, Ambrose lay on his bed quietly, and then picked up the telephone.

"Oh, Mr Usher," said the operator. "There's an incoming call for you. I didn't know you were ready. Are you taking calls?"

"Yes, I am awake. Do tell the policemen. There is a *policeman* down there, is there not?"

"Well, sir, they wanted to know when you were awake. Will you take the call, sir?"

Ambrose said he would. There was a click, and suddenly the receiver seemed to come alive: "Ambrogio!" it yelped. "Wassa matter you in hospital? I-a-come specially to Washington to talk-a with you, and here you sick. Iss an accident? Or are you really sick?"

"Giuseppe! How wonderful. No, just a slight accident.

Nothing wrong with me. But how wonderful that you called. I need your help."

"What? You in trouble again with that stupid Castellano? I tell-a him to lay-a off the picket. I see I must-a get rid of him."

"Oh no, the labour situation's fine. No, this is something else. You may not be able to help. Just a chance though you can. Could you come round to see me immediately here?"

"You betcha-life I come right around. Take me about half an hour. And then we talk, eh? I wanna tell you something new I found in Croce. In his Autobiography. You read it?"

With some difficulty, Ambrose brought the conversation to an end. He found himself smiling as he lay back on the pillow. In the same relaxed mood, he picked up the phone again. Again the operator got the first word in.

"Captain Shaughnessy is here," she said "Can he come up to see you?"

"Let me make one phone call first," said Ambrose. "Can you get me the French Embassy? And please, can you order me some lunch? I'm starved."

In a moment he was talking to Thérèse.

"I wondered if you'd be in jail," he said. "Apparently not. The police are being kind to us."

"Yes. But are you all right?" she said. "No ill effects?"

"I feel wonderful. Slightly incredulous, though. That's really why I called. Did last night happen? I'll believe it when I see you again."

"When shall I come?"

"As soon as possible. Well, give me an hour. Captain Shaughnessy is coming up now. Of course, I may not be here when you arrive. I'm the Number One suspect for everything, you know. The police listen in to all my calls. Are you there, Captain?"

She laughed. "I think you are all right with the police. You trust them with your documents."

There was nothing to say to this.

"Did you speak to Walter this morning?" he asked her.

Her tone changed. "Yes," she said quietly. "He was very relieved. He's flying back to-night."

Ambrose was matter of fact. "Good. Mission accomplished. Oh, there's one other thing. Could you do something for me before you come? Could you phone the Embassy—I mean, of course, the *British* Embassy—and get hold of Miss Turenne? She's Hewitt's secretary—or was. I want to have a chat with her. Perhaps you could bring her with you, if it's on your way."

"Of course. I'll try to get hold of her immediately. Good-bye."

The first knock on the door was the lunch-tray, but Shaughnessy was close behind. Ambrose waved to him cheerfully to sit down. "Do you mind if I eat?" he said. "I'm starving. I can listen while you talk. Can I offer you anything?" He waved at the chicken on his plate.

Shaughnessy looked at him grimly. He was not quite the same genial companion of the night before. "I'm not sure where to begin," he said. "There's an awful lot we want to ask you. Sometimes I wonder" . . . he looked at Ambrose as he muttered half to himself . . . "sometimes I wonder if you're doing all this on purpose. Every time things get straight you seem to get them fouled up."

"For instance?" said Ambrose, helping himself to a copious portion of asparagus.

"Well, I don't mind telling you we had you in the front row in the beginning."

"Number One suspect?"

"Number One hatchet-man, for a special reason. Goldberg had a theory . . . well, no need to go into that. I still don't understand . . . but never mind. Then you got hit on the head while the guard was killed, and your secretary showed up with the guns. Gave us a new angle."

187

"Number One hatchet-woman?"

"Well, maybe." Shaughnessy never took his eyes off Ambrose. He's playing it like a poker hand, thought Ambrose. Trying to bluff it through. What evidence did he have?

"She's got a lot of explaining to do," said Shaughnessy. "Or perhaps it's you who should do the explaining. I guess she knows more about guns than you do, but I don't see any point in it for her—especially with Hewitt—unless . . ."

"Unless she was under my orders?"

Shaughnessy was quite serious now. "It figures."

"Is that as close as you can get?"

"Oh no, closer than that."

"Just because she was shooting up a few burglars?"

"Depends a bit what she was shooting them with."

"Well, what *was* she shooting them with?"

"It happened to be the murder weapon," said Shaughnessy. "We've checked it. One of those two guns she was firing killed Hewitt."

"And Johnson?"

Shaughnessy gave him a sharp look: "Yeh. Johnson too. Same gun. Ballistics people just reported."

"Have you asked her where she got it?"

"Oh yes," said Shaughnessy. "She has some funny story about finding one of the guns in her car yesterday afternoon —it wasn't there in the morning when we asked her to search for it, so she says—and she picked up the other one, so she says, when she chased the burglars. One of them dropped it."

"Well, couldn't that one have been the murder weapon?"

"Yes, it could have been, if you believe her story."

"And that," said Ambrose, "would surely explain everything. The burglars. . . ."

"That's right. The burglars tried to get into the Annex on the night of the fireworks party, and Hewitt got in the way, so they shot him. Then they came back last night with the same gun and this time Johnson got in the way, so they shot him."

"Sounds very good," said Ambrose cheerfully.

"And then they presented the gun to Miss Hope-Little," said Shaughnessy, with heavy sarcasm. "And there's another small point. It happens to be a British Embassy gun. The number shows that."

"Surely the number should show who had charge of it?"

"Oh, sure," said Shaughnessy. "It would anywhere else. In every other place they'd have a list with each gun numbered and allotted. But here everything's just happy-go-lucky. People pass guns around—among the guards, in the gun-range, in the Embassy plane—doesn't make any difference to anybody—until one of them goes off, of course, and we find the body."

"Still, your theory would work nicely if the burglars had got hold of a British Embassy gun earlier. They might have done, if everybody was so careless."

"Oh yes, they might have done. But there's one difficulty there, and that's where you come in again. What about your own little burglary last night?"

"Ah yes. We ought to have a chat about that. I never really thanked you for the police protection. Very reassuring —after the first shock anyway. But where does that fit in?"

"You tell *me*. I got the impression from you this morning that you set out on this little housebreaking job to get some papers that had been left in the cabinet yesterday."

"That's right."

"He'd left the papers there by mistake *that day*. Ross found out and sent the burglars along to get them."

"Right."

"Well, then, why would the same thieves be trying to break in two nights earlier?"

"I agree," said Ambrose. "It's less likely. Perhaps just reconnoitering the ground."

"Or perhaps they had some special account to settle with Hewitt. We've thought of that, too. They were Communists. . . ."

"Or working for the Communists. . . ."

"And they'd found out that Hewitt was an agent. Or he'd found out what they were after, and tried to stop them."

"Sounds plausible."

"Everything's too damn plausible! What about the attack on you. Did they have to get *you* out of the way first? Sounds plausible, too. At least it does now. But that wasn't what we thought at the beginning. We weren't sure at first if the business with you wasn't . . ."

"Don't tell me I let myself get bumped on the head."

"Well, it was all very convenient. Suppose you had been trying to throw us off the trail. It's been heard of, you know. And you weren't as badly hit as all that. Perhaps the burglary at the Embassy was a phoney. All you had wanted was to get the guard out of the way. He may have known too much."

"So you waited for my next move?"

"Yes, and that balled things up again. Why should you go and steal something with a great deal of risk, if something hadn't been stolen from the Embassy?"

"I might have been looking for something else."

"Yes, we thought of that. Suppose you encouraged the Commies to break in last night in order to see where the trail led. We've got to hand it to you about Ross. The F.B.I. never suspected him at all. They think you staged the whole thing. They say that would be a typical British operation."

"Ah, those clever British! Strange reputation. All because they write spy stories. What are the F.B.I. doing with Ross, by the way?"

"Oh, they've picked him up. He's very annoyed. He

particularly wants to find out who telephoned him last night, pretending to be Sanati."

"Yes," said Ambrose, "that was certainly a nice touch. I enjoyed that. And Sanati?"

"He's leaving for Italy to-day."

"So you decided that I'm on the side of the angels."

"Well," said Shaughnessy reluctantly. "The F.B.I. have never had any doubts about that. It's just these murders. The United States isn't some British colony, you know. The British just can't get away with things like this. Trouble is that no one really believes that you'd use a woman to bump someone off, even if she is a Bisley champion."

Ambrose was thinking. "I suppose I'd better tell you something," he said finally. "The gun in Miss Hope-Little's car. Her story is correct, you know. She didn't have it until yesterday. Someone did put it there yesterday afternoon. Mrs Abbot-Hume."

Shaughnessy smiled. "You don't say. Yes, we happen to know all about that. Just waiting for you to bring it up. I *thought* you would know."

"Oh, really," Ambrose spluttered. "Really, this is too much."

"Well, we find things out. As a matter of fact, Abbot-Hume rang us up this morning when he heard about Miss Hope-Little. His wife had found the gun in an old coat of his and tried to get rid of it for him."

Ambrose had now recovered his calm. "But he has a perfectly innocent explanation, no doubt," he said blandly to Shaughnessy.

"Oh, of course," said Shaughnessy sarcastically. "He's on the Pistol Team. Often takes guns back home with him from the range. Perfectly natural."

"But Mrs Abbot-Hume. . . ."

"Exactly. Didn't seem quite so natural to her, apparently. She thought he'd done the murder, and we know why. So she slipped the gun into a car at the parking-lot—just happened to be Miss Hope-Little's car. Very loving wife. She told him yesterday afternoon when he got home. He went back to the parking-lot and was looking for the car to get the gun back, but he couldn't find it in time."

"Yes, he was disturbed," said Ambrose. "Well, where does that leave Miss Hope-Little?"

"I could tell you if we could sort out Abbot-Hume's position."

"Have you talked to him?"

Shaughnessy nearly exploded with sudden anger. "Talk to him! That's exactly the trouble! He's in the Embassy, and the Ambassador won't let us talk to him. Suddenly decided to stand on diplomatic rights."

"So he *phoned*. . . ."

"That's right. He phoned to get Miss Hope-Little off the hook, as he thought. Very chivalrous. But when we want to follow it up, we're stuck. This isn't the end, though," he growled. "The Commissioner is working on this. My God. Wait till the papers get this."

"Has it been given to the Press yet?"

"No," muttered Shaughnessy. "Commissioner's forbidden us to talk. We're having a meeting this evening with the Ambassador. Discussing it with the State Department first. And some people are coming out from Scotland Yard. Oh, my God," he passed his hand over a weary brow. "Give me a nice straightforward pole-axe slaying any day."

"So you've got Abbot-Hume tied up with the first murder, the motive being . . ."

Shaughnessy rose. "We've got it all quite clear, first and second. Plenty of motive. All we need is to ask Abbot-Hume a few questions. . . ."

"Tell me more about Johnson's murder before you go."

"That's the funny thing," said Shaughnessy. "Just the

same as Hewitt. Gun absolutely next to his head. Might have thought it was suicide if there'd been a gun around. Or someone was blazing angry and shot him close to his head—almost like an execution."

"Why wouldn't he resist?"

"Well, there's an explanation. He'd been drinking. Seems to have drunk a whole bottle of whisky. We found an empty bottle on the ground next to him, and he stank of the stuff. They've been doing an autopsy. Probably find he was dead drunk, or close to it."

"And it was the same gun?"

"Yep. Terrible mess. Not just his head. He'd been in a fight. His face had nasty scratches, and someone seems to have kicked him in the stomach—got a horrible bruise."

"What about his own gun?"

"Oh, he wasn't in uniform. His uniform and his holster are hanging up in the entrance room at the Annex. Of course, he could have been carrying a gun in his pocket without the holster."

Ambrose began to say something, then stopped. "Captain . . . I don't know yet. I have an idea myself, but I want to check some things first. It could be quite different, you know. If the Ambassador has started the diplomatic rights business, it doesn't mean . . ."

"I don't care what it means. We're going to follow it through," said Shaughnessy. "He called us in, and he's not going to find it so easy to get rid of us. We've got a few things to ask you, too."

"You will find me willing, ready and anxious to talk. Won't be able to stop me—once I know what to say, of course. But when? When do we meet again?"

"Whenever you're ready. Sooner the better."

"Well, I have one or two things to do," said Ambrose, "and I'm sure you have too. This evening—no, wait. What is to-day, the 7th?—oh, this evening there's the reception

at the Soviet Embassy, their National Day—*must* go to that
—in fact, everybody will be going to that. Doesn't look as
though anyone from the Embassy *or* the State Department
will sit down and talk till after the party. Why don't we
meet then at the Embassy? I'll arrange it with the
Ambassador. Say eleven o'clock. We'll all sit down and put
our pieces together. And now I'm going to shave. Yes, I do
shave. Could you ask them to send me a razor on your way
downstairs? Oh yes, and a clean shirt, size 17 collar. Do you
mind?"

There was nothing for it. Shaughnessy took his leave.

VI

A few minutes to myself, thought Ambrose. What bliss.
But as he thought it, the phone gave its discreet Nursing
Home buzz, and a moment later Cantolli had burst into the
room and was giving him a great hug of welcome.

"Ambrogio! What iss-a happening? You 'ad an accident?
In a car?"

"No, Giuseppe. As a matter of fact, it isn't really
accidental. It's deliberate. I've changed character. I've become a man of action—an adventurer. Of course, it can be
a bit painful." He touched his head wrily.

"Oh, Ambrogio! Iss-a not for you. Adventure. Iss-a not
for a philosopher."

"What about you, Giuseppe? You're a man of action and
a philosopher."

"Iss-a different. Me, Giuseppe, I'm no real philosopher.
I'm an ignorant peasant from Napoli. I like-a read Croce,
he also live in Napoli, he *speak* for Napoli, the beauty, the
history, the sky, the bay—I no understand-a all 'e write,
but I feel, he speak-a for me, like-a my ancestor in the
Middle Ages they look at a beautiful church or painting,
they no understand-a too much, but it's a-beautiful to them.

194

But you, Ambrogio, you are real man of ideas—iss-a not for your adventure. Are you all right?" he added anxiously.

"I'm fine. All I need is a shave. But you know, Giuseppe, all this excitement isn't a bad thing for me. I feel as if I'm living in Florence in Lorenzo's day, with scholars and spies popping in and out from France and Germany and Spain, and cut-throats in the street. It's really quite like Washington."

"Ah, but no room for poor Giuseppe in Lorenzo's Florence."

"On the contrary. You'd be just the same as you are. Trade unions are simply condottieri. . . ."

"Condottieri are more-a like gangsters. You hire them."

"Think so? By the way, do you know any gangsters? That's really what I wanted to ask you."

Giuseppe was incredulous. "You ask-a me to come here to talk about gangsters!"

"Oh, it's important. Do you know any?"

Giuseppe became slightly apologetic. "Well, iss-a natural. I know some, sure. If-a my boys are one kind of condottieri, well, iss-a natural we-a know the other kind, no? Some-a time we fight them, some-a time we get them to help us, you know if an employer iss-a difficult, not now, but a few years ago, when-a we organize."

"Yes, I know. Well, what's happened to the old gangsters? They haven't all disappeared, have they? Some of them are still around."

"Much-a change, you wouldn't a-know them. The Italian ones, I know personally, *very* respectable. Of course, they a-have to earn a living, do a job 'ere and there. But so quiet now. No like-a violence."

The phone rang. Ambrose reached for it, grumbling. "Really, it's worse than my office," but his voice softened when he heard Thérèse at the other end.

"How are you now?" she asked.

"Very well, splendid. Having a pleasant discussion of Italian history, past and present. And you? Any ill-effects?"

"No. I wanted to tell you that I got hold of Miss Turenne. She is coming to see you at four o'clock, if that's all right."

"Excellent. And you?"

"I can't come now. I have some things to do."

"Are you going to the reception to-night at the Russian Embassy?" he asked her.

"I'm invited," she said. "Will you be there? Are you well enough?"

"Well enough? After last night? I wouldn't miss it for anything, even without fireworks. We shall meet there, then, amid the vodka and the balalaikas."

He said good-bye, and when he turned back to Cantolli he saw a mischievous look in his eye.

"In Florence they were-a very fond of the ladies, eh?"

"Now then, Giuseppe. Gangsters. They're more important at the moment. Castellano and your other boys here. They know their way round pretty well, I suppose. Has Castellano been here a long time?"

"More-a than twenny years."

"Do you think he'd remember someone from that time called Umberto Rossi?"

"Rossi? I a-knew him myself. Iss-a no good. He become idealist, and join the Communists. Change his name to Ross. No good. Never like him."

"But he knew his way round? Knew how to get jobs done?"

"Listen, Ambrogio. Anybody can get anything a-done in this-a wonderful country. Ask-a the right person, and pay-a the right price. The mos' that can-a happen, you can be disappointed."

"One big happy family, eh?"

"Not exactly. But people, they know each other. Times

are bad for some people. Have to unerstand-a people's problems."

"Well this is the question, Giuseppe. I think Rossi had to get a job done quickly last night. He wanted some people to burgle the Embassy, and he got them. If this was a straight professional job, could Castellano find out who did it? It's very important."

Cantolli was a little worried. "Iss-a not difficult to find out, but you wouldn't expect-a him to tell the police! Iss-a not healthy. Iss-a not even ethical."

"No, I don't want to tell the police. But I'd like someone to ask the burglars exactly what happened. Someone they would trust, like you. They don't have to say who paid them. All I need to know is what kind of burglars they were, and what happened. You don't have to tell me anything more."

"We try," said Cantolli a little more cheerfully. "Can't tell the police. Iss-a matter of principle. But to find out-a what happened—that iss-a not too difficult. When you want to know?"

"In a few hours, if you can Giuseppe. It's really urgent."

"Ambrogio," said Cantolli seriously. "I no like-a thiss-a life for you. Iss-a too much rush. Why we no sit down and talk about something important?"

Ambrose was saved by a knock at the door. It was the nurse bringing in his razor and shirt. "I've brought you the afternoon papers, too," she said with a smile, looking at the black headlines significantly, as she put the things down on the side table. She closed the door gently as she left.

"Iss-a no good," said Cantolli resignedly. "I can see. Philosophy must-a wait."

"Not long, Giuseppe. As soon as this business is over. Will you telephone me as soon as you have some news? I'll leave here at about 5.30, and I'll be at my hotel until about 9 o'clock. Telephone me there, in any case, to check."

Cantolli rose to go. Small, plump, his bright eyes twinkling with pleasure and friendship, he took Ambrose's hands into his.

"What is the secret of the moral imperative?" he asked him. "I'm-a not satisfied with Croce. I agree that we call-a things good when we desire-a them, but that doesn't mean that we don't desire things because they're-a good. Think about it, my friend." He waved to him and was gone.

Ambrose sighed and climbed out of bed ready to shave and dress. He picked up the afternoon papers, and glanced at the bold headlines, full of the new Embassy murder and burglary. They were going at it from every angle. Then his eye caught another front-page item, not with as bold a headline, but dramatic enough in its own way. ARGENTINE GOVERNMENT OVERTHROWN, it ran. PRESIDENT IN FLIGHT. In smaller headlines, the story ran on: *New Junta Seeks Pact with Britain: British Ambassador in Washington Approached.*

EIGHT

I

As he left his hotel room for the party, Ambrose took a last quick look at the mirror to see if he was presentable. Yes, his white tie was reasonably straight. The red sash of his decoration looked cheerful. The Russians liked one to be well decorated.

He was looking forward to the party. The British Embassy had formally notified the Russian Embassy two days earlier that he was in Washington, and a handsomely engraved card had arrived post-haste inviting him. Matthews, in charge of protocol, had sent it round by hand to his hotel with a little note saying that if rumour were true, this was to be the answer to the fireworks—the party to end all parties.

Ambrose had managed to get everything done in plenty of time—phone calls, interviews, everything. The party, from nine to eleven, and the meeting afterwards at the British Embassy—everything seemed to be falling into shape. Cantolli had telephoned. He had no news yet, but he had hopes that he might have by eleven.

Yes, it was all working out, but it was tiring too, and, once in the cab, Ambrose closed his eyes for a few moments of rest. When he opened them again, it was as if someone had banished care with a wand of gaiety. Alighting from the taxi, he was received by a footman whose gold braid pro-

claimed him to be at least a Hero of the Russian Revolution
—probably a Field-Marshal—and was passed on to two
assistant Generals who relieved him, in one combined
gesture, of his hat and coat. Two dark-eyed maidens in
peasant costume of the period of Catherine the Great
curtsied and swung the doors open for him. In the small
entrance-hall, the glory of Holy Russia lay before him. It
was lit with hundreds of candles, burning in clusters before
a collection of ikons that had presumably been brought over
specially. So much for fireworks, thought Ambrose, as he
walked round looking at the lovely old carvings.

Passing on, the guests came to the main hall. In the centre
was a magnificent staircase, at the top of which Lischev and
his wife stood ready to receive them. But around this hall
was the second surprise. A number of show-cases, all
beautifully illuminated, were displayed, each containing
apparently a scene from Russian history, with little model
figures to tell the tale. In the first, some blacksmiths, in the
costume of Peter the Great's day, were forging some
modern-looking steel girders. "*Scene in Urals, in 1725,*"
said the legend. "*World's first steel girders made here, basis
of all future skyscrapers.*" The next show-case displayed a
busy scene in an engineering shop. A number of figures
were crouched in one corner over a primitive steam-engine
—the first in the world, long before Watt—and in the centre
stood Russia's pride, the world's first locomotive, invented,
as the legend explained, by Terepanov in 1776. Next to this
was the story of electricity. Around a table, Ldygin's wife
and children were looking open-mouthed at a glowing
electric lamp which he had just invented—the year was 1872
—and in another corner of the room Alexander Popov was
twiddling the dials of the world's first radio. For contrast,
the next show-case showed a charming open air scene.
Alexander Mozhaisky, wearing goggles, was about to enter
the world's first aeroplane. The year was 1878. In the back-

ground, a balloon bearing the date 1731 was soaring upward, carrying its inventor, Kraykuteny.

The story went on—the movies, penicillin, jet propulsion —it was all charmingly displayed. At the end of the hall, however, was one empty show-case, and this seemed to be arousing an interest all its own.

Ambrose found Simpkins, the British Embassy's Agricultural Attaché, standing by the empty case among a group of other people.

"I suppose this is Lysenko *not* discovering the transmission of acquired characteristics," he whispered to Ambrose. "The line has just been switched, you know."

"Don't you think it might be someone discovering invisibility?" Ambrose asked him. "An invisible cloak, you know. Russian legend is full of it."

It was all quite delightful, but the crowd behind pressed, and the way was upward, towards Lischev, in his high-collared Russian diplomatic uniform, and his cheerful, buxom wife. As each name was called out, Lischev greeted each guest, bowing stiffly; but when Ambrose was announced, and he moved forward, a flicker of recognition passed over Lischev's face. He greeted Ambrose in Russian.

"Good-evening. I think you speak our language."

Ambrose replied in Russian, with a very straight face, "I am very happy to speak it."

He turned to Mme Lischev, greeted her in Russian too, and moved on.

Was this crowd the same as those who had attended the Guy Fawkes party? Was this the same city, the same week? It was hardly credible. At the fireworks party, before the murder, there had been a feeling of almost schoolboy cheerfulness in the air. Here they were parading, a dense, rather puzzled throng, before the Russian enigma. Was it the vastness of Russia that was so overwhelming, after the cosiness

201

of little England. You felt it even here in the hugely laden tables, the great mounds of caviar and exotic fishes, the hordes of flunkeys with their glittering salvers.

Ambrose took a glass of champagne, and before he had taken a step forward found a Russian on either side of him, ready to talk. Were they his bodyguard for the evening? They certainly knew who he was—and probably knew what he was doing. One of them, small and wiry, addressed him in Russian.

"Have the police made any discoveries yet about your colleague's death? Very tragic."

"I have heard nothing but rumours," said Ambrose.

"Ah, if one listened to rumour!" said the second Russian, a more jovial type, who seemed to be well launched into the champagne. "You are the man of rumour. Rumour says you are a very busy man here."

The first Russian gave his colleague a sharp look. Ambrose waved his hand to imply anything they liked to believe, and was mercifully pushed on by the crowd surging past Lischev. He saw Beauchamp out of the corner of his eye and made his way over to him. A man with an Italian accent, who looked vaguely familiar, was asking Beauchamp about the Argentine coup.

"The newspaper this afternoon says that the new Junta is anxious to make a pact with you," he was saying. "That would be convenient, would it not?"

Beauchamp was as formal as ever. "We cannot go by newspaper stories."

The other man laughed. "Ah, we always look for something in them. We see maybe a little pattern—the events at your Embassy two nights ago—Argentine Government falls—new Government is pro-British. The British have not lost their skill, it seems."

"The British have not lost their reputation," said Ambrose.

"But really, sir," said Beauchamp to the Italian, "you surely do not suggest . . ."

The Italian gave them a very broad, knowing smile. "I am not suggesting anything. Governments come, governments go. But in the history of diplomacy, perhaps someone will one day write a little footnote on fireworks, maybe, eh?"

The crowd behind them stirred. A voice called, "Vincento. Come and talk to me." Pepita had joined them. Suddenly she saw Ambrose. "Mr Usher! Where have you been? The whole of Washington is talking about you. Is this story true that you were attacked? You have a wound still on your head?"

"Well, here I am, hale and hearty, so it can't be so serious."

Pepita was greeting friends to the right and left as she carried on her conversation with Ambrose. "I wish they would let me help to solve the murders," she said to him. "I read palms, you know, and I'm sure it would provide some clues. Oh, Edward, don't be so stuffy. Of course these things help. Do you remember when I read your palm, Hendryk?" she turned to a tall, blond Dutchman standing by. "Wasn't that just before you met you know who, and didn't I tell you?"

Hendryk spluttered a little.

"Listen, Mr Usher," Pepita took Ambrose's arm and steered him away. "I have a plan. You know I'm reading palms at the Embassy Bazaar on Monday. Suppose we got all the suspects there—the murder suspects, I mean—there must be lots of suspects—and I read their hands. I could tell you who the murderer was. As a matter of fact, I've got something very interesting to tell you that I discovered just yesterday. Not about the murders. But it's important. Come over here, I don't want anyone to hear this."

They moved over to the side. Ambrose kept his eyes open for his bodyguards, but they did not seem in evidence.

Pepita was now whispering in a truly conspiratorial

voice. "Do you know the Rumanian Minister, Paretscu? He's here somewhere, of course. I'm sure he's planning to break."

"How do you know," asked Ambrose.

"It's just what I'm telling you. I read his palm."

"Well. . . ."

"Oh, you're as bad as Edward. Don't you see, it's not *just* his palm. There's been a rumour recently. Last night we were at dinner at the Van Eyrick's—he was there too—and we got on to palm reading afterwards. Everyone falls for it, you know. I told him—it was quite true—that there was a sudden break in his lifeline, after which it got very much stronger. He gave me a terrified look, and begged me not to say anything to anybody about it."

Ambrose was keeping an eye on the room while Pepita was whispering, and suddenly saw someone who should have been in London. "Good Heavens," he exclaimed. "Hepworth! You know him, don't you? The new Under-Secretary. What on earth is *he* doing here? I must go and talk to him. Will you come?"

Pepita, however, had spotted someone else and moved on. Hepworth had seen Ambrose and was bearing down with a brimming champagne glass in his hand. "What a life, Ambrose! What a life! And you didn't want to come." He was tall, elegant and lackadaisical, the Englishman that looks like a permanent undergraduate.

"Herbert! What are you doing here?"

"Have to keep an eye on you, old boy. Besides, can't resist parties."

"Something to do with Hewitt?"

"Partly. Send you here, and look what happens. Besides" —he hardly changed his tone—"I found out something myself. Most odd. When shall we talk?"

"After this, if you like, at Throttle's. We're all meeting. You say 'partly'? Anything else?"

"Yes, I'm *en route* to the Argentine. Don't you read the papers?"

Ambrose broke in. "Hold it. Here come Hengist and Horsa. My bodyguards. Can you take them off me? Something I want to do."

Ambrose introduced them to Hepworth, who immediately swept them off to the food table, proclaiming his love of caviar. Ambrose had caught a glimpse of Auguste Flantin strolling by and moved quickly in his direction. He had not seen Flantin since the cocktail party at Beauchamp's on his first day, and there was a little unsettled business in his mind.

When Flantin turned, he found Ambrose at his elbow, and greeted him with the greatest cordiality.

"I'm so glad to see you again, Mr Usher," he said in his carefully clipped English. "How sad it was about Mr Hewitt. We had such a pleasant time with him the other night. It doesn't seem possible."

"No," agreed Ambrose. "It is very sad, and so puzzling."

"There are no clues yet?" asked Flantin.

"Nothing that we have heard. Just a mystery."

"And then the guard being killed. You have your share of troubles."

"Yes, it's very sad. I hope it can be solved, though."

"You have confidence in the Washington police?"

"Well," said Ambrose, lowering his voice slightly. "I heard that someone is coming out from Scotland Yard. A really top man. Halibut."

"Halibut? And he is a top man?"

"Perhaps it's just a rumour, but they say he's absolutely superb."

They chatted for a few moments more, but the essential point had been made. Halibut, eh? When he mentioned the name, he had seen the flicker in Flantin's eyes. Only for a split second, but he had recognized it. He felt pleased with himself for a moment, but Flantin had the last word.

"If we could help in any way, we would be glad to," Flantin was saying. "I, or Mme Marot . . . anything we can do . . ." He waved his hand cheerfully to Ambrose as he turned aside.

II

I need a breath of air, Ambrose thought. There was an open window close by. He moved over to it and stood there looking out at the rustling trees of Massachusetts Avenue.

As always, when he could stop to let nature speak, the magic of autumn filled his mind. The clatter of the party faded away. He heard nothing but the sighing trees.

Standing there, he recalled his first meeting with Thérèse —could it be only three days ago—when they had stood in the garden at the Beauchamp's, breathing in the autumn air. . . .

Autumn was not a dying season. It tautened you, invigorated you. There was so much promise in that exhilaration.

As he stood there, he heard behind him a deep, musical voice begin to recite softly in Russian the Pushkin lyric:

> *"And with each Autumn*
> *I flow anew,*
> *The blood plays buoyant in the heart . . ."*

He turned quickly, and smiled happily at Lischev. He felt close to him at that moment.

"You still learn Pushkin by heart," he said.

"There is all too little to learn," said Lischev. "Too short a life. Suppose Shakespeare had died at 37."

Suddenly the name Lischev rang a bell in Ambrose's mind. "Are you descended from Alexei Lischev?" he asked.

"My grandfather."

"I remember his essay on Byron and Pushkin. I never

206

could read Byron again. Cannot we meet and talk some-time—about Pushkin?"

"About Pushkin? Yes. Pushkin, and Shakespeare, and Hardy. I admire Hardy."

"And perhaps about other things?" said Ambrose.

Lischev looked at him quietly before replying. "It is more difficult to talk of other things," he said finally. "We have a proverb in Russia: *An ox is caught by his horns, a man by his tongue.*"

"I was born in Serbia," said Ambrose. "We say it differently there. We have a proverb: *If a man burns his tongue, he must tell the company that the soup is hot.*"

Lischev smiled. "We are after all wiser in Russia," he said. "We avoid serving hot soup. Champagne, iced champagne"—he waved his arm towards the room—"it is so much pleasanter. . . ."

They turned away from the window to mingle with the guests, but the few words with Lischev stayed with Ambrose as he wandered on, looking for Thérèse. Suddenly he caught sight of her, standing talking with a group of people. She was wearing a lovely grey gown, of stiff brocade, her shoulders bare, her iron-grey hair glittering with light. She introduced him to her companions, and it was hard for him to get her away for the talk he so much wanted. Time was getting on. Admiral Throttle passed by and signalled to Ambrose to come over to him for a moment. They had a quick word about arrangements for the rendezvous later. When Ambrose was free again, Thérèse had gone.

He wandered through a doorway into the adjoining room to see if she was there. All was still very cheerful. In a group of people in the middle of the room he recognized Pepita's friend, Paretscu, the Rumanian Minister, and walked across to hear what was being said. Simpkins was with the group, and introduced him. Paretscu was medium-sized, dark and stocky. He had apparently been drinking rather heavily, and seemed to be in an aggressive mood. One of the people there was Tragocz, the Hungarian Minister, and Ambrose had the impression that it was Tragocz' manner—he was tall, blond, and arrogant—that poor little Paretscu was taking so heavily.

Yet they were only discussing sport—the latest Hungarian victory over England at soccer. Tragocz was receiving congratulations from Simpkins rather patronizingly.

"I can't explain why we are so good at sports," he was saying. "Perhaps it is our military tradition. Or perhaps the mountains, our beautiful Carpathians. Our best footballers are from the mountains. They are sure-footed, and they have courage."

Paretscu seemed to find this too much to take. "I believe you are the world champions at ping-pong," he said. "Ping-pong and *courage*? I would say a certain agility. You have to think quickly, no? You win by your wits. Is that correct English?" He appealed to Simpkins.

Tragocz looked down at Paretscu. "I speak of our tradition," he said, rolling his words. "The Magyar people have always been unconquerable. From King Stephen on, a thousand years. This is a long tradition. It creates pride. Other countries have not always been so fortunate. The People's Republic of Rumania is a great country to-day, but, after all, to be a province of Turkey for so many centuries . . ."

"We must all study a little history," said Paretscu sharply. "How far back shall we go in Rumanian history? To John Bessaraba? You remember him, I am sure. He defeated King Charles of Hungary in 1330, or perhaps 1230—I forget exactly." He took a glass of champagne from a passing footman, and took a long drink.

Tragocz kept his temper excellently. "Well, now we fight only in the sporting stadium. The U.S.S.R. has shown us..."

"We have fought invaders from all directions," cried Paretscu, with increasing heat. "And we will always fight. You cannot make a . . . a *goulash* of Rumanian history."

Tragocz stiffened. "Do you find something wrong with goulash?" he asked frigidly.

"No, no," cried Paretscu. "Goulash is the perfect dish, the Magyars are the greatest people. Long live the People's Republic of Hungary!"

He was waving his glass insultingly at the Hungarian as he spoke. With an uneasy smile, Tragocz backed away, and turned to leave. He had, however, to pass close by Paretscu, in whom the devil suddenly entered. Ambrose saw Paretscu put his foot out, and neatly knock Tragocz' feet together. Tragocz stumbled, almost fell, and looked round furiously for the culprit. Paretscu was looking upwards, with an innocent but beatific smile.

"Sure-footed, eh?" Ambrose heard him mutter. "Braggart! *Satellite!*"

There was an urgent whisper in Ambrose's ear. Eldridge was standing by him, outwardly as poised as ever. But he was saying quietly: "Let's get out of here, quickly, Ambrose. There's trouble."

"Trouble?" murmured Ambrose, as they moved away.

"H.E.'s having a show-down with the police." Eldridge maintained the polite smile on his face as he exchanged bows with the guests. "And the Embassy's going to be blown up. No connection of course."

III

In the Bentley, racing back to the Embassy, he told him what had happened. Before the party, Hepworth had been down to the State Department discussing the real thing that had brought him out—a really big thing on which the British needed American co-operation. The Americans had been more than obliging. They had agreed to everything that Hepworth had asked for, and on which he had brought out instructions received personally from Winston himself. He had been feeling very cheerful as a result, envisaging, no doubt, the aura of Churchillian good humour that would envelop him when he reported back to No. 10. At the end of the interview they had brought up the Abbot-Hume business. It would look very bad, they said, if the British stood on their diplomatic rights over a thing like this. Make it very hard to carry the Senate along over the other agreement, which really mattered. Couldn't the Foreign Office agree to allow Abbot-Hume to be questioned by the police? Couldn't do any harm if he was innocent, and would make a very good impression. Hepworth, full of bonhomie and gratitude, had instantly agreed. He had scribbled a little note giving permission, which they were to show to Abbot-Hume.

"Well, you can imagine what happened," said Eldridge. "The police drove up about half an hour ago. They demanded to see Abbot-Hume. Needham refused to admit them, and sent for the Admiral. He's gone tearing off there in an absolute fury. Says it's a trick doing it behind his back. He's told Dennis to stay in the Residence, and not to appear under any circumstances. I suppose you know, there are good reasons why he shouldn't."

"What about the Embassy being blown up," asked Ambrose.

"Oh, that's just a joke—at least I suppose so," said Eldridge. "It's one of those routine threats from oppressed Colonials with a new angle—Guy Fawkes—a little late, of course. We got a letter this afternoon with a New York postmark from some group that wants independence for the Mermaid Islands. Cheap note-paper, and the message scrawled in pencil—not too literate. Says something like: 'We have warned you for the last time. To-morrow we strike. Guy Fawkes will succeed this time.' And underneath is the slogan: '*Independence for the Mermaids!*' It's really a beautiful mix-up. The message is dated November 4th, so they presumably meant it to arrive on Guy Fawkes Day, when they would strike. But the postmark is November 6th. I suppose the ringleader put the letter in his pocket and forgot to post it."

"But isn't British colonial policy marvellous," said Ambrose wonderingly. "We send out schoolteachers to an obscure collection of islands off the coast of South America to teach them English history, so that when they want to blow up the Embassy they can do it in the name of Guy Fawkes. Wonderful!"

"I suppose it's a practical joke," said Eldridge.

"Do you think so?" said Ambrose. "Nothing will surprise me at this point. What time is it, by the way?"

"It's a quarter to eleven," said Eldridge. "We were going to meet at eleven anyhow."

They went straight to the Ambassador's study. Throttle was standing there with a brow like thunder, talking to Matthews. At the other end of the room Shaughnessy was talking to McDonald of the F.B.I., with Goldberg in the rear. McDonald smiled politely at Ambrose. Shaughnessy gave him a curious look, almost conspiratorial. They had shared too much in the last few days to be enemies.

Ambrose went into the small room next door where the Ambassador's secretary was on duty. "Has there been a phone call for me?" he asked. There had been no call, and it was now eleven. What had happened to Cantolli?

He thought for a second and then went over to Shaughnessy. "Can Goldberg wait in the next room," he said. "There are some people coming that I may want to bring in later, and I'm expecting an urgent phone call. He would be useful there if you can spare him." Shaughnessy agreed instantly, and Goldberg went out.

At this point Rawlins, the Assistant Commissioner of Police, was shown in. The Ambassador went across to greet him with a fair semblance of politeness.

"Where's Hepworth?" Ambrose whispered to Eldridge.

"He went off from the party with someone from the State Department. God knows where he's got to. Probably has no idea what's going on."

Rawlins had apparently heard of the threat from the Mermaids and was trying to be co-operative. "Would you like us to send some police up here and to patrol the grounds, just in case?" he was asking the Ambassador.

"Certainly not," said Throttle. "Quite unnecessary. I have ordered the police to leave the grounds, and that is final. I am waiting for the arrival of our own people. Their plane was grounded in Iceland, but they will be here soon."

"But in the meantime, this threat?"

"Nonsense. You don't think we take any notice of that. In any case, you might as well know that since the murder of Johnson last night, and the burglary, in which the police were remarkably un-useful, I have set up a rota of special patrols in the grounds, drawn from our own Embassy staff."

"But are they armed?" persisted Rawlins.

"That is our own affair. Of course they're armed. We've drawn rifles and machine-guns from the Military Liaison Commission upstairs. They're studying new weapons. So if anyone does try anything on, they'll get the very latest in weapons and ammunition. Useful practice." The thought seemed to amuse him slightly.

Rawlins shrugged his shoulders. "Well, can we discuss the other business?" he said.

"I can't see what there is to discuss," said the Admiral brusquely. "I might as well say right away that there will be no waiver of diplomatic immunity while I am Her Majesty's Ambassador here. When the first murder occurred, I asked the police in. I know. But it was a mistake.

And it didn't do any good, as far as I can see. The very next day Johnson was killed, a very valuable man, while the police were actually in charge. No, I'm keeping things here just as they are until our own people arrive."

Nobody spoke for a moment. There was the feeling of the quarter-deck in the air. The Admiral had spoken. No one cared to contradict.

Shaughnessy fidgeted and looked to Rawlins. Rawlins looked back at him and then seemed to decide to assert himself again.

"We don't think it's quite as simple as that," he said. "We can't understand why we can't ask Mr Abbot-Hume a few questions. Mr Hepworth seemed to feel that that was reasonable."

The Admiral bristled. "What sort of questions?"

Rawlins looked over to Shaughnessy, who then spoke. "It's simply this," he said, calmly and slowly. "We think we know how both murders happened, motive and everything. Even if he has to stand trial in England, we'd like to get the record straightened out here."

"And you want to put the case to us now?"

"That's what we'd like to do."

"Then go ahead. We're listening."

Ambrose looked at his watch. Quarter-past eleven. If only Cantolli could come through with something in time.

"It seems simple to us," Shaughnessy began. "Abbot-Hume was the most likely candidate for the first murder—we thought so as soon as we found out that Hewitt was his wife's lover."

"What's that?" barked the Admiral.

"We know it. And we know that it preyed on Abbot-Hume. He made all kinds of excuses, pretending to be out of town while he followed them round. He was in a great state of tension—anyone could see that. But we had no way

213

of connecting him with the murder until his wife tried to get rid of the gun."

"You don't know that that was the murder gun," said the Admiral.

"We do, sir. We know that a gun from Abbot-Hume's home was dropped into Miss Hope-Little's car yesterday by Mrs Abbot-Hume. He told us so himself. And we know that Miss Hope-Little was found with two Embassy guns, and that one of them was the murder gun."

"How far does that get you?" asked the Admiral. He was determined to heckle to the end, it seemed.

Shaughnessy maintained his calm. "It's a process of exclusion," he said. "Suppose the Abbot-Hume gun wasn't the murder gun. Then the other one must have been. Well, how could it have been? It was an Embassy gun, and on the morning after the murder there was only one Embassy gun missing—namely the Abbot-Hume gun. This second gun was in somebody's possession that morning, someone who couldn't have committed Hewitt's murder."

"Who?" asked the Admiral.

"Johnson," said Shaughnessy simply. "Johnson was wearing his gun when he and the other guard heard the shots and ran to the body. He must have been carrying it the night he was shot himself, even though he wasn't wearing his holster. It was probably knocked out of his hand, and later Miss Hope-Little was found with it. Whether she picked it up herself or whether the burglars picked it up is irrelevant."

The Admiral broke in. "But if you think you can prove that the gun Miss Hope-Little found in her car was the murder gun, that not only ties Abbot-Hume to the first murder, but it ties Miss Hope-Little to Johnson's murder."

"That's right, sir," said Shaughnessy. "There's no way out of it. She must have shot Johnson."

"But why?"

214

"Oh, there's a motive there—not rational, but quite effective. We know that she was completely distraught over her cat's death. She had said publicly to several people the day before that she suspected Johnson of kicking her cat. If she found a gun in her car and was carrying it when she ran across Johnson, something could have snapped in her mind. She mightn't even be aware that she had deliberately shot him. Guns are second nature to her. And she's been in a state of acute shock ever since."

There was a knock at the door. Goldberg came in, saying that Ambrose was wanted urgently on the telephone. It was Cantolli.

"I have your information, Ambrogio," he said triumphantly. "Iss-a very interesting."

"Tell me in Italian," said Ambrose. "It will be quicker." They talked rapidly in Italian for a few minutes. "You are sure?" Ambrose asked him finally.

"No question about it," said Giuseppe firmly.

"Splendid. Bless you. Come up here and wait for me. We may need you." He rang off and went back to the Admiral's study. As he entered, Hepworth came in by the other door. For some reason he seemed to be bursting with cheerfulness.

IV

Yes, Hepworth was in a very good mood as he walked round shaking hands with people. As far as one could see, he regarded this gathering as one of those transatlantic occasions on which it was his duty, as a visitor newly arrived from England, to say how much he liked being in the United States. He was one of those innumerable English politicians whose mothers or aunts or something are American, and who never miss a chance to bring it up.

In his case, his grandfather had been one of the original building engineers of the Chesapeake and Ohio Railroad.

He discovered in a second that Rawlins came from Cincinnati. The bond was obvious. They shook hands with renewed warmth. Anglo-American relations had been restored.

Whether under his influence or not, the Admiral seemed suddenly to decide that a little refreshment was indicated. He offered drinks, which were gratefully accepted. There was the pleasing sound of ice clinking, Scotch gurgling, and soda squirting. In a few minutes the hostility seemed to have been lowered several degrees.

Hepworth was most amused to hear of the bombing threat. Everything made him cheerful. "I suppose our friend Ambrose has been solving the murders," he said brightly. "Well, who dun it? No use looking at me. I have a perfect alibi."

"Usher has not told us much yet," said the Ambassador, "but he told me he would have some facts by to-night. Well," he turned to Ambrose brusquely. "What are the facts?"

Ambrose waved his hands rather helplessly. "If only I were a detective instead of a philosopher!" he sighed. "Yes, I have some facts. I even have what Croce would call a 'construct' of the case in my mind. But somehow I can't be sure that this is 'reality' any more than Croce can about *his* constructs. There seem to be some other facts lying round. Maybe they should affect my 'construct'. Maybe they shouldn't. I don't really know."

"I see you're bringing Croce in again," said the Admiral. "Is that your Italian friend? . . ."

"Yes, my old Italian friend. He solved our labour problem," Ambrose explained to the company.

"Damned useful fellow," said the Admiral. "Well, what does he say this time? I suppose he can prove that the police idea about Abbot-Hume and Miss Hope-Little is all wrong. It *is* wrong, isn't it?"

"Oh yes, it's wrong," said Ambrose. "But not in the same sense of black and white. A lot of the right facts, but somehow in the wrong order. . . ."

Shaughnessy looked grimly at Ambrose. "Well, what's the right order?"

"My trouble is that *I'm* suspicious of Abbot-Hume too," said Ambrose, "but in a different way—in a larger framework. Yet that doesn't fit in with my construct. Look, suppose I start at the beginning." He looked round, and plunged in.

"I was sent out in the first place to have a look at Hewitt. They were afraid he was a leak instead of a conductor. I wasn't sure about him. I'm still not sure. Never really had a chance to find out before he was killed. But he was very suspicious of me—which was perhaps natural—and he seemed to have a very active private or secret life—two different things. I wasn't sure how to separate them.

"The danger seemed to me to attach too much importance to Hewitt, especially after he was killed. After all, it wasn't only Hewitt that I was checking. It was the leak—things coming and going. After he was killed, it seemed more important than ever to try to establish the overall thing, not just the murder details.

"There was plenty going on. I wasn't sure how to connect them all. There were things right here in our Embassy. Apart from Hewitt, Abbot-Hume seemed to me to be playing a strange role. Seemed to be away a lot on secret missions. There was trouble in another quarter too, which has now been attended to—at least some of it has. Had to do with scientific papers being passed on.

"It all seemed to have further ramifications—and a lot of it seemed to lead to the French Embassy. Now, that interested me because the very first night I was here I ran into a member of the French Embassy staff called Auguste Flantin, who said something—or rather *didn't* say something—that seemed a little odd. Maybe I was a bit on the qui vive about the French Embassy. I'd heard in London that something funny was going on in the French secret service.

"Anyhow, Flantin puzzled me. May I tell you one specific thing? It may have been small, but, after all, even the tiniest thing has to have a reason. When I was talking to Flantin, he mentioned quite casually—quite spontaneously—that he'd been at Oxford after the fall of France working with the de Gaulle intelligence group there—he called it the 'information group'—and when I asked him whom he knew, he rattled off some names, all quite authentic—Meakers, Abbott, Hopkinson, Derzhinsky. But there was one funny thing. He didn't mention Strickland, and that seemed very peculiar to me. You see, St John Strickland was actually the leading member of that group, but later on, after the war, we found out—well, you probably know this, McDonald—dear St John had been a very active Communist agent all the time. He's disappeared now. Nothing was ever made public.

"Now why should Flantin have not mentioned Strickland's name? There was only one good explanation. I felt that it was an unconscious suppression. He felt the need to conceal not his public but his *private* link with Strickland. Rationally it wasn't the slightest slur on him to mention that he'd worked with Strickland. During the war, Strickland was thought to be first-rate and thoroughly reliable. It was a slip, an unconscious slip. What people call a Freudian slip. That's an absurd way of describing it, of course."

They were all listening closely now, except that Hepworth sprawled in an armchair, seemed to have slipped away into another world.

"I thought I'd better check," Ambrose continued, "so I got a signal across to London after Hewitt's murder to send a message across through the usual channels to the effect that Halibut of Scotland Yard was flying out secretly to take charge of the investigation. That message was top secret.

We put some other stuff in it too. Of course, Halibut wasn't coming at all. There's no such person as Inspector Halibut.

"I met Flantin to-night at the Russian party. I managed to work in a mention of Halibut. I saw a flicker in his eye instantly. It was unmistakable. He'd seen that message, and he shouldn't have. It just confirmed that Monsieur Flantin is very much mixed up in all these affairs.

"There was something else, too. Archaeology. But I won't go into that now. He just seemed to know things too quickly for my liking.

"Well," said Ambrose, "all this raised a number of possibilities. Originally I had thought that perhaps Flantin was secretly linked with Hewitt. But the Halibut message came through after Hewitt's death, so he must have had some other link with our Embassy. Could that mean that Hewitt had discovered that Flantin was an undercover agent for the other side, and that Flantin was sufficiently threatened to have to have him liquidated? Then Mrs Abbot-Hume turned up with a gun that could have been the murder weapon. That shook me. Did it mean that Flantin was working with Abbot-Hume? And if so, where did that leave Abbot-Hume?

"One thing came to my mind immediately. The night I got here I went to a cocktail party, as I said, and Mrs Abbot-Hume was there without her husband. He was supposed to be out of town lecturing, but in fact he was *in* town. Then we all went to dinner, but Flantin excused himself and went off. I wondered later whether Abbot-Hume and Flantin had met that night. Maybe, I thought, that was when they decided about Hewitt. Abbot-Hume knew about the fire-works party. Suppose he had suggested that they lure Hewitt away during the fireworks, when no one would hear the shots, and get rid of him."

Hepworth came to life. "So, on your theory," he said in his cheerful way, "Hewitt was on to something really deadly about Abbot-Hume and Flantin, so deadly that he had to be killed."

"No," said Ambrose quickly. "I don't say he was. I only say that if I went by *some* facts, this seemed a possible construct."

"Well, there's just one snag, old boy," said Hepworth casually. "I'll have to bring this out, though I hoped not to. You see, Abbot-Hume is one of our agents too—works for Military Counter-Intelligence, C.I.6 they call it. I only discovered it yesterday. That's one of the reasons why I came out."

v

Ambrose hardly dared look at the Ambassador's face. It had gone red and then purple. "Do you mean to tell me," Throttle said to Hepworth slowly, "that C.I.6 keep a man here without telling *me?*"

"It's a little hard, sir, isn't it?" Hepworth replied. "I quite agree. Very awkward. But that's what I'm discovering about the Foreign Office. Oil and water aren't the only things that don't mix. I just discovered this thing yesterday. You probably knew about this kind of thing from the Service side before, but I'm just a new boy, as I said before. They came over and told us after Hewitt's death. Apparently C.I.6 have their own system of agents, and they like to keep it all to themselves."

"And no one at the Foreign Office knows?" said the Ambassador uncomprehendingly.

"Well, no one at the ordinary operating level," said Hepworth. "*I* didn't know, and, of course, as you are for the time being an F.O. man, they didn't bother to tell you either. But there is one little section of the F.O. in a back room off Mount Street that keeps track of everything, or tries to."

Ambrose was listening to the exchange enraptured. So

nobody here knew, he thought to himself, except, of course, old Needham. That's what he was hinting at the other day. *He* knew about Abbot-Hume, but he wasn't sure if *I* knew. Good old Needham.

"You see," said Hepworth, "it's supposed to be a good thing to keep all these activities running side by side, even if it looks like overlapping. The little chap from Mount Street that I talked to called it 'lamination'. Much better than one vast centralized organization, he said. But, of course, it creates problems."

Ambrose turned to Hepworth. "And I suppose you knew all about Flantin too."

"Well, funnily enough I did know something," said Hepworth, "but I didn't want to interrupt you. Quite true that he has a secret connection with all this stuff. He's all right though. You see, they mentioned to me that he's been Abbot-Hume's contact in the French military intelligence ring, under Bergeot. I spoke to Bergeot myself. Very clever of you to dig it out, though. He must have been very amused to hear you bring up Halibut. Knew it was a try-on, I suppose. No, we'll have to look elsewhere for the murderer, I'm afraid. Any more ideas?"

For some reason, Ambrose, far from being disturbed, was smiling cheerfully. "Oh, now it's all plain sailing," he said. "Once I can leave Abbot-Hume and Flantin out of it, the whole thing falls into perspective."

Shaughnessy began to growl. "I'd still like to ask Abbot-Hume a few questions," he muttered.

"I wonder if you will when I'm finished," said Ambrose. "I see nothing wrong in your theory—it's certainly one way of fitting the facts in—but perhaps there's more than one way. It's as bad as philosophy, isn't it? No such thing as a simple proposition: the thing has meaning only with what one brings to it. That perhaps explains a lot. You began by looking for an explanation of the facts. Very proper. I indulged in the philosophic luxury of asking myself if things were what they looked like. Wasn't quite so eccentric as it sounds. Somehow everything seemed too pat. If things *weren't* what they seemed, I could see a possible 'how'. But I couldn't see 'why', or rather I could see too many 'why's'. Then Abbot-Hume's gun showed up as the possible murder weapon, and I had to suspend judgment until I knew where we stood on Abbot-Hume and Flantin. You see, even a philosopher has to take *some* account of facts. But now Mr Hepworth has told that we can disregard all those strange goings-on with Flantin, which certainly makes life much simpler for us all."

Glancing round, he caught Eldridge with a mysterious smile on his face. Or was it just Eldridge's usual quizzical, rather sceptical look? He went on.

"Gradually I had come to see a possible 'why' to go with my 'how'—a very simple 'why'—tragically simple— nothing to do with high diplomacy at all—but once again I had to suspend judgment when the burglars showed up. I knew what they were after—the Captain here knows that too now—but it was all mixed up with the guns. Suppose the burglars had been on the scene two nights earlier, bringing the murder gun and perhaps using it. A little far-fetched, but one could visualize a link-up. There was only one way to get it clear. I had to find out about the burglars, and now I know. They weren't involved with the gun, so we can get back to a really simple explanation after all."

Shaughnessy had leaned forward aggressively. "How do you know about the burglars?" he growled. "I asked you particularly a few hours ago, and I don't recall you giving me any information."

Ambrose smiled. "Now, Captain, you mustn't be angry with me. I just found out myself about fifteen minutes ago when I got that telephone call. It was from a friend of mine —the student of Croce I told you about."

"Damned good man," muttered the Ambassador.

"Yes," said Ambrose, "he's a good man. Believes in the moral imperative. I set him a little problem this afternoon. He's an Italian by origin, and he knows his way around Washington's underworld—or should I be polite and say other world. It was all based on a hunch. I 'intuited', as I explained to Captain Shaughnessy in the early hours of this morning, that the burglary at the Annex last night might have been done, as it were, under contract. Not really very hard to guess. I'd worked out that Ross—well you know all about that—wanted something stolen from the Annex, and I guessed that he would certainly know where to hire the right people. So I asked my friend if he could—in an anonymous way and as a personal favour—find out who got the contract."

"And he did?" asked Hepworth. "Fascinating."

"Yes," said Ambrose. "He says it wasn't too difficult. In that world, people tend to be specialists, and a few enquiries in the right quarters produced the answers about who were available and who finally landed the job. What is more important is that, at my request, he interviewed the participants to find out exactly what happened."

Shaughnessy had a strange expression on his face, looking at Ambrose. "I suppose this is all a private affair. The police don't come into this at all."

"Surely we can keep the two things separate," said Ambrose. "For the moment, we are agents of Truth, not Retribution. Shall I continue, or leave it to the police?"

Shaughnessy said nothing, and Ambrose resumed.

"It is just a piece of luck," he said, "that the character of the people who did the little job last night helps us to determine about the guns."

"The character?" asked the Ambassador incredulously.

"Yes," said Ambrose. "It's as simple as this. The head burglar last night doesn't like guns."

"Is this supposed to be funny?" asked Shaughnessy.

"Deadly serious," said Ambrose. "There were two people on the job last night, a father and a son. You won't want me to use their real names."

"Oh, of course not," said Shaughnessy, with heavy sarcasm.

"Well, suppose we call them Filippo and Filippino," said Ambrose, warming to his story. "I am told that Filippo is very well known and highly respected in his profession. He is expert on tidy jobs, smooth in effecting entrances, very good in extracting particular items, special papers, photographs and so on. He used to conduct a thriving business, specializing, I believe, in blackmail, but, as I am told it, he has one peculiar foible. He just won't carry fire-arms. Hates them. Always has. Famous for it."

Shaughnessy grunted.

"Business has not been too good lately," said Ambrose, "and this was presented as a very simple two-man job. They had to slip into the Annex—which, they were told, would be quite easy because there was only one guard and lots of ground-floor windows with flimsy wooden bars—go up-stairs to the second floor, and get some papers from a particular filing-cabinet, if they were there. If not, there was no harm done. $500 if they brought back the papers, and $100 if the papers weren't there. It was because the job was so easy that Filippo decided to take Filippino along, and keep the fee in the family. He has a large family, and is trying to give them some training. Filippino is none too bright, but his father has not given up hope that one day he may make the grade."

Ambrose looked round at his audience for a little encouragement. Shaughnessy's face was set grimly. Hepworth had collapsed into his armchair again. He, at least, was enjoying it.

"Now we come to a little psychology," said Ambrose.

"Filippo has been very strict with Filippino about one thing He has always absolutely forbidden him to play with guns— to own them, to have anything to do with them. The result is what you would expect. Young Filippino has always longed to carry a gun. They are his dream. And that is the keynote of our whole story. Can anyone guess what happened?"

No one offered to guess. Ambrose resumed.

"This is the story as I am given it," he said. "They came along last night, reconnoitered in the grounds, and stumbled across the body of a big man lying on the ground, apparently dead, with a whisky bottle and a gun near him. Filippo had a cursory look and decided that it was none of his business. He told Filippino to leave everything exactly as it was, and off they went to carry out the real business of the evening. But temptation was too much for young Filippino. As his father moved on ahead, he slipped behind and picked up the gun. At last he would have a gun of his own.

"They did the job. There was no guard around, so they calmly opened the front door and went straight upstairs. It took them a little time to find the room they wanted, but in the end they did, opened the filing-cabinet, and there, right in front, were the papers. They took them and left. They were just clearing off through the Annex gate when the head-lights of a car suddenly flashed on them, and someone jumped out of it and began firing a gun at them.

"I can visualize the scene very clearly. It was Miss Hope-Little, of course. She had driven up to the Embassy feeling distraught about her cat, wondering how she could find out about its death, but mostly just feeling distraught. Sitting there in the car, she had found a gun in the pocket of the door—the Abbot-Hume gun—and was holding it, when suddenly she saw these two furtive figures slipping away.

225

"I can see her leaping into action, and I can sympathize with the effect on young Filippino. With bullets whistling by, he felt pursued by the guilt and danger of the gun he had picked up. All his father's warnings swept over him. Guns were dangerous. They led to the electric chair. He threw the gun away and ran. Miss Hope-Little picked it up and started firing it as well as the other. But the burglars were too fast for her. They jumped into their car and were off. By the time people began running out of the Residence to find out about the shooting, all they found was poor Miss Hope-Little, with her two guns, in a state of near collapse.

"Filippo and his son arrived at Ross's, collected the $500, and as far as they were concerned the incident was closed. Of course, I don't know how the police feel about it. It's part of the rules of the game that my informant won't talk to the police, but we had to find out what happened for Miss Hope-Little's sake."

Shaughnessy stirred himself. "I don't suppose you expected confirmation from me, but I happen to know Filippo, as you call him. I remembered him when you described him. Eight children. Real family man. Lives in Baltimore, and won't touch a gun. Well, I suppose he'll go to earth now for a bit, but if he ever comes into the District of Columbia. . . ."

"Quite," said Ambrose. "But he would expect that, presumably. Have to watch his step."

"And you think this destroys our theory?" continued Shaughnessy. "To my mind, it's exactly the contrary. If Filippo didn't bring the gun that killed Hewitt, how did it get there at all? Obviously it was the one that Mrs Abbot-Hume had put in Miss Hope-Little's car."

"There is one other explanation," said Ambrose.

"What's that?"

"It was there already."

"What do you mean?"

"Why, you told us yourself before. There was only one other Embassy gun that it could have been. Johnson's."

"Johnson!" cried the Ambassador. "You mean Johnson's gun killed Hewitt! You mean Johnson . . ."

Looking at their astonished faces, Ambrose was particularly struck with Eldridge's expression. He had somehow stiffened from his usual relaxed attitude. He said quietly to Ambrose: "Are you suggesting that Johnson was an agent?"

Ambrose shook his head. "No. I thought so at first, but then I discovered something much simpler. All around Hewitt there was this great political whirl"—he waved his hand to indicate them all—"and in the middle a simple personal equation. Johnson was a man in love. Yes, it was tragic enough."

The Ambassador was staring at Ambrose open-mouthed. "But how could Johnson have killed Hewitt!" he asked.

Shaughnessy was bursting with the same question. "It's ridiculous," he growled. "Johnson was standing with Wilmot when they heard the shots. The chauffeur heard them too, and they all ran and found the body. We got that quite clear from the beginning."

Ambrose smiled. "Not really." he said.

Rawlins broke in. "And who killed Johnson?" he asked. "Was that revenge?"

"In a sense," said Ambrose slowly. "Life took its revenge. It all adds up in the end."

VI

The Ambassador looked at Ambrose blankly. "Do you mean it's all clear to you now about both murders? I don't get it."

"Well, sir," said Ambrose. "Let me explain. One can start anywhere, but suppose we start with this. As soon as I was sure that the burglars *found* the gun next to Johnson and didn't bring it with them, I was struck by one thing. This gun killed Johnson, and it was the same gun that killed Hewitt. The first question we all must ask is: did the same person kill them both?"

He looked round. They all seemed to agree.

"If that is what happened," continued Ambrose, "there's one odd thing. Why did the murderer take the gun away the first time and leave it the second? On that ground alone you'd think that there might have been two murderers. Someone killed Hewitt and took the gun away. Someone else got possession of it and killed Johnson, and left the gun there for some unexplained reason.

"Of course," he went on, "there is another possible explanation. Suppose the gun was left behind the second time because there was no one to take it away. In other words, suppose Johnson shot himself."

Now he had their attention. Even Hepworth was sitting up, listening closely.

"The police were puzzled about Johnson's death from the beginning," said Ambrose. "The gun had been held so close to his head that they would have put it down to suicide except that no gun was found there. They decided that it was murder and that someone had held the gun right next to his head."

"Wait a minute," said Shaughnessy. "You say Johnson shot himself. All right. But you won't say how Johnson could have killed Hewitt. Wilmot was standing with him when they heard the shots. He said so quite clearly, and so did the chauffeur."

"Not really," said Ambrose. "What Wilmot said was rather different. I went over it with him and the chauffeur very closely the day after the murder. They were standing together when they heard sounds that they interpreted immediately as shots. Of course, if you ask Wilmot directly, he won't allow himself to admit that it was all suggested to

228

him. And when they found the body, clearly shot, it all fixed the picture firmly in his mind. Same with the chauffeur. But I put together a rather different story. They heard sounds, and Johnson said they were shots. They all ran into the wood, following Johnson. It was all suggested to them. Appearance and reality."

"But if it wasn't those shots, what *did* they hear?" asked the Ambassador.

"They heard three of your hand-made fireworks, sir," said Ambrose with a smile. "Can you think of any that would have sounded right?"

"Why, yes," said the Admiral slowly. "The ones I call my *startlers*. Yes, they would sound just right. But how could Johnson have worked it?" He was a little reluctant to concede that his fireworks could have been guilty of anything, and yet not entirely unhappy to have them brought into the picture.

"It seems to have happened like this," said Ambrose. "Johnson shot Hewitt about fifteen minutes earlier, probably. Nobody heard the shots because the fireworks were in full spate. It was not a planned murder. There was probably a struggle at close quarters. I'll tell you in a minute why I think it happened. Johnson was confronted with the need for an alibi. He thought of the fireworks. He was thoroughly proficient in their use, as you told me yourself."

"Oh yes," said Throttle. "He was more than proficient. He understood the whole thing very thoroughly. Understood theory, too. I never could understand how a man who was so intelligent would be content with a job as a guard."

"I can tell you about that," said Ambrose. "Anyhow, he was an expert, and he must have had a few extra startlers and fuses in his pocket. Were you working late on the pieces, sir?"

"Yes, as it happens we were," said the Ambassador. "The Falkland piece. We were adding some extra startlers and rattlers to simulate more gun-fire. Different kinds of sounds, you know, for different guns. He may easily have had a few extra ones in his pocket. Most unfortunate, it seems."

"That's what I thought," said Ambrose. "He quickly decided that he could give himself an alibi if he were standing next to somebody else when the gun shots seemed to emerge from the wood. He fixed up three startlers with very slow-burning fuses on a tree. I would guess that he fixed them up much nearer the Annex than the clearing was. He wanted to make sure that they were distinctly heard.

"The fact is that we *all* heard them. I remember hearing some sporadic fireworks after everything was over, but since all the sound came from in front of us, and we were looking at the fireworks stands, we couldn't think of them as anything but odds and ends of fireworks that got delayed. In fact, I recall one rocket going off still later, after the announcement that Hewitt's body had been discovered.

"I doubt if Johnson worked all this out. All he needed was an alibi, and not just an alibi in time. Much more important was the bullet. He knew that if they just found a body with a Colt 38 bullet in it, all the guns in the Embassy would be examined. The guns they wouldn't examine would be those carried by Wilmot and himself, since they had heard the shots and run back to the scene. So while the police were examining all the guns next day, he was walking round with the wanted gun nestling in his holster."

Ambrose looked at Shaughnessy to see how he was taking it. Shaughnessy was listening, saying nothing.

"The rest was easy for him," said Ambrose. "He left Wilmot and Watkins with the body, and ran back to the Embassy. On the way he recovered the fireworks cases from the tree where he had fixed them. There was absolutely nothing to connect him with the murder until he committed suicide and Filippino picked up his gun."

"But why did he commit suicide then?" asked the Ambassador.

"Oh, that was after he attacked me in Rock Creek Park," said Ambrose.

Shaughnessy rose from his chair. "Attacked you!" he exclaimed. "You mean that you knew all the time who it was and never told me."

"Oh yes, I knew. I knew a lot of things much earlier on. But I couldn't get them into the right perspective until you supplied the missing clue."

"Me!" cried Shaughnessy.

Ambrose smiled. "Suppose I try to tell you the story from the beginning as I think it happened."

VII

"I was pretty slow about it," Ambrose began, "because I suppose I was afraid of an anticlimax. I'd come out here sure that I was going to deal with the big public things—and that the big private things were somehow in a separate compartment. What was most important about Hewitt? Was he a public or a private person? Were there any clues? I'd felt when I first met him that his character lay open to one. I should have stuck to that. But the other things—the involved things—were happening, and they misled me I only got it clear when I came back to him as an individual. He was like an open book. I don't mean that he didn't have things beneath the surface, but there was a more obvious thing about his character. It couldn't be a pose that he pursued fun and excitement wherever he found it. And if this was so strong an element in him, it would be the element that would account for his fate. That's what fate means to me.

"Well, what were the things close to him? Mrs Abbot-Hume was one—that was pretty clear. But I felt it to be a symbol, not a factor. He was enjoying it. I couldn't sense any desperation in it. There has to be desperation for murder, don't you think, and desperation has a way of coming with futility, not with happiness. Was there anything enjoyable that might have petered out and so become dangerous? There was, but I only found it out by accident." Ambrose paused, and said slowly: "Hewitt had been having an affair with his secretary, Miss Turenne, and it was all over."

Shaughnessy broke in. "You say you found out through me?"

Ambrose nodded. "Yes, indeed. I'll tell you how in a minute. He had been having an affair with Miss Turenne. It's sad, isn't it? She's a charming girl, and was very much in love with him. He was, after a time, much less involved, I would guess. Probably never took it seriously even at the beginning. But for Miss Turenne it was serious enough to make her refuse the man who was desperately in love with her—yes, Johnson.

"We all felt that it was a bit odd to find a man like Johnson in the job of a guard. He was obviously well educated and intelligent. I found out about him when I looked up his personnel file. He was a Scot who had emigrated to Canada and had taken a course at the Technical Institute in Toronto. When I looked up *her* file, I discovered that she had been in Toronto at the same time, taking a secretarial course. She must have been quite friendly at that stage, because the files showed that when she went back to her home town, a little place in Quebec, he worked in the same town for a year. A Scottish Canadian wouldn't normally do that without a special reason.

"I could see the whole story in the files, even before I asked her about it. She came down to work here, and he followed, taking a job as a guard, which was the only job he could get quickly. I don't really know if she'd already got tired of him—he was pretty surly as a person—or if the break happened when Hewitt began to flirt with her. Anyhow, she wouldn't have anything of him, and he wouldn't give up.

"I saw her the day before the murder. She was terribly unhappy. She'd always accepted the fact that nothing permanent was going to come out of the affair with Hewitt. Now at last she'd realized that he was putting an end to it at any level. She must have told Johnson that Hewitt was not going on with her. To Johnson this was the last straw. If *he* couldn't have her, he was determined that Hewitt should treat her properly.

"At the fireworks party, he must have waylaid Hewitt and made him walk over to the clearing. He probably threatened him with his gun. Anyhow, Hewitt went. Johnson must have tried to intimidate Hewitt, and if I know Hewitt, he would be completely supercilious—probably taunted him, and told him it was none of his business. They probably fought, and the gun went off, at least twice. There was a witness to it all—dear old Palmerston, who spent so much of his spare time in the oak tree there, resting and watching. A stray bullet must have got him. Another got Hewitt. Palmerston was badly winged and managed to stagger some distance away. Hewitt collapsed instantly.

"Well, we know what Johnson did. He was intelligent, quick-witted. He rigged up the fireworks alibi, and got away with it the first day. Miss Turenne was prostrate with grief. She had a kind of suspicion, but didn't let herself think. I was a bit slow myself, and played it wrongly. Typical bungling amateur. I had tumbled to the idea of a fireworks alibi because I was suspicious of the way they had heard the shots and found the body so easily. Let's say that I entertained it as a possibility. But I knew nothing, of course, of any private relation between Hewitt and Johnson, and thought that if Johnson was involved, it must be part of the espionage story. If so, it was far too important to spoil by just getting the police to examine Johnson's gun. I wanted to see where the trail would lead.

"It was on the afternoon after the murder that I was suddenly presented with a clue that could link Hewitt with Miss Turenne. If I could find something that could link Miss Turenne with Johnson, I thought I might have something. That's when I decided to look up their personnel files. It didn't take long. I soon saw the connection.

"I didn't know how much the files would show, but I deliberately let him overhear me on the telephone asking for them. I thought that if he was involved, it might be the only way in which we could startle him into the open. It worked a bit too well. I was wandering about in the clearing later, and thought I heard footsteps. He may have been thinking of attacking me then, but nothing happened.

"But he was desperate, and he got his chance later when I walked back across the Park. I didn't see who attacked me, but it makes sense, doesn't it? I put up quite a fight, and I'm told he was quite bruised when they found him later.

"But what did he feel after the fight? He'd left me lying— perhaps dead. He went back to the Annex and phoned Miss Turenne. She told me this earlier this evening. He tried to talk to her. She wouldn't talk. Then he knew it was all up. He took a bottle of whisky from the liquor store in Miss Proudfoot's room, and screwed up his courage—or his despair—with it. And that was how they found him."

There was a silence when Ambrose finished. It was a sad tale, all too human.

Shaughnessy was the first to speak. "We had quite a talk this afternoon at the Nursing Home," he said slowly. "You could probably have told me something then."

"Ah, but there was a big gap at that time, Captain," said Ambrose. "Don't forget that I'd had no chance to check with Miss Turenne and find out if the whole basis of my guess was right. I did that later. Nor had I a chance to find out if the burglars had after all brought a gun with them. And Miss Hope-Little: I had to make sure, through finding out about the burglars, what gun she'd picked up. I thought it was easier to find out these things unofficially, so I needed a few hours."

Shaughnessy grunted. He was far from satisfied or pleased.

"You said I helped you find out about Hewitt and Miss Turenne. How was that?"

"Why, yes. I got the idea from you, and it worked."

"When did I give you the idea?"

"It was our friend Billy," said Ambrose. "We were all puzzled to know who Hewitt broke a date with that first night. We didn't know anyone called Billy. It seemed a dead end.

"Well, the afternoon after the murder I was in your office, and you mentioned to me that your nickname 'Don' was short for 'Donegal'. While I was driving away, it occurred to me to wonder if Billy was a geographical nickname, like yours, or like Tex for Texas. Billy suggested something to do with William—Williamsburg, Williamstown . . . didn't make sense.

"Then I tried William in French—Guillaume. And I immediately connected. I remembered that Miss Turenne came from St Guillaume, in Quebec. I recalled the picture of her sitting in Hewitt's office, before his death, telling me sadly that she didn't know what she was going to do. I could see the whole thing. I could even hear Hewitt giving her the nickname: '*Don't like Betty as a name, doesn't suit you. I'll call you Billy, after your hometown.*' It seemed worth trying. That's when I went back to the Embassy and looked at the personnel files, and the rest followed."

"So it was through me," said Shaughnessy glumly. "I'm glad I was such a great help. Goldberg will be delighted."

"Goldberg! Goodness, I forgot! I left Cantolli with him. I must . . ."

No one heard him finish. A tremendous explosion filled the air.

VIII

It was a great boom, with a crash of splintered glass.

"Get down," cried the Ambassador. "It's the Mermaid Islanders." They all fell flat on the floor.

There was a second of silence, then two more booms in quick succession. The floor seemed to rock with the force of the explosions, but nothing inside the room was hurt.

It had all happened in a second. They were still prostrate on the floor. In the silence they heard shouts from outside. "Take cover! Put those lights out!" The Embassy Home Guard was on the scene.

Eldridge leapt to his feet and switched out the lights. Again there was an explosion, and again they all lay flat.

And now the firing started. First some rifle shots, and then a rattle of machine-gun fire. It was all very close. The raiders seemed as well armed as the patrols. Rifle shooting was mixed now with the sound of machine-guns. The noise was deafening. Then it seemed to die down. A few more shots were heard. Then complete silence.

The Admiral was on his feet. "They've got them!" he cried triumphantly. "Come on!" He ran to the door and switched on the lights.

At that moment, the door opened and Goldberg came in with three Embassy men carrying rifles. Ambrose noticed that Beauchamp was one of the men.

"Well?" barked the Admiral.

For some reason, the patrols looked hesitant, almost sheepish.

"Don't tell me they got away," said the Admiral fiercely.

"It's all over, sir," said Beauchamp.

236

"Haven't you captured them?" cried the Admiral.

"It was your lab downstairs, sir," he replied. "It's all blown up."

"My lab!"

Beauchamp looked more hesitant than ever. "There must have been a lot of fireworks there," he said.

"You don't mean . . ."

"Yes, sir. Something must have started them off. . . ."

The Admiral said slowly. "I looked in an hour ago . . . perhaps my cigar . . ."

"Probably, sir. Once it started, it all went . . ."

"All my beautiful rockets, my startlers, my trouncers, my Falklands . . . and my powder bins. . . ."

"It was quite a bang, sir."

The Admiral looked at him, and then began to smile slowly. "Quite a bang. It was, wasn't it? Small room. Tremendous repercussion. Quite a bang." He stopped. In the distance they all heard the wailing of a siren. "What's that?"

"It must be the fire-engines, sir," said Beauchamp. "We put in a call as soon as we found out." Now they could all hear the engines roaring along Massachusetts Avenue.

"Must have done a bit of damage, eh?" said the Admiral cheerfully. "Well, we can soon put it right. It was quite a bang, wasn't it?"

Eldridge murmured to Ambrose. "I suppose you feel you've proved your point. A little elaborate, wasn't it?"

"Independence for the Mermaids!" said Ambrose. "They deserve it. And I must go and see what's happened to Cantolli."

NINE

"Neque semper arcum
Tendit Apollo."

HORACE, Odes

(Apollo does not keep his bow strung forever)

I

So it was all over. Ambrose felt relieved, yet still puzzled, as he walked slowly up the hotel drive before going to bed. There were still a lot of loose ends somehow.

Was it really all over? The deaths had been explained, and unexpectedly they had had a lot of fun. But was this all? What had really gone while this little exercise in life and death had been played out?

With the Mermaid invasion to round things out, tension had completely relaxed, and the whisky had flowed cheerfully for quite a while. The Ambassador had ended up delighted at the impromptu fireworks party, and he was full of confidence about his future. He told Ambrose that he had counted a great deal on Johnson's help, and had started work with him the very night of Hewitt's murder to see if they could track down what had gone wrong with the fireworks. He had continued the next morning, and between them they had practically solved the problem. "It was the way the compound was sprayed," he explained. "You see, I have four little electric motors up there on the stand spraying out a fine gas while the other parts are actually exploding. Looks now as if it was just coming out too fast. That's why we got that smoky effect that annoyed Ilano."

Hepworth had persisted to the end in treating the whole things—murders and all—as if he didn't take it quite seriously.

238

But he had a private word with Ambrose, suggesting that now this business was cleared up, he might like to go to South America with him the next day, or follow in a few days.

"It would be such fun," he said. "Some special things going on there, you know, and not just in the Argentine. We could use you."

"Peru?" Ambrose asked him.

Hepworth looked at Ambrose affectionately. "I see you've been doing a bit of homework," he said, "catching up on your reading. Yes, Peru. Archaeology and other discoveries. Interesting place."

"And we think that prolifium . . ."

Hepworth looked round in mock anxiety. "Don't mention the word, my boy. We're just interested in archaeology, and so are others. Lots of friendly rivalry. We might have a little trouble—your kind of trouble."

"I'm no expert on archaeology."

"Oh, Pulsifer will teach you. Think about it."

Ambrose had talked with the others too, but while they talked, he had wondered. They seemed to have some common ground when they talked, yet they were still in different compartments—Shaughnessy with his hate-love for the British, the Ambassador with his strange fireworks compulsion, Eldridge and McDonald, the two institutionalists. They were still moving round, so to speak. None had come to rest. Except perhaps Cantolli and Goldberg. Yes, *they* had found something really satisfying. Ambrose had run into the waiting-room to apologize to Cantolli for keeping him waiting so long and had found him deep in happy converse with Goldberg, and quite indifferent to the other excitements of the evening. He had been telling Goldberg about Croce; Goldberg in return had been initiating him into the mysteries of anthropology. They had decided that they must bring the two subjects together.

"Iss-a one subject, Ambrogio!" said Cantolli. "Iss-a part of history, but history iss-a deeper if we bring in anthropology."

Goldberg was equally excited. "You see, Mr Usher," he tried to explain, "what I missed in anthropology was some way of linking it to the world around me, but with Croce you bring in the anthropological experience to stimulate your own consciousness. . . ."

Cantolli was very thrilled to have found so apt a disciple. "Iss-a wonderful," he said to Ambrose. "He has natural gift for Croce. I make him a proposition. I need an assistant. You call-a him bodyguard; I call-a him assistant. Why Goldberg here no give up the police and join the union. We go round together all the time and we talk and read. How much-a you make with the police, Goldberg?"

Goldberg told him.

"I double-a that. You join me. We travel. We discuss . . ." —and Ambrose left them happily discussing their future together.

Perhaps that was, in some mysterious way, the object of all that had happened. The world had spun round, a man had killed and died, and the result was that Cantolli and Goldberg had discovered in each other the perfect foil for philosophic enquiry. Well, that was something.

And what of himself? Was all this as remote from his own self as his other Government work had been, or was the wall crumbling? Why had he built the wall in the first place?

I wonder what happened to Thérèse at the Russian party, he thought, as he turned to go in. She just seemed to disappear. He looked at his watch. It was 1.30 a.m.—exactly twenty-four hours since he had woken her up to go and burgle Ross's house. Well, this time he would let her sleep. And off he went to bed.

At nine precisely he phoned Thérèse. She said hallo very dreamily. He must have woken her up. But when she heard who it was, her voice became soft and warm.

"How *are* you? How is everything?" she wanted to know.

"Highly satisfactory, splendid, all cleared up. I'll tell you when I see you. When *do* I see you? What happened to you last night?"

"Oh, I went off to meet Walter," she said. "I promised to meet him at the airport at midnight with my car when he got in from Toronto."

"Walter?" Ambrose had quite forgotten about him. "How is he?"

"Oh, he's wonderful," she said. She sounded suddenly enthusiastic. "It's rather miraculous. This whole affair seems to have had a wonderful effect on him. He seems to have got rid of something. He's thought things out, and it's changed him. He had such a lot to tell me about himself. We sat and talked until after two."

"After two? No wonder you were still asleep. I'm sorry I woke you."

"Oh no, I'm glad. I wanted to tell you. I know how much you like him."

Ambrose felt a slight twinge. This wasn't quite the conversation he had been expecting.

"Ah, dear old Walter," he said nevertheless. "I must see him this morning. So he's changed?"

"Oh yes. It's so noticeable. I'm so happy. It's something I've been waiting for." She did sound very happy.

So there it is, thought Ambrose. Thérèse and Walter. Why was he so surprised? He had felt this at the beginning. It had taken root a long time ago, and grown. Ah, well. "Yes, we must meet, we must all meet." He hardly knew what he really wanted to say. "I'm going up to the Embassy to do a little work—clean up a few odds and ends. Don't know my plans now. I will telephone you."

"Please do," she said. "I think I'll get some more sleep. I'm awfully tired. Good-bye."

Ambrose put down the receiver. Well, he told himself, isn't that nice? Then he smiled wryly. Would everything just fade like this? Probably.

He felt rather flat. Wandering round the room, he picked up the *Washington Post* and glanced at it. An item caught his eye, and at first he hardly took it in. He read it again, and this time he understood it. Bergeot arrested for passing secrets. The evidence was strong. The Government seemed likely to fall. Bergeot! Hadn't Hepworth said that Bergeot had vouched for Flantin? And if now Bergeot . . .

This is really fascinating, he thought. I must go up to the Embassy. Let's see what's going on.

III

Hepworth had already left by plane for the Argentine. Ambrose had a brief word with the Ambassador, but Throttle was too busy to see him for long that morning. "Now that the murders are all cleared up," he said to Ambrose, "I've got to concentrate on this Argentine business myself. Fact is—but don't mention it to anyone yet—I've just had a cable from the Exporters Federation of Britain—the E.F.B. you know—to head a mission to Buenos Aires. Seems that I'm very popular suddenly with the new Government in the Argentine. They think my fire-works thing on Ilano helped to ridicule the old gang. As a matter of fact, I heard this morning that Ilano has been exposed as the head of a 'ring'—you know what sort of thing Buenos Aires is famous for—and they think I knew. Of course I didn't, but still . . . I'm probably going to resign this job—had a word with Hepworth about it—and go into the export business, manufacturing fireworks. They sell, you know. . . ."

He was very happy.

Ambrose wandered off to Eldridge's room, and found him sitting there, as calm and impassive as ever.

"Have you seen the thing in the papers this morning about Bergeot," Ambrose asked him.

"I have indeed. Interesting, isn't it?"

Ambrose looked at him. "Well, it's a little more than interesting, isn't it Hugh? Bergeot was the chief of military security who told Hepworth that Flantin was a trusted agent. If, as they now say, Bergeot was a Communist agent, where does that leave Flantin?"

"Well, you told us last night that we had to have a flexible approach to all these things," said Eldridge calmly. "I think you could argue quite fairly from this that Flantin was in it with Bergeot, and that would make Flantin a Communist agent. If Dennis trusted him, it would have been a mistake. Of course, we can all make mistakes, you know."

"But Hugh, isn't it a little more serious? I was suspicious of Flantin myself, you remember, and I thought that either Dennis was wrong too, or was being taken in. But I ruled the whole thing out because of Hepworth's assurance that Flantin was all right."

Eldridge smiled a little enigmatically. "I might as well explain. Hepworth was just being a little ingenuous, you know. It was really the other way up. Dennis was in the clear because he'd *discovered* about Flantin, but we didn't want to put it that way last night. As a matter of fact, I could easily have scotched the whole Dennis business from another angle if H.E. hadn't decided—at my request—to go in for nonco-operation with the police. You see, Dennis had a perfect alibi if we wanted to bring it up. He was in the cipher room during the last part of the fireworks, sending an urgent message. He came straight out just when the lights went up and they announced Hewitt's death."

"Did you say at *your* request, Hugh? Why did you ask H.E. to keep Dennis out of things?"

"Oh, I thought it was better not to let him get involved in questioning. You see, some other things might have had to come out."

"Such as?"

"Well, my own position, for example." He smiled modestly. "You see, I'm in C.I.6 too. I'm really in charge of it for the whole of the Western Hemisphere. Dennis was just doing things for me."

Ambrose looked at him. Eldridge smiled back, saying nothing.

"But Hepworth did tell us all about Dennis's work quite openly," Ambrose said finally.

"Yes, no harm in that. In fact it was rather useful. Just threw up a little smoke-screen for the F.B.I. and the police. Dennis was going back to England anyhow. No need for them to know about me, though."

Ambrose began to see things. "The idea is just to acknowledge anything that happens to come out, and just let the rest run on, no matter who gets fooled?"

Eldridge smiled. "Well, we do try to keep out of people's way."

Another glimmer came to Ambrose. "Was there something more about Johnson that you didn't choose to mention?"

"Well, there was really. Dennis had got his eye on him for a job with one part of C.I.6—a surveillance job with what we call *The Centipedes*—fifty people in it, you know—a hundred feet—just a little joke of ours. Johnson had that nice earthy look, and he was quite intelligent. Dennis had given him a couple of test jobs to do. One of them was . . ."

"Don't tell me. I know. He followed me the night of my arrival. Was that it?"

"That's right. And the next day too. He didn't find out very much, but Dennis gave him full marks for the crucial point—he wasn't spotted. You didn't see him—at least he thought you didn't—and neither did the ordinary F.B.I. trailers. And he did a very good job tracking Flantin down. Gave us some good leads."

"And he was going to be trained for higher things?"

"Yes, he would probably have done very well if he hadn't got involved in this awful private mess. His electrical training was especially useful. He hadn't had much of a formal education in Scotland—left school at fifteen—but he'd taken a diploma in electrical work at the Toronto Technical Institute—well, you know that—and as long as a candidate has some kind of higher education, they're prepared to admit them. Dennis was very keen. It's part of the job to turn in several recruits a year."

"Well, Dennis was wrong to give him full marks about me. I spotted him. How do you know the F.B.I. trailers didn't."

Eldridge smiled genially. "Well, you'd expect us to have our own sources of information there, wouldn't you?"

Ambrose found himself getting out of his depth. "You are really impossible, Hugh. I don't know whether to take you seriously or not. What else was going on?"

"Oh, the whole Flantin business. Dennis had been collecting stuff on Flantin, and only got it quite clear that night. As a matter of fact, that's the message he was sending from the cipher room during the fireworks."

"And they needed a couple of days in London and Paris before they pounced on Bergeot, I suppose?"

"That's right."

"And you let me just fumble along. . . ."

"Well, you were doing quite a useful job in your own field, you know, Ambrose. Very useful indeed. Couldn't have managed without it. We all have to work in our own way, and it all adds up. That's why we call it lamination."

"Well, why are you telling me all this now?"

"Oh, Hepworth thought I should. Especially if you're thinking of going down to the Argentine and Peru. He told me before he left to tell you all this. Help you to make up your mind."

Ambrose sat looking at Eldridge. "You know," he said, "I'm beginning to wonder if the Americans are right after all. I never thought so, but now I begin to wonder."

"Oh, what about?"

"I heard Alistair Cooke tell this story at a lunch once when he was receiving some award for his radio talks to England on the American scene. There's a great difference, he said, in the way each country looks at the other, especially in diplomacy. If an American diplomat stationed in London gets drunk at a party and starts walking about on his hands, his host will take him quietly to the door and put him in a cab to be taken home. But if a British diplomat in Washington gets drunk at a party and starts walking on his hands, everybody says: 'Now I wonder why the Foreign Office sent him over here to do that.'"

Eldridge laughed. "And you are beginning to wonder. . . ."

"Well, really, Hugh, what am I to think?"

"Now, now," said Eldridge soothingly, "don't take everything too seriously. But I do hope you'll go to South America. What do you think?"

"I think I ought to go back to Oxford, where I belong," said Ambrose. "No one ever gets drunk at cocktail parties there. It's nice and safe." He smiled at Eldridge and left.

IV

Yes, I think I'll get back, Ambrose said to himself. It's safe there. No jolts to the ego. The mind is its own place—makes its own rules. . . .

Back in his own room to clear up such papers as had accumulated, he came across the notes that Miss Hope-Little had typed out for the review he was doing on the existentialism book. He looked at them, rather bewildered. I'm not sure, he thought, whether I've stopped understanding all this or am just beginning to understand it.

He wandered rather sadly down the corridors towards the front door of the Embassy. Only four days since he had met Miss Hope-Little in these corridors, and Palmerston too. He sighed heavily.

At the door, Needham was waiting. Ambrose looked at him with considerable curiosity. The talk with Needham in the nursing home, and now the talk with Eldridge. These Foreign Office people. It was too much.

As usual, Needham knew everything. "I hear you're leaving us, sir," he said. "Quite a short visit this time. I hope you'll enjoy your next post."

"No more posts, Needham. I'm going home. Back to Oxford."

"Oh, I see, sir." He raised his eyebrows slightly. For some reason, he seemed somewhat puzzled. "Well, I hope you will be back soon."

"I hope so," said Ambrose. "Or do I? I don't really know. But if I do, you will be here, will you not? Forever and ever."

"I trust so, sir," said Needham. "Good-bye, sir. Shall I telephone for a cab, sir?"

"Oh no. I'm in no hurry. I think I'll walk back across the Park. No danger this time."

All was sunny and peaceful in the Park. Back in his hotel room, Ambrose got out some paper and decided to write the review. I must have at least one concrete souvenir of the visit, he thought ruefully.

He had just settled down, when the phone rang. It was Thérèse. Thérèse. . . . Yes. Where did she fit into the

Flantin business? He had not asked Eldridge. Perhaps he didn't want to know.

"I'm so glad I caught you," she said. "I've been waiting for your call."

"Oh, I've been rather busy. So much to do, you know. Winding up."

"Are you going back to Oxford?"

"Yes, I think I'll go in a day or so. Perhaps I shall see you there?"

"At Oxford?"

"Well in the British Isles, shall we say. I had a vague idea that maybe you might be finding your way to Scotland."

"To Scotland?"

"Well, Walter, you know. . . ."

"Ah, that's it," said Thérèse. "I thought that that was it after you rang off this morning. I was so sleepy that I couldn't think very clearly, but when I woke up I wondered if that was what I heard in your tone."

Ambrose felt himself beginning to smile. "So you're staying here?"

"No, as a matter of fact I do have some news, but not about Scotland." She laughed. "It's a long way from Scotland. I have just heard this morning that I'm being transferred to a new post."

"Oh, where?"

"To South America, this time."

Oh dear, oh dear, thought Ambrose. So that is it. "Not to Peru, by chance?" he asked her.

"Yes, Peru. How did you guess?"

"Oh, I'm good at guessing. And I suppose they want you in a hurry."

"Yes, it's always like that in the French Foreign Service. Is it the same in yours? They leave you without a word for months, and then suddenly you have to leave the next day for your new post."

"So this move is quite unexpected?"

"Yes, I had no idea. Of course, I do know Spanish. I suppose that helps."

"Oh, I'm sure that will help," said Ambrose. "Everything will help. Don't forget to take lots of wire along with you."

"Wire? Oh, I see. No, I don't think I need any wire. My wire days are over. I've opened my last lock."

"Have you?" said Ambrose. "I wonder. And what more news? This seems the day for news. How is our friend Flantin?"

"Auguste? Yes, you do seem good at guessing. I've just heard that he's been recalled to Paris unexpectedly."

"Oh, I see. Just recalled. Quite simply."

"So it seems."

"But *you* are going to Peru."

"Yes, I believe it may be a very interesting post."

Oh yes, thought Ambrose. Very interesting indeed. But really, how was he to take all this? Was it just a game? Flantin was the big wheel, and they had got him. Thérèse would just go on working on simple jobs where they needed her . . . or—wait—suppose it was the other way round. Could Thérèse . . .

I don't really want to know, thought Ambrose. I'm better off really at Oxford, expounding the moral imperative to my undergraduates. That's where *I* belong. Cantolli is right.

"And you are really going back to Oxford?" she was saying. "I can't believe we shan't meet any more. It seemed to me . . ."

"Yes, I know. Lots of unfinished business. . . ."

"Can I see you before you go?"

"Of course, of course. We *must* meet. It's essential. I will telephone you."

So it will all go spinning on, thought Ambrose, as he put the receiver down. Wheels within wheels, and lots of excitement, and plenty of "immediate objectives"—wasn't that

249

how she had defined it? And I will be back at Oxford. Yes, it's better that way. It's safer.

He picked up his notes and thought for a few minutes on how he would tackle the review. He felt tranquillity descending on him. What a relief it was to get back to something he understood.

He began to write:

If, as a disciple of Lotze is reputed to have remarked in later life to a friend of Husserl, the only universally acceptable test of any system of philosophy, and particularly of moral philosophy, might be to envisage it as subjected to the assessment of a David Hume—relying presumably not on the traditional pugnacity of the Scottish temper (which was felt, however unjustly, by the Emperor Hadrian no less than by Dr Johnson to condemn its possessors to a place beyond the Chinese Wall of civilized society) but rather on that other Scottish quality of plain sense, which allowed the natural sceptic in Hume to draw as firm a line as Dr Johnson himself drew in one swift kick between the disconcerting implications of empiricism and the comforting reassurances of the natural world around him—one might still hesitate to submit the (to adapt a phrase of Kant's) "weariness and complete indifferentism" of existentialism to such a judgment, since even a man of "mild disposition" (which Hume claimed for himself) and "little susceptible of enmity" (as Rousseau, in a famous passage of the *Confessions*, confirmed) might still find something unbearable in the thought that two hundred years after he had composed his own *Treatise*, living on the soil and nurtured by the spirit of France, the heirs of disciplined Enlightenment could surrender to self-indulgent Obfuscation. . . .

He broke off for a moment and stretched his arms luxuriously. Yes, this was the world where he was at home, the world where you could define things, qualify them, the safe world. . . .

He got up and walked over to the window. How pleasant it was to be bathed in this bright sunshine. So much to do, so many ways to do it, so many, many ways. . . .

He moved back to the desk, and, standing there, looked down at what he had written. How ironic, he thought, that the existentialists should draw sustenance from Spinoza. But perhaps not. Hume had talked about "the hideous hypothesis of the atheist Spinoza". Almost as if he had anticipated what could happen to it as time went on.

The sunshine drew him to the window again. Term at Oxford had four more weeks to run, and then there were six weeks of vacation. Did he really have to go back so quickly? There was the book, of course. The publishers were pressing.

Somehow it was hard to get on with the review. What was bothering him? I must do something more energetic, he thought. All at once it came to him. I wonder if the swimming-pool is open. A nice, relaxing swim. Just what I need.

v

He telephoned to enquire. The pool was open for the use of guests, and in a few minutes he was down at the pool's edge, clad in a pair of trunks that the hotel provided.

He stretched his arms luxuriously, looking at the cool, green water. Just what he wanted. A long, relaxing swim.

He was going to climb in, as usual. But suddenly, for no conscious reason, he felt the desire to *dive* in—to let go—to lose himself. Could he? He had never dived. He raised his arms and plunged.

For one agonizing second, he wondered what was happening. The water struck him all at once, on the stomach, the face, filling his ears, his mouth, choking him. He sank, then rose, filled with a marvellous exhilaration. He had dived. It was wonderful.

He swam to the side, climbed out, and without waiting dived in again. This time he kept his mouth shut and went in head first, feeling, as he plunged, the sense of throwing himself out into the water—losing himself.

He swam up and down for a little while and came out glowing. How absurd to be so pleased, he thought, with something any child could do. But that was just it. That was why he was so pleased.

The sense of exhilaration stayed with him as he rubbed himself dry. What was it? Something struggling for expression.

He smiled cheerfully to the lift man. "Nineteenth floor!" he proclaimed, as though he was to fly to the moon. The gate clanged, the lift soared up, and at that moment he recognized what he was going to do. Miss Turenne's sad little remark came back to him. *One has to take a decision.* Yes, that was it. *How can the prisoner reach outside*—Oh dear, how long had he taken to understand it—*except by thrusting through the wall?*

As he came into his room, he glanced at what he had written, lying waiting on the desk, and smiled. That was fine, but there were other things too. He stretched out his hand to the telephone, and gave the operator the number of the British Embassy. He was through in a moment to Eldridge.

"Oh, Hugh," he said, "this is Ambrose again. I've been thinking about Hepworth's invitation. He left the arrangements in your hands, did he? No problems? Well, I think I might accept it. It sounded fun. The Argentine and other points south. Yes, I think I might go. No point in rushing back to Oxford, really."

They talked for a few minutes about arrangements, and then Ambrose put the receiver down. There was another call to be made, but it could wait for a minute or two. Yes, he would enjoy making this call, but he didn't want to rush it. Where would it take him? How could he know in advance—how could he know anything—except that he had to go on?

He was ready now, and picked up the receiver to make the call. While he waited for the girl to answer, the words came unbidden into his mind:

> *Fair stood the wind for France*
> *When we our sails advance,*
> *Nor now to prove our chance*
> > *Longer will tarry.*

"Your call, please," said the girl.
"Can I speak to the French Embassy?" said Ambrose.

TEXT SET IN MONOTYPE FOURNIER.

PRINTED BY THE MURRAY PRINTING COMPANY,

WAKEFIELD, MASSACHUSETTS.

PAPER MADE BY S. D. WARREN COMPANY,

BOSTON, MASSACHUSETTS.

BOUND BY H. WOLFF, NEW YORK.